I0613532

The Epic Catalog

By: Denise L. Gadreau

Denise L Gadreau

ISBN-13: 978-0615719030 (Inner Light
Journeys)

ISBN-10: 0615719031

This book is dedicated to Josh Downing

Thank you for being you!

A Brief Synopsis...

Jeffery Turner is a man who does not realize he is from a parallel world. He finds this out on a planned trip in the 1950's. He is about to embark on a voyage to the Bahamas from England and meets an extraordinary stranger who sets the mystery in motion.

"The Epic Catalog" is the title of this adventure. As the story develops, two fourteen year old cousins, Anna and Desmond, find out about a book which Jeffery Turner has given account of. It is a tale that dates back from the 1950's to 2011, and as the two cousins read the book on the computer; they somehow find themselves part of the mystery.

Additional characters are an entomologist and his wife, an archaeologist, school teachers, a perpetual student with seven degrees, an antiques dealer, a plane taxi service, flyer's who are also known as fairies in our dimension, a museum professor and Mrs. Perpecuwitz who owns a summer attraction called Rose Cottage.

Anna and Desmond meet many extraordinary people and characters as the book unfolds. There are dimensional twists and turns, plane encounters with a UFO, a rescue at sea, open portals, and a 73 year old confirmed bachelor who finally gets married....

The book goes back and forth to the present and the past and a parallel world. The story involves England, The United States, a sea in Italy, France, Brazil, and a parallel world.

Near the end, does a 73 year old Jeffery Turner finally return to his parallel world? There is a surprise ending which branches into a compelling sequel.

For the Reader ~

A glossary of French phrases and interpretations are located on pages 394 – 395.

The Epic Catalog

Chapter 1

"There is no rhyme or reason for what just happened. It was a sequence of events that seemed inevitable. Sort of the calm before the storm, miraculous or not, I shall recount all in detail as I remember it.

It happened in my seventh year of practicing medicine, I was looking forward to a month of respite, and it couldn't have come soon enough! One of my good comrades was seriously injured in a horrific plane crash a week before, and I had to tell his family after my team and I had tried to save him that he was gone, it almost undid me.

The occurrence that led up to a series of incidences which I am now about to tell you, happened long ago. I was on a pier in London, ready to board the Queen Mary, anxious to be on my way. What happened here initiated a spark to set the account in motion, bringing conformity to it all. Like the schools of fish darting here and there, a charade of going nowhere, yet still have a purpose.

How was I to know it would happen in this way? How was I to know about the turn of events causing me to respond in such a way? We never truly know ourselves, until we genuinely examine our own part in it all. Is it coincidence or just a string of circumstances that authenticated the measures I exhibited? I am not sure. We fight our conflicts within our own minds, although others appear to blame it on chance, I cannot say I had this luxury, for I willing knew there may be consequences, consciously or not for the events unfolding within the course of my life proclaiming to be my destiny."

"Hmmm," read Anna Belk. "This is interesting; I wonder what year it was written in."

Anna loved to research old books and to investigate phrases and wording, and it didn't matter how peculiar they seemed. She happened to be on the internet, looking up a book from a series of words delivered to her in passing at Rose Cottage. "Hmmm, here's the copyri...oh great, Mom's calling."

"Anna, AAAnnnaaaa," heard Anna Belk, somewhere interrupting her thoughts. Anna was complex for her age of fourteen, was especially gifted in mathematics, and dreamed of being a world famous author, the more theatrical; the better. She had been interested in the 1930 - 1940's era lately.

"Drat's! Just when I was reading something really dramatic," Anna looked over the contents one more time.

"AAAANNNAAA!!!" The voice bellowed.

"Coming Mom," yelled Anna. She pushed print for this segment of script on her computer and ran downstairs to see what her mother wanted.

"Anna, didn't you hear me calling you"? Her mother gave her the look. "We're going to be late for the airport.

"Why are we going to the airport?" asked Anna "Oh, I forgot," said Anna without enthusiasm. "I was reading a really great story, Mom! And....I forgot about Desmond!"

Hmmmm, Desmond, Anna reflected. Ever since they moved to the center of nowhere, Desmond had been coming over for a month during summer vacations. Aunt Lenora goes on tour for her books usually during the month of July, but this year, she went a few weeks earlier. She's was a best selling author, as Anna hoped to be someday.

"But Mom, I'm working on a new story, and Desmond will want to write the story with me. He'll never leave me alone, and bug me to do stuff with him while I'm concentrating and coming up with new phrases and ideas!" replied Anna.

"You mean, like getting into trouble?" asked Ellen Belk.

Anna was about to reply, but knew it wouldn't do any good so she frowned at her Mother. It was an accident, she thought. I mean, I didn't actually intend to crash the car into the gate last year, so she sighed.

"Anna, we went over this before," said her Mother exasperated as Anna frowned. "If I know you, you'll find an enormous amount of things to do, having adventures before the week is over."

Anna loved her cousin Desmond, but she was in her writing mode and didn't like to be distracted from the creative ideas she came up with when she was on a roll. That's just how it was.

They drove to the airport and had to wait an agonizing hour for the plane to arrive. Anna was exploring language and pattern phrases for her story and she wanted to try them out. When she thought of something, she would write it in her small note pad so she wouldn't forget it. The flight was delayed because of fierce wind torrents over a neighboring city. Finally, groups of people were coming in through the gateway.

There are a lot of people coming to the city of nowhere, thought Anna. "Better get this over with," Anna complained under her breath.

"What was that Anna?"

"Oh nothing, sure is a lot of people, I don't see Desmond maybe he is not coming this year," Anna smiled precociously.

"Oh he's coming all right...there he is," Ellen Belk waved her arm in the air.

"Desmond," yelled Ellen Belk with arms out stretched. "How is my favorite nephew"?

"Hi Aunt Ellen," Desmond Shay hugged his Aunt. "Didn't think we were going to make it with the fierce winds and all," He scanned the area for Anna.

"Well you are here now, and in one piece I see. Glad you are alright!" Ellen smiled.

"Yeah, thanks Aunt Ellen"

Anna resigned to focus now on Desmond instead of her story, turned away and gave one of her mother's looks to no one in particular. She put her small notebook away and said: "Hey Desmond, how are you? Heard you had some bad weather up there, almost didn't make it, huh"?

"Hey Anna," Desmond gave Anna the official summer handshake. "Yeah, it was a little scary."

They walked to the baggage collection area and retained Desmond's belongings and started toward the car.

"Whoa, Anna, did you just see that?" A flash of light appeared with an image that came as quickly as it went. Anna didn't see it; she was scanning the shelves of the bookstore in the terminal as they passed by it.

"See what, Des?" Anna brought her focus on Desmond.

"Ahhhh, nothing, maybe it was jetlag in combination of the sun coming through the window."

"Hmm," Anna adjusted the strap of one of the carry bags as they walked out of the terminal to the car. I wonder, she mused.

As it turns out, Desmond and Anna both turn fifteen this year. It was the 10th of June, and soon on July 11th, Ellen Belk would throw a double birthday party for Anna and Desmond. Anna's birthday was two days before Desmond's. His birthday was on July 12th. Anna never let him forget that she was the older and smarter one.

The ride home was talkative and uneventful. Desmond told them all about the plans his parents were making for going on a family road trip during the second week of August. This year they were traveling to one of the Great Lakes and staying for two weeks. It did sound exciting.

Anna had a very good mother, but she didn't have a father. A fatal car accident occurred nine years ago and her father didn't make it. She was 5 years old. Sometimes snatches of memories would come, so she held on tight to them. Occasionally Anna would write what she did remember down, trying to fill in as much of the blanks as she could. She hoped that one-day, wherever Henry Belk was up there, he would be proud of her when she became a world famous writer.

Anna envied Desmond, every time he talked about the things he did with his Dad. She listened reflectively, but never let Desmond know she really cared. So as Desmond finished talking about his other vacation, Anna's Mother replied: "You're going to like it, Desmond. You're Mom and I use to go to the Great Lakes when we were kids. I'll bet she will show you some of our old haunts."

"Hmmm," Anna quietly looked out the car window.

It wasn't until last year that Anna and Desmond bonded. He was always a klutz, almost like he had too much energy for his body. Anna made a quick decision. Maybe she and Desmond could work together like last year. She was willing to try again.

As soon as the car pulled in the driveway, Desmond's cell phone rang. "Hi Mom, yup, I'm here. We just pulled into the driveway. Okay. MOM, I WILL...OKAY! Love you too, Mom. Bye." Mom wants to talk to you Aunt Ellen and he handed her the phone.

"Geez," said Desmond rolling his eyes. Anna helped Desmond carry his bags upstairs into the guest room, just across the hall from Anna's room. "What are you working on now, Anna?" Anna was always trying to write something dramatic and creative, and as Desmond recalled, some of them were entertaining.

"Nothing yet, Des, I found some great phrases from some old book I was reading on line, just playing around with it."

"Like what?" Desmond's curiosity was up. He sat on her bed.

"Oh you know the usual stuff."

"Did you write about what happened last year? I wrote some notes when I got home"

"Well not exactly, this story is something completely different, besides, I don't know if I have enough material to write about it." Anna hoped this would dissuade Desmond.

"I brought my note pad," Desmond was getting excited, "We could write it together!"

Anna just smiled….great, she thought, just what I needed!

"What do you think Anna, should I get my notes?"

"ANNA, DESMOND, come down stairs for lunch," yelled Ellen Belk from the foot of the stairs.

Anna thought this was perfect timing…..Saved!!! Thank you Mom!! "Maybe later Desmond…"

"K"

Anna set the table with the dishes and flatware, while Desmond got the cups and placed them on the table. Ellen Belk filled the plates with steaming macaroni and cheese. Let me tell you, this is not your ordinary box type. Anna's mother was very particular when it came to food, and most everything was from scratch.

Ellen Belk had thought of opening a gourmet catering service years ago and went to cooking school, but found she didn't really want to cook full time, so she continued teaching at Rydner's Elementary School. Besides, she enjoyed having the summers off and spending time with Anna, and tried to make up for her not having a father. She made delicious desserts also, and was the envy and delight of the parents when there were school functions.

Rydner's Elementary School went up to the fifth grade. Ellen taught fourth grade and was a dedicated teacher. Anna and Desmond just completed their last year of middle school, and the latter week of August they would enter high school. Anna would attend Rydner High and Desmond Trigonal High School in his hometown. Anna was looking forward to the move into a new school; Desmond had some apprehension about it. He was tall, slender with sandy blond hair and lanky. He was a real computer genius. In some ways he was reticent, he wasn't into sports, but he loved to hike and bike ride.

On any given weekend, Desmond would pack a lunch, mostly P & J and go off for the day with his friend Rhodes, and they would explore the caves and trails for mysterious artifacts. What had started it all was the fossil Desmond and Rhodes discovered in the Costonian Cave near an old mine shaft. Studies resulted from top paleobiologists coming to the area and examining the indigenous peoples, environmental biology, archeology and geology of the land mass the cave rested on. He was on national television and both he and Rhodes received an award. That was three years ago. Desmond tasted the first bite of his lunch, pure heaven he thought. He loved Aunt Ellen's mac 'n cheese.

During lunch, Ellen Belk asked Desmond questions about what he was going to do for the rest of his vacation. While Desmond told his aunt all about his plans, he seemed a little preoccupied. Anna, deciding to make the best of his visit, was a little concerned.

"Something's up," she thought, "and I intend to find out later!"

Chapter 2

My story is rather an incredulous tale, quite unbelievable, with unexpected twists and turns along the way.

The whistle blew for the last call to board the ocean liner. I reached for my suitcase, I was on Holiday you see, and found to my utter amazement, a man dressed in strange clothing suddenly stood right before me fading in and out and said: "I believe Lorien, this is for you." His hand went forward and an envelope materialized right before me, and as I reached to take it, he disappeared, right before my eyes. I was quite taken aback, shocked to be more precise!

I did not know what to make of it, was there a something wrong with me? Was I going senseless? And yet, there was the envelope in my hands. I needed someplace to go to quiet my nerves, and quickly followed the throng to my room on board the ship. As I placed my suitcase down, I looked for something to steady me. I found a small bar in the other room and poured myself a small drink. That seemed to sooth me. I am not an avid drinker. In fact, I rarely drink at all, but I was pretty shaken.

Then I opened the envelope. In it were three odd looking keys, a piece of anomalous fabric, and a folded piece of paper or something like it with number codes on it. The sequence of numbers and letters looked like this:

ϑυλψ Ελεϖεν, τωο τηουσανδ ελεϖεν

ΑΒΔΣΥΣΑ ΡΧϑΤ2011

"What in the world is this?" I was mystified. The whole contents of the envelope had an iridescent glow. Was I mistaken for someone else? It was uncanny! And who was he referring to... Lore... Loran... Lori-n? "Well, wonder if there is a chap on board with that name." I was baffled. Although, I had to admit, the name sparked something in me. What was it? The thought pervaded me, it was gone!

Clouds had rolled in and it started to rain. I heard distant thunder. Lightening lit up the sky. All of a sudden, I found myself in a cave which was fading in an out. It felt like a daydream. "What in the world?" I heard strange sounds, voices, scared me out of my wits. The air was sweet, like perfumed flowers. I still had my glass in one hand and the envelope in another. I drained the glass of its contents and just stood there, dazed unable to comprehend what had happened. Then I was back in my room.

After that episode, I decided to lie down. I thought I was losing my mind. The storm outside was brewing. "Just a little rest, for the nerves," I thought as I lay on the bed.

I found I was utterly exhausted and recalled the strange events that had just transpired. Sleep over came me at last. I am not sure if I was still in the dream state or not, but, here I was, back in that cave again!

This time I heard people coming, almost urgently. I did not know where to run. I turned around and they were dressed in the same way as the man who disappeared from the pier.

Anna adjusted her computer screen. "This is getting really interesting," she murmured. She read on:

"What's going on"? I demanded!

"All will be revealed in its time," said the man who delivered the envelope. "Ah, the others are here."

I turned around and there was a group of people all of similar dress. The eldest of them spoke. "You are Jeffery Turner, yes?"

"How do you know my name"? I asked.

"We have been waiting a very long time to reach you, and now you are here among us, like a hologram, but for a limited time, so I will try to explain as quickly as possible," said the elder man.

There was a knock on Anna's door. "Anna, you busy"? Desmond entered her room.

"Mmmmn, ah, just reading this book on the internet, what's up?"

They had a late night out to see the newest movie at the theater, and now they both had gone to their rooms for the night.

"What book on the internet"? Desmond couldn't help asking with his curious nature, so Anna scrolled to the title page. "Ohhhh, it looks, well sort of, ah, well interesting." Desmond scanned Anna's room.

"What are you doing, research, on vacation"?

Anna sighed; she didn't want to tell Desmond she was going to write another story. He would be in there for hours, wanting to know the plot, trying to put his two cents worth in, so she said, "Just happen to come across it, and it seemed interesting, that's all. So, Desmond, what did you want"?

"I was playing a game on my computer, and this grouping of numbers kept flashing up, look what do you make of it?" Desmond turned his laptop screen so Anna could see it. "Have you played this game before"?

"Yeah, I have, but never saw that!" Wait ...a...minute! Look at this."

Anna scrolled her computer window to the page of codes in the story before Desmond came in. They were exactly the same set of codes.

"Desmond, you were preoccupied at lunch today, did you get the codes before?

Desmond shook his head, "no, It was something I forgot to do at home. I called Dad and he took care of it." He looked at the numbers, then back at his frozen game screen. "This isn't a coincidence is it, Anna"?

"I'm not sure," Anna said cautiously.

They both stood there amazed and perplexed, looking at the numbers on the game screen, and the numbers of the codes in the story. Part of it was their birth dates. "This is weird," thought Anna.

"Anna, how did you come about getting the story on the computer"?

"Well, if you must know, I was researching different word groupings for...a... well," Anna sighed; "another story, and this one came up on the tag search. It had an interesting title so I clicked on it. I found some cool words and phrases I thought of filing until later."

"What do you think it means, Anna"?

"Again, I'm not really sure, but there may be some clues with the codes."

Just then, the game went blank, and then Anna's computer also went blank. "That's weird, let's figure it out in the morning," said Anna.

"Okay," Desmond yawned, "I'm sort of tired any way!"

ϑυλψ Ελεϖεν, τωο τηουσανδ ελεϖεν

ΑΒΔΣΥΣΑ ΡΧϑΤ2011

7101999-7121999-7112011

ABDSUSA RCJT2011

Chapter 3

A storm was brewing through the night and Anna dreamed of being in a cave of sweet perfumed flowers, and strangely dressed people. There was a man who seemed older aside a group of people in the cave, but regal in a sense. He was addressed as Guardia, The Seer. He looked right at her and smiled. Then he spoke.

"Hello, dear child, please do not be afraid. We have come in your dream state to talk to you about the manuscript you are currently reading on your computer. Your name is Anna, am I not correct?"

"Yes sir, but who are you and why are you in my dream?"

"We are of the parallel world that Jeffery Turner is from, the man in the book. We have come to you because we desperately need your help. You are one of select few who holds the key to an event that will take place soon, but in your world, a long time has past. A long time ago, a portal was opened which connected two worlds, your Earth, and our world, Neia. A man named Jeffery Turner came through many years ago and we are trying to help him remember who he is and to come back into our world. He is an important person here and our destiny depends on it. Little beings called the Flyers have shown us who you were in your world. It is through their help that we have been able to come to you in your dreams tonight.

"Anna, you too have an important role to play in this story, yet truly it is not a story. We have astal traveled in your dreams to your world, and your time. Soon an important event will take place. Are you afraid"?

"A little, the book, the numbers, it isn't a coincidence, is it?"

"No, Little one, it isn't. We have come back in time to your world and dimension, because we need your help. Your cousin plays a major role in this, also. There is a holographic doorway that allows us to come into your astral world for a limited time. That is why you see us in your dream state. It is very unpredictable and we may fade out at any time."

 "But, why us, and what does it have to do with the man in the story"?

"Ahhhhh, yes my dear, the man in the story. You and your cousin have a connection with him, which shall be revealed eventually. You are curious about Mr. Turner?"

 "Yes, it is a little strange, especially the codes in the book." Anna tuned her head and saw Desmond.

"Anna!" Desmond looked surprised.

"Desmond, you're here?" Anna asked in amazement.

"He has been here all this time, but unseen, like a spectator in a dream, but now I wish to speak to both of you."

"I'm not sure if I understand how this is happening, I mean, seeing each other in our dreams," said Desmond.

"We have a special way to communicate differently through sound waves, but in your dreams, we are using the theta waves to appear in this way."

The Seer pondered for a moment, and then looked at them both gravely. He had to complete his mission before he faded from their dream state. He sighed and began to tell Anna and Desmond some information for them to remember when the time is right on Earth.

"Mr. Jeffery Turner is actually from another dimension, a parallel dimension. Lorien is his rightful name. One day, he crossed over into your dimension, but without any recollection of it. How this happened, we can only speculate. He was 10 years old. He could not remember who he was. He is the direct descendent to become the next Elder in our world, when he turns thirty-five. There are many rituals and much learning before this event would take place. It has been

14.9 years in our dimension and now time is running out."

We must bring Lorien back to our time, and have succeeded only minutely. We thought we had advanced thirteen years ago, but it was not the right timing. Much must come to pass; and we have learned each world must be lined up in similar progression. Soon an adjustment will take place in both universes which will make the translation possible."

The Seer looked at both of them intently. Then he continued.

"There would be only 10 years and three months for Lorien's training, which should have started when he was 13 years old. Sixty-three years have passed in your world.

Lorien would be reaching the age of 25, in our parallel world. It is not a coincidence that his birth date is the day between both your dates of births, there is something significant on July 11. A portal will open on this day only between the two dimensions. If we cannot get him back between the segments of time available, then Lorien may be lost from us forever."

He paused, then asked; "Will you help, Anna and Desmond?" Will you help us to get him back?"

"But how can we"? Anna asked. "It was just a story. He's just a character in a book!"

"It seems already impossible," said Desmond.

"Ah, my friends, He is alive in your world. In your dimension, time progresses slower in our world. Here he would be 25 years old, and in your world, he is 73. If we could somehow recapture the past, it would be possible to bring him back. As we perceived Anna, you have been reading the book?"

"You mean, it's true," asked Desmond?

"Yes very factual," said the Seer. "Anna, you know the contents of the envelope, and Desmond, you understood the sequence of codes to be your birthdays?"

Desmond and Anna looking at each other then slowly agreed.

"The process of the numbers, the three keys and the piece of fabric will bring him back to us through time. At 11:45pm of July 11, the planets and stars will be in direct alignment and conjunction to the planets and stars of our dimension. At that precise moment, a great shift through the window of a portal will allow him to pass through. We call it translating. Lorien will regain his memory and will still remember the years from this world. If it is successful, he will come back to us at the age of 25."

"Now, Anna and Desmond, you must continue to sleep. The signal is getting weak. We will meet again when you dream the next time if the astral doorway opens again."

The Seer vanished from their dream state. Anna and Desmond went back into their own dreams, until they woke up in the morning.

Chapter 4

"What do you mean, come back to you? I don't understand! Who are you, and how did I get here?" asked Jeffery.

"Do we not look familiar to you in any way? Do you not remember us"? The Seer asked.

"Is this some kind of joke? Did Russell put you up to this"?

"Ah, Jeffery Turner, no, you would not understand yet," the Seer mused.

"Do you not remember us in your dreams then"?

Jeffery looked at them, searchingly; he was a little uneasy.

"I... ah, I'm not sure," said Jeffery slowly. "I remember dreams of when I was a child, never thought much of them, but... how do you, how can you…..you have not really answered my question!"

"You are in a sleep state; we are in your dream sleep. We were able to use a mechanism of theta waves that forms an astral hologram projection in your brain.

"I do remember lying down, exhausted and done in.....but I was in a cave before I went to sleep," Jeffery queried.

"Because of the urgency, we were able to bring the environment temporarily to you, but only momentarily, there is a holographic gateway that opens for a few seconds, we cannot keep you in our dimension, our parallel world for long because you were only a three dimensional being in the Earth plane. Even though your body make-up is different from those of the Earth plane, you have retained some of their energy throughout your existence while on Earth.

It is very similar to a hologram. You were able to process our dimension, but not your whole being, or body, just through your mind. We may have found a way to bring you back. The procedure will take years to finish, you may have aged in this world before we can accomplish it," the Elder emphasized. "Do you remember any part of your childhood, before you were adopted by the family who found you"? The Elder asked.

"How do you know I was adopted....oh, right...this is a dream!" said Jeffery. "Hmmm, I'm not sure, I remember in a dream thinking I had lost something, and I was searching for it. I remember seeing places that seemed... umm, a bit unfamiliar, strange. I was frightened, started running, I bumped into some people. They were hard to understand, in the dream I was crying. I was taken to their home. I remember their kindness. I was eventually adopted by the people who found me, because I hadn't any parents, so to speak. I did actually in real life, get adopted by the people in my dreams. Quite peculiar really, and I stayed with them until I went to College.   I have a job, a good one, now I'm on holiday, I was ready to board the Queen Mary and then a bizarre man approached me, and gave me an envelope, and disappeared."

"Jeffery, your real name is Lorien, you are from our world, somehow you slipped into this dimension, a parallel world when you were a child, you have not been able to get back," explained the Seer.

"Lorien? Dimension? Parallel world? I don't understand….."

"You have become acclimated to this dimension more and more and before we lose you for good that is if you die before…"

"Before…I die….what is going on, am I going to die," exclaimed Jeffery.

"No not now, it is just a fact in the dimension you are in at the moment, it is different where you are originally from. Lorien, we are your people; we have come back to this dimension to help you get back to us."

"This is just a dream…wait, where are you going," asked Jeffery?

The Seer flashed in and out for a second, and then he replied, "I cannot stay, think on my words, Lorien. Keep the envelope in a safe place. Do not lose any of the contents. We will try to contact you again." With these words, the Seer vanished.

Feeling perplexed, I awoke with a start. I found I was still on board the Queen Mary, and it was late afternoon.

Chapter 5

The rain was falling in such astronomical force; I had a hard time keeping focused. I needed to get out of the cabin, mingle, and take in some fresh air....

Anna and Desmond looked at each other. They had been up for hours. Desmond read the previous chapters, so he could get a better idea of the story to analyze as he recalled the events of his dream during the night.

"Well," said Desmond, "it is starting to make a little sense. What are we going to do, Anna? How can we help Jeffery? We don't even know where he lives and if he even lives in this country."

"I know," Anna said thoughtfully, "we have a little less than a month to find him. We can search for him on the web, or try to contact his publisher,"

"How long ago was the book published? He sounds British from some of the wording he's using and he seems a bit aggravated."

Anna scrolled to the beginning of the book and looked at the copyright page.

"Hmmm, 1958, presuming that he was about 20 years old in 1948 or so, which would make him about 71 or older now."

"I bet the library will have a copy, Anna and we can get the author bio and other information of, um...maybe where he lives from inside the dust jacket. Lots of times they put that stuff in the back of a dust jacket cover."

"It's a start," Anna lost in thought began a series of views, creating a fascinating adventure in her mind. "We can ride over later; we brought your bike upstairs a few days ago from the cellar and put it in the garage."

"Did you fix the flat?" Desmond was almost afraid to ask.

"Actually, we had it repaired the day after you left last year. Mom was a little mad about what happened."

"Yeah, I over heard the telephone conversation one night not long after I got in from the flight home last year," reflected Desmond. His parents were not too happy about the incident.

"Look, Mom just thinks we were coming home from the lake with the Taigas' and rode our bikes home."

"Well, that's basically what we did."

"She wasn't too happy about the gate."

"But you had to move the car in order for the quest stones to appear. It was the only way," interrupted Desmond, "bout how mad was Aunt Ellen?"

"I lost my computer for two weeks, remember?"

"Oh, yeah, I forgot." Desmond was sympathetic

Anna looked back at the computer, scrolling down to where they left off.

"Let's read a little more of the story."

Chapter 6

I made my way to the deck, the wind had died down and the rain felt good on my face, I just stood there clinging to the rail, looking far into the distance thinking for quite some time, trying to put some pieces of the puzzle together. The storm was rallying, so I collected myself and went back to my cabin for a hot shower and a change of clothes.

The Dining Room had the remains of a buffet. I looked longing at the stuffed lobster and sat down to enjoy a generous portion. I needed to replay the incidents from midday. In all honesty, were the episodes authentic or just periods of delusion? Was I going over the deep end, and what was all that business about the envelope anyway?

I could hear a low rumbling in the background as the orchestra played on. Three keys, a piece of fabric and a small piece of paper with codes on it. What does it all mean? I was deep in concentration when I happened to look up "What the world?" I mouthed in pure horror, to see a woman slip on the carpet with her high heels and flounder across my stuffed lobster!

I helped her out of my dinner, each of us brushing ourselves off. She was very apologetic, new heels and stumbling on something on the floor, and then she took a real good look at me full face and exclaimed; "You're him!"

Lifting one eyebrow in puzzlement, thinking she was a little daft, she said again, "You are him, the man I keep seeing in my dreams!"

Now I knew she was daft and thought just for the benefit of doubt, may have bumped her head in some way on the table. She nearly finished off my meal, except for the wine. I quickly picked it up, gulp down the rest before she had any other ideas of destruction. It was a waste of mouthwatering stuffed lobster.

"I'm very sorry about that; I've ruined your meal and your dinner jacket. My name is Rachel, Rachel Carde," she said holding out her hand. What an exquisite hand it was, indeed.

"Jeffery Turner," I said standing shaking that beautiful little hand. "I can't say I'm glad to meet you; not when you murdered my lobster and all." Just a little humor added to break the tension. We both smiled.

"I am terribly sorry."

Did I detect a slight accent?

"I mean I'm not use to wearing such high heels. I think my shoe caught on a snag of the carpeting," Rachel explained hesitantly while brushing the last piece of lobster from that lovely hair. Light brown with auburn highlights. Hmm. Curious what comes to mind when you really look?

"I'm really very, very sorry."

"You just said that."

"Oh."

"Look, what did you mean when you said you saw me in your dreams?" I thought I would be direct. I was curious.

"Oh, I don't know why I said that. I was startled when I saw you up close."

What did that indicate? I thought.

"I mean for the past month, may I?" Rachel said pointing to a clean chair.

The waiters had come around and did a capital job of cleaning my table, and offered Perrier to damp clean our attire. Out of the corner of my eye, I happened to notice another waiter come into the dining room. He placed two plates of stuffed lobster on my table, and poured two goblets of wine. I was almost blissful.

I nodded my head, thinking it was a little pretentious of her, but looking into those hazel eyes, hmm, very hazel as she chatted on. And, noting there were two plates of stuffed lobster on the table, "Of course, allow me," I said holding out her chair.

"I had these very peculiar dreams," she continued. She took her fork and started jabbing the lobster almost tenderly. She placed the fork delicately into her mouth, "mmm, very delicious she murmured.

"I dreamt of a group or tribe of people in strangely dressed costumes in a cave. And you were there talking to a very old man."

I did a double take, purely stunned, thinking I was a specter now in an illusion.

"Mmm, this is very delicious," she whispered taking another bite. "Well, as I said, Hmmm, I really haven't had a bite to eat since breakfast."

Get to the blooming point, my thoughts thundered, but quickly dissipated as she looked up into my eyes, searching.

"In one hand, you were holding three antiquated keys, a piece of unusual fabric, and something else; I never could make it out. The other hand held a glass of some brown liquid."

"A drink", I interjected.

"Oh," Rachel looked questioningly my way, "How could you know?"

"It just happened, I mean the dream..."

"What do you mean?" Rachel took another delicate jab at the lobster.

I had to make up my mind quick, and sorted out the details with my own story or vision, or what ever you would call it with her.

We talked for another hour, and questioned each other like detectives investigating a case. Rachel stifled a small yawn. I glanced at my watch it was 10:05.

"Look, what are your plans, I mean why are you on this cruise? This is not a coincidence. There must be a reason we were both here together."

"I'm an archeologist," Rachel explained. "I am on my way to a small village near Saintes-Maries-de-la-Mer, along the French coast, I mean after a little respite. I'm meeting my team for a new discovery in one of the underwater caves. The tides have been especially low the past five months and some divers found a few rare coins, some other relics and ancient writings on one of the walls." We were fascinated," Rachel continued, "the pictures sent to us seemed genuine. We were given a grant to go to the location and examine the walls and dig up anything else we could uncover." I am due there in two weeks. This is the beginning of my vacation.

I smiled as she talked on, nodding my head, saying little ditties, looking into those beautiful earnest eyes murmuring, "of course, ah yes, hmm, ah jolly good" and all of that.

Rachel quietly stifled another small yawn. ".....and the pamphlets sounded wonderful, I always wanted to go to the Bahamas and of course the Florida Coast. I've been working extremely hard on the last dig and..."

"Wait a minute, you're Dr. Rachel Carde. Well this is trump! I have been following you along with the London Times. The papers really do not do you justice, couldn't really make you out. Are you with someone, I mean, well, could we meet tomorrow to talk some more. I'll show you the envelope and..."

"Oh, yes, I mean no, I'm not with anyone, if that is what you mean. I'd be delighted to meet with you tomorrow. Say, oh-mm," Rachel stifled another yawn.

Om, I thought?

"Hmm...," Rachel calculated the time in her head, "probably about two in the afternoon? I have some paperwork I need to finish in the morning."

What in the world was I going to do until then? I felt a little distraught, but realizing that time didn't matter all that much while on the ship; I began to think better about the whole ordeal. "Two o'clock is fine with me, Dr. Carde."

"Rachel, please call me Rachel, we're practically friends, and with the lobster incident and all..."

"Alright, Rachel, I'll meet you on deck at two o'clock near the pool. I'll bring the envelope," I said again, shaking her hand goodbye.

How fortunate to run into Rachel Carde, I thought as I made my way to my cabin, an archeologist fancy that! My step began to feel a little lighter.

Chapter 7

Desmond looked up from the computer screen, "I think I hear Aunt Ellen calling us."

"Okay, let's go to the library and get a copy of the book, I know Mom won't mind."

"What's it called again?"

"The Epic Catalog,"

"Hmm, kind a weird named for a book, I wonder what it means, the title....look Anna, the screen went blank and the book is gone."

Great, thought Anna, "hope the library has a copy!"

"DESSSMOND, AAAANNA, I'M LEAVING NOW...WHAT ARE YOU BOTH DOING TODAY?" Mrs. Belk called from the bottom of the stairs.

Anna and Desmond ran downstairs to give her Mom a hug goodbye.

"Mom, we're thinking of riding our bikes downtown to the library, and then just ride around, you know the usual stuff."

"Thanks Aunt Ellen for fixing my flat tire." Desmond hugged his Aunt goodbye.

"You are certainly welcome, Desmond. Okay, please, please be careful. You have your cell phones incase I need to get in touch with you? They're charged?"

"Yup!" Anna and Desmond both replied simultaneously.

"Good, I'm off, Have fun and no trouble!"

"MOM!"

"We'll be okay Aunt Ellen," said Desmond reassuringly.

"Alright then, be home for supper, See you both then."

"Let's pack a lunch," Anna said looking out the window and waving as her mother drove away. "Did you empty your backpack yet?"

"Not yet." Desmond ran upstairs, tripping as he went.

Anna shook her head walking into the kitchen. "Some people never change." Anna said under her breath.

Desmond met her in the kitchen in almost two minutes.

"That was fast."

"I dumped it all on the bed; figure I'd put it away later. What's for breakfast?"

"Mom left a plate of waffles on the table. We may have to microwave them."

Desmond was on them quick. "I am a little hungry."   Uncovering the waffles, he said, "They're just a little warm. I'll put the plate in the microwave and get the butter and syrup in the fridge. What are you making for lunch?"

Desmond peered into the refrigerator looking for the syrup, butter and milk.

"P & J, the usual." Anna started two piles. Each pile contained a sandwich, fruit, chips, juice boxes, bottled water, and string cheese.

They both quickly ate their breakfast and placed the dishes in the sink.

"Shouldn't we wash them first?" Desmond had located the sponge.

"No, leave them, Mom won't care. We'll wash them later. It's just a few dishes. Here's your backpack."

"Do we need a flashlight?" Desmond peered into his backpack.

"No, we're just going to the library and ride around," Anna hurriedly picked up a spare house key and put it in a small pocket of her backpack.

They rode like the wind. The sun was shining through the trees. The air was a little brisk for the middle of June. It was a 7-minute ride to the Rydner Public Library. After parking and chaining their bikes at the bicycle posts, Anna turned to Desmond.

"There is a chance the book may not be here, should I bring it up on one of the computers and print it?"

"I think it would be expensive. I could bring it up on my iPod if we need to."

"Might not be able to upload it at all if we lost it on my computer...it was a little odd though in the first place how it just appeared in my Google search when I was looking for something else, but we still may be able to bring it up on the computers inside the library."

Anna thought about it as they entered the building. "I think we either need the book or a printed copy, how much cash did you bring? I have $11.00 in my pocket."

"Why do we need a printed copy?"

Anna turned and whispered to him. "Because, we may find clues in the book, the story might have some hidden codes for us to figure out. We can write on the printed copy as we go along."

"Hmm," Desmond was taking out his wallet. "I got a visa cash card and twenty five dollars cash, you know, for spending money, 'cause I'm on vacation."

Anna looked at the visa cash card. "How much did Aunt Lenora put on the card?"

"Only $100.00, that's for the whole 6 weeks." Desmond was at the information computer. "Do I type in Jeffery Turner's name as the author?"

"Yup, and if it doesn't come up, try the title, The Epic Catalog," Anna peered over Desmond's shoulder. Desmond, a good researcher would never give up until he had viable answers. Anna liked that about her cousin.

"The book is not in the catalog. What do we do now Anna?"

"Good Morning Anna, why hello Desmond," smiled Mrs. Jacqueline McFinn as she was passing by to the circulation desk. Is it that time already? Welcome back. What are you two planning this year for the summer?

"Hi Mrs. McFinn!" Anna and Desmond really liked the Librarian. "We're looking for an older book, Desmond answered."

"You look a little frustrated Desmond, what book are you looking for?

Desmond looked at Anna she was nodding okay, "The Epic Catalog by Jeffery Turner."

"And it was written in 1958," volunteered Anna.

Well, to tell you the truth Anna and Desmond, it is a dated book and we wouldn't have it in our catalog. In fact, none of the libraries in the county would carry a book that old unless it was a literary classic and an up to date copy."

Anna and Desmond sighed.

"However, we do have several old books in the bookcases down in the upper cellar. We go down there periodically to bring donations for our annual sale. We did get several loads from an estate in Windham County and they did donate some older books about 6 months ago. Would you both like to look? Our sale won't start until the Thanksgiving Holiday, which is about 5½ months away. You may buy the book now if you find it."

Anna and Desmond's spirits lifted and both nodded yes.

There were three rooms lined in bookcases. The rooms had large windows. Two rooms were full and the third had five full bookcases and boxes of books ready to be placed on the last four bookcases.

"If we don't find the book on the shelves Mrs. McFinn, do you want Desmond and I to place the books on the empty shelves as we go through the boxes?" Anna asked looking at all the boxes on the floor.

"Only if you and Desmond want to, I'll check up on you two in about an hour."

"Thank you Mrs. McFinn."

"Oh you are very welcome, Desmond and Anna."

Desmond and Anna turned to the bookshelves as Mrs. McFinn climbed the stairs to go back to the main library.

Chapter 8

Anna took one side of the first bookshelf, while Desmond began to search around the corner. They both continued like this for about half an hour.

Anna could hear Desmond talking to himself. "No, not this one, hmm this looks like an interesting book. Etc., etc.," Then she heard; "How are you doing Anna?" So many books, I'm not sure we'll find it."

"We're almost done with this room," Anna said peering around the corner. Mrs. McFinn will be back in about a half hour.

"K ...I did find a couple books with the beginning tile 'Epic,' but not with 'Catalog,' and, not by the author Jeffery Turner." Desmond continued looking.

Anna and Desmond were halfway through the 2nd room when Mrs. McFinn came in. How are you both getting along?

"Okay," Desmond stood up. He was peering at the tiles on the bottom row.

"No luck yet Mrs. McFinn," Anna came around the corner.

"I see a few books I'd like to buy in November, but not the one we're looking for today," Anna said still looking at her row of books.

"Yes there are a few I saw also. It's almost noon and we close for an hour. Did you pack a lunch today? You are certainly welcome to eat at the picnic tables in the park section on the library grounds."

"I am a little hungry," said Desmond.

Nothing new here thought Anna, he's always hungry. Wonder how come he doesn't gain any weight? Anna was thin also. Desmond grew a few more inches since she last saw him. Now he was slightly taller than she was.

"Thanks Mrs. McFinn, We'll be back at one o'clock." Anna replied as she picked up her backpack from the first room. Desmond followed.

Outside the sunshine was a welcome sight from the fluorescent lighting in the book cellars.

Anna and Desmond settled near the far end of the library walk. Desmond tore open his backpack and started to eat his sandwich.

"Mmm, crunchy peanut butter, thanks Anna. You make the best!"

"It's all we had in the pantry." Anna unzipped her sandwich bag and took a bite.

"What'll we do if we can't find it in the library cellar?" Desmond asked between bites.

"I'm not sure, there may be other options." Anna was looking at the details of the design around the border of the library sign. Inside were the words: 'R. intro exterioris hominis Unum!' For the summer months, a quote was posted using any language for the patrons to solve. The first correct submission for this quote won a gift certificate to Rydner's Book Barn.

Anna looked at Desmond. "If we print out the copy from the internet it's almost 300 pages. That's about 30 dollars, oh, wait, I forgot. Remember last year the Antiquities Store at the end of Sephia Avenue?"

"Is that where we brought the quest stones?" Desmond's curiosity was aroused.

"Yeah, I forgot about that. Mr. Edis may have a copy of the book, if not; he may even be able to get a copy." Anna picked up the trash from her lunch and threw it in the receptacle nearby. Desmond quickly followed.

"He's pretty cool," Desmond was looking at the puzzle. "May...May....the...out...ward, no, in...ward...May the innnn...ward and out...ward mem...ma...mane...man...b...be...ah...Uno...one,

MAY THE INWARD AND OUTWARD MAN BE AS ONE!"

"SOCRATES," Anna joined in. "Yeah, and I know we can trust him. Look, it's almost one. Let's head back to the front and see if we were the first ones to figure out the quote. I think it went up just a little while ago."

Chapter 9

Desmond followed Anna to the circulation desk. Sam was sitting at one of the computers working on a newsletter publication.

"Hi Sam," Anna waited until he looked up from the computer screen.

"Hey, Anna, what can I do for you?"

"Desmond and I figured out the puzzle on the billboard outside."

"Hey Desmond, Ahhhhh, vacation time?"

Desmond looked up and smiled. "Yeah."

"Good to see you, well about that quote, hmm, which one is it?" Sam flipped through the papers on his desk. "Okay, what's the quote? Remember the rules?"

Anna nodded her head in agreement. "R. intro exterioris hominis unum!" Desmond repeated the quote slowly in Latin then the translation. "May the Inward and Outward Man Be As One."

Anna followed with, "Socrates."

"Yup, that's it." Congratulations. Then softly over the intercom, Sam announced that there was a winner for the quote.

"Okay, where is the certificate, hmm, oh here it is." Sam lifted it from under the desk blotter. "A ten dollar gift certificate for Rydner's Book Barn, you know that you can only win once?" They both nodded.

"Anna and Desmond, here you both are." Mrs. McFinn appeared from around the corner. "Are you both ready to go back down to the book cellar?"

"Thank you Mrs. McFinn," answered Desmond, "yes."

"Thanks Sam," Desmond waved the gift certificate in the air.

No prob! Good seeing you Des, have a good summer, Anna." Sam turned to the next patron in line

"I see you figured out our first quote. How long did it take you? Was it too easy?" Mrs. McFinn opened the door to the book cellar and turned on the lights.

"I was still trying to figure it out, but Desmond got it first."

"I see the Latin is paying off, Desmond."

"Actually, Mrs. McFinn, I like it very much."

"I am glad to hear it, Desmond." Mrs. McFinn unlocked the book cellar doors.

Ann just smiled.

"I don't suspect you both will be down here very long. Oh by the way, we have some student workers coming in later this afternoon. After you go through the boxes in the third room, leave the books. I would like the students to reorder the books in the rooms, and then they will put the others on the shelves. Well, good luck."

"Thank you Mrs. McFinn," Anna and Desmond said.

With that said, Mrs. McFinn smiled and went back upstairs to the main library.

Chapter 10

Anna looked up from her stack of books, Desmond saw and felt her disappointment.

"It's not as easy as I thought," Anna looked into the last box. Desmond put the pile of books on the floor, as they shifted through each title.

"I thought it might have been in the estate boxes," Desmond looked at all the piles of books on the floor.

"Yeah, me too," Anna followed as her eyes scanned all the books on the floor. "We'll have to put the books back in the boxes, and then find Mrs. McFinn."

They put the last of the books carefully back into the boxes. Some of them were delicate, and it took a little longer.

After they found Mrs. McFinn and thanked her, Anna and Desmond decided to go to Mr. Edis' Shop on Sephia Avenue.

Clouds covered the midday sun, the sky was getting dark. The air felt humid and a slight breeze rose up from the East.

Anna involuntarily shuddered.

"What's wrong, Anna?" Desmond had unlocked his bike and noticed Anna shudder.

"I'm not sure, Desmond, Hmmmm….Let's ride to the Antique Store"

Anna saw the detour sign as they came up to the end of Sienna Street. The clouds over head were getting darker!

It took Anna and Desmond 25 minutes to cross traffic, take the Detour, and find the right road that connected to Sephia Avenue. The Antique Store was near the end of the street.

Desmond felt drops of rain as they parked and chained up their bikes to the post near the entrance to the shop. They dashed through the door as the rain came rushing down and claps of thunder boomed outside. The lights flickered off and on. They were greeted by Elise, the resident cat, who lived in the shop.

Charles, a shop employee and relative, smiled as they came around a corner of one of the isles. Anna looked up, smiled back, and asked if Mr. Edis was in.

"Oh, I'm sorry, he's on vacation, and should be back this weekend. Hmm he's at the end of his vacation though, but maybe I can help. Haven't I seen you in before, maybe a few months ago?"

Anna nodded her head. "Yes, I bought a present for my Mom on Mother's Day."

"That's right, is it Allie?" asked Charles.

"No, it's Anna, pretty close though! My Mom loved the box. She said it reminded her of the box her grandmother gave her when she was a girl. She put it on her dresser."

"Yes, the 1938 lacquered box! I remember now! So what brings you and your friend into the shop today?"

Desmond looked up from the old airplane replicas. "I'm Desmond, Anna's cousin."

Charles went over and shook Desmond's hand. "Pleasure to meet you, Desmond; do you want to know about the replicas of the planes?"

"Actually, we came in to find a book, we tried to find it at the library, but it was out of circulation," Desmond shifted from the plane replicas to the inner isle.

"How old is it?" Charles straightened a lamp on an Italian baroque writing table, circular 1870.

"It was printed in 1958, it's called: The Epic Catalog." Anna felt a little hope.

"Let's take a look in the rare book rooms." Charles made a gesture to follow him.

Besides being an Antiquities Shop, there were two rooms downstairs dedicated to rare and first edition volumes. The upstairs housed a used book stored called: "A Treasured Friend," and the Café Umbria, a very posh café of the most desired delectables.

The building shook with the last booming of thunder. The lights danced on and off again, dimly at first, then became brighter as they climbed the stairs to the second floor.

"How about a cup of tea before we start and you can tell me why the book is so important," said Charles glancing at their dampen clothes. "You both look like you could use it. "

Anna nodded. "Yes, please," answered Desmond.

Desmond took out his Visa card, and Charles stopped him, "Part of the perks of being with an relative here, Desmond, you won't need any money today!"

"Thank you," Anna & Desmond said. Anna had a huge smile. She liked Charles. Even though he was almost nineteen, he looked much younger and Anna liked how he was considerate of her choices the last time she came to the shop.

They made their tea and settled in an area of a huge stained glass window emerging from the first to the second floor. The building, an old church sold to Mr. Edis after the members built a new one across town to accommodate all the people who attended. Finally he had the building of his dreams. Mr. Bartholomew Edis had collectors from all over the world contacting him for his antiquities and the building definitely made the shop contents more desirable.

Anna started. "I guess we became interested in the book after I found it online and started reading it….."

"You better tell him why Anna," interrupted Desmond.

Anna disclosed some of the information leading up to when Desmond came the other day.

"So you like literary classics," Charles inquired.

"Sort of, I love phrases, and well, I like using them in my stories."

"And you want to some day become a writer?"

"Um, well yes, but this book had codes in it…."

"And…?"

Desmond decided to tell Charles about his video game and how it would freeze up and show the codes, his confusion, then seeking out Anna to see if she knew anything about it.

"That's when Anna showed me the codes at the beginning of the book on the computer."

"Hmm, it sounds like a good mystery. Is there any more?"

"This is the weird part, in our dreams, ouhhh...!" Anna had just kicked Desmond under the table.

Charles smiled again. "Divulging secrets, Desmond? It's ok if you don't want to tell me the rest, but it is interesting and I may be able to help."

Desmond gave Anna, the look. "Okay, but this will sound weird. You tell him, Anna, you're much better at remembering everything than I am."

Anna sighed, all credibility she felt she had with Charles may just as well go out the window, she told him about the Dream, and the rest of what they read so far, their failure of uncovering the book in the library basement, and then their ride to the Antiquities Shop.

Charles looked searchingly at them both. "And you know for a fact this book is in print?"

"Yes, we both saw it!" Desmond sat on the edge of his seat.

Charles made a quick decision. "Well, then, it's all settled we have to find that book for you before it's too late......wait a minute! I know why you looked so familiar when I first saw you Anna, the time you bought your Mother's gift? You brought something...to the store, hmmm, Desmond I didn't see you that day."

"I remember! My Mom telephoned me and I had poor reception inside the building," recalled Desmond, "I had to go outside for the duration of the call and Anna came out when I was almost through talking to my mother."

Charles put his hand to his forehead and frowned. "Stones... yes that's it, the stones."

"The Quest Stones," said Desmond"

"Are they... safe," asked Anna?

"You know, Mr. Edis is my Grandfather?"

"You sort of look like him in a way," Anna observed.

"Thanks." Charles laughed. Yes, they are safe. But now they are the size of a very large egg, they have an agate look to them, sort of orangey brown."

"I wonder why they shrunk." Desmond remembered carrying one in his backpack. It was really heavy; Anna carried the other one in hers.

"It seems to be a mystery. But they're safe here. Grandfather never told me why, but someday, maybe you will tell me, but now we need to search the shelves for your Epic Catalog."

Charles drew back his chair and started collecting the mugs, Anna and Desmond cleared away the rest.

Chapter 11

They began the search in The Treasures Friend Book Store, after an hour, Anna was losing hope. Charles came around through the doorway of the fiction room. He had two employees from The Treasured Friend looking for The Epic Catalog in the paper back section.

"Nothing yet," Charles looked over at the non fiction and walked over to the history section. Anna covered another area, while Desmond and the two other employees continued to search the paper back books.

The Antiquities Shop had all the rare and first edition books cataloged in the computer, but not in the Used Book Section.

Finally after another hour, they all met on the landing. Anna and Desmond looked and felt discouraged. Charles brought them each a brownie and colas and sighed.

"Let me call Grandfather, he won't mind. He may have some contacts where he is vacationing and may be able to get a copy."

"Where is he vacationing, Charles?" Anna asked.

"London, England, and Saintes-Maries-de-la-Mer, the French Coast," said Charles. There was a rare artifact, coming up for auction, and he was going to bid on it and then go on to visit his sister in England. He should be in there, later today.

Desmond dropped his brownie, and Anna looked at Charles, eyes wide and gaping.

Charles raised his eyebrows...."ok, there's more to this, isn't there? Let me close up the shops. It's about that time. I have a double wide jeep; you can put your bikes in the back and fill me in on the ride home. Where do you live?

Anna and Desmond talked nonstop on the drive home. Charles was enjoying this immensely; it was like old times for him, bringing back memories of his older brother, who after getting his doctrine in England, taught classes on Environmental Ecology in France. It turned out that Charles lived with his father two streets down. Lawrence Edis was a Professor of Antiquities at the Phieleon Cultural Museum the next town over.

"My Dad is a Professor at the Museum not far from here, the next town over; he may have some connections," said Charles. As he opened the back of the jeep, Mrs. Belk came home and he introduced himself, mentioning that his Grandfather owned the Antiquities Shop on Sephia Avenue. Bits of sun came through one of the clouds.

"It was nice of you to give Anna and Desmond a ride home; I hope you didn't go out of your way."

"My pleasure, Mrs. Belk, I live two streets down and it was still raining."

"How will we find out if you can get the book?" Anna asked. Desmond looked at Charles.

Charles drew out two business cards from his wallet, and gave one to each of them. Then he grabbed a scrap piece of paper from the front seat of the jeep and extracted a pen from the glove compartment.

"Okay, "A-n-n-a B-e-l-k is that correct?" Anna nodded. "And your telephone number?" Anna told him her telephone number. "Okay, well Anna and Desmond, I will help you find a copy of the book any way I can, and as soon as I find out, I'll call you."

"Take my number too," said Desmond, "just incase Anna doesn't have her cell phone with her." Charles wrote it down and placed the paper in his front pocket of his shirt.

Charles drove away as Ellen checked her box for mail. Anna and Desmond put their bikes in the garage. Ellen Belk walked into the kitchen, while Anna was pouring two glasses of iced tea. "Mom, do you want a glass of iced tea?"

"Oh, Anna, I would love a glass of ice tea. Do we have any ice?"

"Yup," Desmond opened the freezer door and located the ice tray. He plopped a few ice cubes into each glass, and sat down with Anna at the kitchen table to talk to her and Aunt Ellen, while she shifted through the mail.

Mrs. Belk looked up from the letters on the table. "What a nice young man, Charles is. So tell me about your day, you two."

Anna and Desmond told her a limited amount of information about the book they were looking for.

"And did you find it at the library? Did you see Mrs. McFinn?"

"No and yes, Mrs. McFinn asked how you were and said to say hello, and that they have the new issue of the Chef's Magazine you were looking for, and do you want her to save it for you. She said this is one of their late nights and you can call her."

"I think I will do that later, thank you Anna. Charles couldn't find the book either?"

Desmond shook his head. "No, we searched The Treasured Friend Bookstore and the books in the Antiquities Shop, and..."

"Nothing," said Anna. Anna put her empty glass in the sink with the breakfast dishes. Desmond followed suit.

"Anyway, Mom, Charles is going to check other resources and then let us know if he comes up with anything. We're going upstairs, on the computer, Mom. What time is supper?"

"I've got it already prepared in the fridge; just have to heat it up in the oven. Hmm, should take about 30 minutes. You can set the table a few minutes before.

"Okay Aunt Ellen." Desmond and Anna ran up the stairs. Mrs. Belk just shook her head and smiled.

Anna fired up her computer; Desmond brought in his laptop and sat on the bed. The book was gone from Anna's computer. She was puzzled, and checked all her files … nothing! It didn't even print earlier.

"I got it!" Desmond jumped up from the bed.

"You got the book?"

"No, but I think I know why you can't get it on the computer all the time. A hologram, I bet the book was a hologram."

"That does make sense, Desmond. Maybe because it isn't something tangible and dense, like us, our bodies, it stayed longer than Jeffery Turner did in the cave, I mean Lorien.

Let's do some research on Rachel Carde, and find out what country she was from.

Chapter 12

"Dr. Rachel Carde, renowned archeologist, retires from the field at age 71." Anna looked up from the computer screen.

"Let's read this article, the 3rd one down, Anna."

"Dr. Rachel Carde began her career in The United States at the age of 15, where she attended excavations with her parents during the summers of her school holidays. It was at this time she decided to follow in the footsteps of her parents, Dr.'s Winston and Maria Carde, who are renowned for their work in Turkey, Peru, Botswana, and North of the Great Lakes region in the United States. Among many other excavations, the Cardes are world renown."

"Numerous articles have been written about the Carde's, but the ones they will always be known and remembered for are the artifacts found near Saintes-Maries-de-la-Mer, along the coast of Southern France,"

Anna looked up from Desmond's computer. "Another coincidence, Anna ...there is something important about that place in France..."

"And Mr. Edis is or was there a few days ago. I wonder what the artifact was, the one he went to bid on during his vacation?" Anna went to her computer to bring up the article. "Let's print it and start a file, we may need it to find out if there is any more information about helping Mr. Turner."

Desmond took the sheet of paper from the computer and read the rest of the article.

"Dr. Rachel Carde's last excavation proved to be a major highlight for The United States and Great Britain. The relics will be on display November 5, 2001, at the Peabody Museum of Archaeology and Ethnology Harvard University, in Cambridge, Massachusetts, and the following month at the Petrie Museum in London, England."

Desmond paused, "I wonder what the artifacts were..."

"Read the rest of the article, Desmond, it might be in there."

"An a Address and Reception will follow on November 19, 2001, at the Science Museum of Natural History in New York City, where Dr. Carde and her husband, Dr. Jeffrey Turner reside. Admission proceeds will benefit the Archeology Department of the Museum. "

"They lived in New York City, Anna!" Desmond was excited. "It's only about 4-5 hours from here."
"I hope they still live in New York City or maybe near there." They could hear a telephone ring

downstairs. After a few minutes, Anna's Mother called from the bottom of the stairs.

"Annnaaa, the telephone is for you. You left it in the foyer. Come downstairs to set the table after."

"Okay Mom, thanks." Anna retrieved her phone and ran upstairs. Desmond sat on the bed waiting.

"Hello? Yes, Hi Charles, Oh no bother at all! ....Oh, yes we can meet you Thursday....at 3:15.... No, that's okay, either Mom can bring us or we can ride our bikes down, we can take the bus if it rains...thank you so much....Ok, bye."

Anna, all smiles, and slightly blushing relayed the message to Desmond. "Charles talked to his grandfather, Mr. Edis. He wants to see us. Charles said he's coming in late from his flight tomorrow, and he is seeing a client Thursday morning. So, Mr. Edis can see us around 3:15."

"Why Anna, did Charles say?"

"He said that his grandfather wanted to talk to us in person. Let's go downstairs to set the table before Mom calls us again."

"K' Desmond shut down his computer, and they both went downstairs to set the table for dinner.

"Anna," said her mom, "Charles got back to you quickly. Did he find the book you're looking for?"

"Not really. Mr. Edis wants to see both of us on Thursday, at 3:15."

"It has to do with the book, Aunt Ellen," added Desmond.

"I called Mrs. McFinn and I am going into town Thursday to pick up the magazine. Hmmm, what a coincidence, I could go in the afternoon."

Ellen Belk placed three stuffed pork chops with a good helping of a healthy salad onto the three plates in front of her, while Anna poured the water into the glasses and Desmond placed the utensils on the table.

"Let me drive you down, I'll drop both of you off, then I'll shoot down to the library. I may stay a while, and chat with Jacqueline. What time would you like me to pick you both up?"

Desmond shrugged his shoulders as Anna lifted her eyebrows in question?

"We're not sure Mom, but can we call you, or you can call us when you're ready to leave."

"I guess that will work," said Ellen Belk. "Alright, let's eat."

After dinner, Anna and Desmond stacked all the dishes into the dishwasher.

"It's been a long day, Anna, and I'm kinda tired, Desmond yawned."

"That's because you probably have jet lag."

"Hmmm....maybe" Desmond wiped down the counter, as Aunt Ellen put the leftovers in the refrigerator.

"Want me to start the car for you Aunt Ellen?"

They were getting ready to go to the Dairy Queen in town.

"Just in one moment Desmond," Aunt Ellen handed Desmond the remote on the keychain. "I need to make a note for tomorrow," and she went into the den for a piece of paper.

Chapter 13

The air was stifling, it was hard to breathe, and Anna looked around. Where was she? It felt like she was somewhere in between. In between dreams? Nothing seemed right. Everything around her felt distorted ...someone ...calling ...her, someone who was familiar ...Desmond?

"Anna, Anna, I can almost see you, where are we? This doesn't look like the cave, are we in a dream? Anna...I can't see you anymore...An, oh Anna, are you there? Desmond was alone, it was hard for him to breathe, then quickly the air seemed to diffuse, and everything was in perfect proportion. The air became breathable and he could actually see Anna.

I can see you now. "

"I can see you too Desmond, I am not sure where we are..."

Then someone spoke. "It is I, the High Elder of our planet. You spoke to The Seer before in your dreams, but now you are in my trance state. Because of the polarity in the weather, we found this was a safer way to contact you. It is still a hologram, but different in our world. I am sorry to cause each of you confusion. We do not mean to frighten you, Desmond and Anna.

"It was a little frightening, I couldn't breathe at first," said Anna.

"I am very sorry about that Anna. Anna, have you found the book of Lorien's yet?"

"No, but we are trying to find it. We may have help. Mr. Edis' grandson Charles said he would help us search for it."

"Ah, yes. Mr. Edis does play a significant part in all of this."

"How?" Desmond inquired.

"Again, the Flyers were very instrumental in relaying the past to us. Mr. Edis may have the book. He is a collector of rare antiquities, even though the book is not a rare book, he does have a connection, we are most certain of this fact... In our trance states, we can see into your world, but little portions at a time. He is a kind man, which we know for certain. This man, Mr. Edis has knowledge of Lorien. The stones he has in his possession, we have been told by the Great Seer, may hold important value to what the keys are intended for. Lorien's book holds this information."

The Elder was fading in and out. "The weather has changed suddenly here, children. We wi... tr... to trans... the b...to....I am afr... we may n... be able to contin..."

Desmond and Anna were alone, and then they faded back into their dreams.

Desmond awoke suddenly. He felt cold and shivered for a few minutes in his bed. It was warm outside, the latter end of the second week of June. He drew the outer bed blanket up over him, and walked into the hall and quietly opened Anna's bedroom door.

"Anna," he whispered, "are you awake?"

"Yeah, come in and close the door so Mom won't wake up." Its cold, isn't it?"

"I was freezing, but my body is starting to warm up now," said Desmond."

"That was freaky," Anna said. At first, I couldn't breathe..."

"Me too, everything was distorted. The Elder said there was a lot of important information in the book. We got to find it Anna. And he knows about the quest stones."

"Yeah, it's weird; especially how they came to us last year...I thought once we brought them to Mr. Edis, he would know what to do with them."

Anna yawned. "I'm really tired Desmond."

"Yeah, I'm bushed, let's talk about this tomorrow. G'night."

"See you in the morning." Anna yawned again and fell fast asleep."

Desmond quietly closed Anna's door, and walked into his bedroom. He climbed back into his bed. Even though he was tired, he had a hard time falling back to sleep. Something about Mr. Edis...hmmm...

Chapter 14

Charles Edis was getting into his jeep, when his cell phone rang. It was early morning, and he was going to the bakery for some morning pastry...

"Hello? Oh, Hi Grandfather. Oh no...I was up, it isn't too early. Yes, I did speak to Anna and her cousin and they can come to the shop by 3:15, you want me there too? No problem, I can rearrange my schedule. Yes, you too Grandfather...see you later."

Charles looked at his watch. He had planned to go kayaking later, but his grandfather said it was imperative for him to be at the meeting also. Hmmm, I wonder why.

It was interesting, no exciting really to have another adventure, thought Charles. I miss Anthony. We used to go on many quests together, hmm, gave Mum and Dad a real fright a few times.

Charles drove down the road reminiscing and humming to himself, when his jeep suddenly stopped right in front of the old quarry. Overgrown hedges and rose bushes hung over the antiquated fence. Usually Charles would love to come here and think, walk around the property, it was peaceful and serene. Sometimes he would take his lunch break here and sit on the huge flat rock to eat his sandwich. The quarry was within a few minutes driving distance from the shop. It was hard to believe that this place of serenity was so close to the main road, yet far enough to block out the main hub of traffic.

But why had his jeep stopped here? What was the significance of this place, now? Charles opened the door of his vehicle and climbed out. He opened the hood to check if any wires had come apart. "Hmm, seems to be in order here, no wires out of place." He checked his fluids..."Okay here. The water and antifreeze are leveled, and the oil light didn't go on, unless there was a fault in the engine light, hmm, I don't understand it."

On the left side, near the gate, to the entrance of the quarry, he thought he saw just a slight flash of light, while he checked his fluids under the hood. There was a second flash as soon as he closed it. Charles cautiously looked around. He went to grab his cell phone from the front seat, when he saw distortions around the rose bushes. It looked like heat rising on a very hot day in the desert.

Charles went to take a closer look. The gate looked strange. Instead of one lock, there were three, and beyond the gate... "it still looks hazy, and where is the quarry? Never saw a lake there before, nor the dense woods, and look at the flowers along... does it look like a path?   What odd colors."

He went to touch the gate to open it, and felt a slight static of electric charge.

"Yeowwww," yelled Charles.   "That smarted. What is going on?" He was perplexed.

Charles went along the side of the fence, to where there were more bushes, grasses and an old crumbling brick wall covered in brambling roses. It wasn't hazy over here. He hesitantly touched part of the wall. Nothing! Walking back to the gate entrance, he saw the haze become brighter; pictures were forming in and out. He could barely recognize them. There was a very old man dressed strangely standing inside. The wind started to gather and gain strength around the what, what was it? Was it a portal of some kind? A sphere? The man seemed to be saying something. It was too windy around it, Charles couldn't hear. It was the oddest thing to see. The inside of the sphere, for lack of a better word was calm, and serene, but on the border of the sphere, was chaos. Where Charles stood, it was sunny out and peaceful. He had never experienced this before.

"Who are you, do you need help?" Charles yelled. The man lifted his hand showing three fingers. He was saying something. The wind was dying down around the haze, the old man was vanishing. Charles thought he said, "Eee..."

"I didn't hear all of it. What do you mean?" Charles was getting anxious. "Who are you?" He shouted again, "Can I help you?"

The haze was gone, along with the view inside the gate, and the old man beyond.

"What did he mean: eee...?" The engine started running again..."Strange," said Charles. He was reluctant and unsure of what to do next. Was it a hologram? The occurrence was mystifying. Almost like a UFO phenomenon without the spaceship, unless the haze was the spaceship... Charles would have to think about it.

"I think I need to tell Grandfather about this. He knows about stuff like this. Charles put his hand out tentatively to where he was electrified earlier... He didn't feel any tingling in his hand; he closed his eyes and touched the leaves on the gate. "Nothing..., nothing at all," he murmured.

Chapter 15

Anna heard a slight buzzing noise. She was almost awake, but not quite. The noise was fading in and out.

"What is that noise?" Anna yawned. It didn't sound like the alarm clock; she looked out from under her covers.

Her alarm clock said 6:06 am, and then she looked at her computer. "I don't believe it," Anna was astonished! She flung the covers off, rushed out of bed and hurried out of her bedroom across the hall to Desmond's door.

She quietly knocked and opened the door. Desmond was asleep. Anna walked over to his bed and gently shook him, whispering; "Des..., Desmond..."

Desmond, opened his eyes, "What is it Anna, is it time to get up? Did I over sleep? Did I miss breakfast?" Desmond was scratching his head, sitting up yawning.

"The book Desmond, The book is back on the computer."

"Wow, Anna, are you sure?" Desmond was getting more alert.

"Yes, come on, before we lose it again."

Desmond and Anna quietly crossed the hallway into Anna's room. Anna took the laptop and sat on the bed, Desmond was beside her in a flash. Anna scrolled down to where she thought they left off from the other day.

Desmond adjusted the screen. They read on.

When I awoke the next morning, I felt refreshed and ready to go. I had a date with Rachel Carde...or I should say meeting. Dash it all, she was elegantly refreshing. She didn't look much older than I'd say hmmm twenty-two, twenty-four? And she was beautiful. What was I going to do until two in the afternoon?

Anna said, "I think this is where we left off."

"It is." Desmond nodded.

The clock read 7:57. I quickly bathed and dressed. I went to the room where I found the breakfast buffet. Hmmm, Rachel wasn't here. I remembered she had a lot of paperwork to catch up on and I certainly knew all about that. I chuckled to myself...

"Well. What have we here, Eggs Benedict I presume?" I scanned the buffet table with delight.

"Oh yes sir," said the Waiter. We have fresh lox, oysters, and smoked kippers. Potato fries, or as they say in America, sir, home fries!

"Yeeess," I cajoled

 "There are a variety of eggs, toast, waffles, creamed and dry cereal, fresh fruit and fresh fruit salad, nothing but the best for our passengers' sir."

Anna and Desmond looked at each other and wrinkled their noses. "Oysters, smoked kippers for breakfast," Desmond emphasized. They read on.

There was a slight tapping on the door. "Anna, Desmond, since you are up, I am going to make breakfast, what would you like me to make?"

"FLAPJACKS," Anna and Desmond said in unison. They looked at each other laughing.

"Sounds good, I am going to shower, come down in about forty minutes."

"Ok, Mom."

"K, Aunt Ellen."

"It's still on, Anna, lets read some more."

"Let's get dressed first, Anna said, and I'm going to try and copy it, Mom got ink for my printer yesterday."

Desmond quickly went to his room to change his clothes.

When Desmond came back, Anna was dressed looking perplexed.

"What's wrong Anna?"

I don't understand this Desmond; the pages are coming out blank. The printer is registering ink, but it is still blank.

"That confirms it's a hologram, Anna!"

"Let's read more before it's gone again, Des."

"K."

I carried my plate of food to the deck, where tables were elegantly set up for breakfast. Ahhhh, I took in the fresh ocean air. A slight breeze, warm sun, and later Rachel Carde...this will be a capital day, I thought!

After breakfast, I sat in the sun, the air felt a little brisk, the month only being May, but the sun felt quite warm and comfortable. I was settling down with a novel I brought with me. I must have dozed off...

Did I have a vision, or was I dreaming. Who were the two children that are riding bikes? Their ages, maybe 12, or 14, the bikes, the cars, they look a little modern, perhaps? The other person looked familiar...can't quite make the whole thing out. Where is this place? And, how did I get here?

Oh, here it goes yet again, I was back in the cave. There was the same man standing in front of me, similar to the dream I had the other night. He was by himself. He looked anxious and spoke to me.

"Lorien, we only have a few moments, the energies are higher and I must speak quickly, since you are not quite in a dream state. Beware of your twin; yes you do have a twin. He was with you when you went through the portal many years ago. He may be your brother, but he does not have good intentions at this time in his life. He thought he was rid of you, until his spies found out you have a possibility of coming back to us. This is why you were chosen. He has a different destiny that he is unaware of and has strayed off his path. There are others who he is in allegiance to and they will try to stop you from coming back to us. He has been heavily influenced. We know there are those who want him to be the next Elder. He has gone over to the Anoa, who have made promises to him we know they will not keep. It is because of his nature, that he does not see their treachery. In our parallel world he is very much younger than you are in the earth dimension you are now in, but he could still cause damage. Here our spies, the Flyers are observing his every move."

There are some secrets only an Elder can control; the knowledge of this is only transferred to the next elder."

The Seer paused...

I did not know how to respond, a twin brother? Treachery? Secrets? I let him continue.

"Lorien, you saw a vision of two children?"

"Why yes I did, what does that have to do with me?"

"They are in your future, 2011, by then you will be much older. They will help you get back to us."

"That's us!!! Desmond yelled out...

"That's incredible, Desmond, were in the story!" Anna said excitedly.

They both looked back at the computer screen to continue.

"Aaanna, Desmond," yelled Ellen Belk from the stairs.

"Oh great, is it time for breakfast already? ...Coming Mom."

Anna and Desmond met Ellen Belk at the top of the stairs. She had her purse in her hand.

"I forgot to get eggs last night; I'm just going to Mercer's Grocers to pick up a few things before breakfast. Your breakfast will be delayed, are you both really hungry?"

That's okay Aunt Ellen., we're not really hungry yet."

Anna was shaking her head no. "We're reading something on the computer, Mom."

"Honestly, has Anna roped you into one of her stories Desmond?" Aunt Ellen laughed, "I'll be right back!"

"K, Mom, we'll be up here, Bye!" Anna and Desmond were smiling.

They ran back into Anna's room to read as much of The Epic Catalog as they could before breakfast.

Chapter 16

"And my twin...?" Jeffery asked

"Your twin is known as Thereon. He is still in our world. Your father in our world is The High Elder. Thereon had thought since you were gone; he would be the next elder, because of the lineage, but now he knows differently."

"The Anoans do not understand the Nature of our world. If they gain control, the balance between our world and yours may be lost. The Anoa may have found a way to create chaos in the portals and we suspect that their control may infiltrate some types of energy in your world, so beware of this Lorien; this League will bring chaos to both our peaceful worlds."

"All is not lost yet, if we can get you back in time Lorien, then we have a chance. It is your power within your lineage that will hold the balance of the seven atmospheres of Neia. Your DNA and body system contain the right elements that correspond to the peace and tranquility here."

"I am known as The Seer. I am able to go into your time zone on earth, through your memory and the work of crystals; we can travel in this way, but not bodily. It is known as astral travel in the world you are in, only we are fully conscious when we travel, we are not asleep."

 "But," Jeffery hesitated, "What? Not again! ...he's gone!"

Then the vision or dream switched off. Another picture was forming, the sun was glaring. I was hearing voices, "Sir, sir? Are you Mr. Jeffery Turner? Sir?"

I awoke with a start. My sunglasses must have fallen off. I looked up and saw someone in between me and the sun, bright light all around the head, kept saying: "Sir, sir..."

As I became fully awake, there appeared to be some slight confusion. What in the world? "Is everything all right, I asked? Is there something the matter?"

"Sir, are you Mr. Jeffery Turner?"

"Yes, yes I am."

"Sir, I have an urgent telegram for you. I am to await your reply."

Chapter 17

I hurried to the Ship's Bridge, to send a telegram. The message was upsetting and urgent. Father had been struck by a vehicle and was in hospital. I needed to get back to London.

Captain Parlae' was very kind. He sent a telegram back for me. The ship was due to dock in the Bahamas by early evening, around 7:19 pm. I had to book a flight to England. Captain Parlae' telegraphed the international airport, and reserved a flight home for me scheduled at 9:45 pm on the Trans World Airline, or known as TWA.

With the flight secured and a telegram sent to my Mother, I was rest assured that I would be able to get on the next flight scheduled once we reach the Bahamas.

It was 10:45 am. Since it was early enough, I decided to walk around the deck of the ship. I had to think, put all of the unusual in order of perception. It was curious, how…, what was he called the, hmmm, The Seer, how I felt when The Seer said I had a twin. I sort of identified with it. It was if I had known, what is that saying? Oh yes, out of sight, out of mind. "Out of sight, out of mind, hmmm"

"I beg your pardon," said a woman standing next to me.

"Whhaat, "I asked absentmindedly? I looked down to ...what in the world was that? Is she walking a mini powder puff?

"Did you ask me a question?" The woman looked concerned.

"Oh, I am terribly sorry, I was just thinking out loud." Just then the powdery waif came around the other side of the lady and barked, danced a little and barked again.

"Oh, What a dear, my little mootsie wootsie wants to play. How sweeeet!"

"Again, I am terribly sorry...." I walked away as fast as I could. Mootsie wootsie, egads!!! I took special care of my surroundings from then on.

After some introspection, I came up with a conclusion. There is more to this anomaly than I understood and Rachel Carde may put some of the pieces of the mystery together. I had looked forward to spending some time with her, especially today. But now... the Bahamas, talking, swimming, dining...hmm, very unfortunate, but I must go to London, I am worried about Father.

Rachel and I met on the deck, near the pool at two o'clock. She was carrying a sheaf of papers and I was a little distracted, which she noticed right away. We sat at a table near the pool, at that time I was ready for a beverage, but had a cup of tea instead.

During our respite, I told Rachel about my father's accident.

"I am very sorry Jeffery, Is there anything can I do?" she asked.

I shook my head, "I have to fly home as soon as we dock in the Bahamas; it looks like my holiday is over, for now. I don't mind really. My parents are more important, but I would like to go over some new developments before I leave in the evening."

Rachel looked up, she met my eyes, and I told her about the vision or dream after breakfast. I showed her the contents inside the envelope. I didn't want to take them out. The contents had an illuminating glow about them. We stared into the envelope for about a minute, touching the keys, cloth and paper.

"Amazing, I've never seen anything like this." Rachel's instinctive side was cautious. "Are we safe?"

"Well ...it appears so. I've been looking and touching them periodically." As I fastened the envelope securely, I remembered my dream or so called dream, and relayed it to Rachel.

"Funny though," I told her, "I didn't dream last night about any of this, just the dream came when I dozed off while reading my novel earlier."

"Jeffery, would you mind if I came with you? I could go to France from London."

Was she kidding? I could only hope, "but Rachel, what about your holiday? What about your rest from your last dig?"

As I read in the paper, she had been there for at least seven months!

"Oh, I am getting rest, and there are some things we need to discuss and figure out, I had a strange dream again last night. The location, I didn't recognize, it was, well, dramatic, and the vehicle, I had never seen one like it before. It was about a young man, who appeared to have been electrocuted from an old fence covered in roses, although I could not make out where and why. An image of an elderly man I saw in my first dream suddenly appeared on the grounds fading in and out. I am very curious though to hear more from you, Jeffery, but first, could we book an extra flight to England tonight? I would like to go with you, if you didn't mind," Rachel looked earnestly into my eyes.

That did it! We went to see the Captain. He was making the rounds to see if everyone was comfortable and if they were in need of anything.

Rachel and I followed Captain Parlae' to the bridge of the Queen Mary, he radioed International Airlines in the Bahamas to inquire about the seating on TWA. There was room on the plane.

By then it was 4:00 in the afternoon. Rachel went back to her cabin to pack and I followed suit in my own cabin.

There isn't much to tell about the evening. I was very troubled about Father, but resigned to enjoy the food and the conversations around our dinner table. After dinner, Rachel and I walked along the promenade, of the ship.

At 7:01 pm, Captain Parlae' announced the ship was arriving in the Bahamas costal waters. Rachel & I went to our cabins to get our luggage ready for the Porter; we said our goodbyes to some of the people we met at dinner and during the day. The Queen Mary made it into the harbor by 7:16.

We were driven to the International Airport from the pier. I was beside myself with joy. I looked at Rachel as she looked out the window of the car. Her facial features were very petite; beautiful...I was feeling something, a schoolboy crush perhaps; I looked away, to view the sights from my window.

"Jeffery, I've been thinking about the conversation regarding this afternoon. What if my vision has something to do with the future also? I mean, what if I am involved in some way too?"

"I'm not sure, it is possible, and why else would we be having comparable dreams?" It is still new to me also, Rachel, and a complete mystery."

"Hmmm, we need more Jeffery, more information, more clues as to how this is really happening…I've heard of portals before, it has the makings to be a science fiction, but we know it is real. It's happening to us."

"Yes, Rachel, it does appear to be a science fiction story, but I am starting to remember incidences and things I had forgotten completely as a child. Rachel, it's starting to come back!"

We arrived at the International Airport at 8:15. Now we waited to board the Trans World Airway for 9:15 pm.

"Uh-oh," Desmond groaned; "The page is fading in and out." Then the computer went blank.

"Hmmm," Anna looked at her watch. "Let's go downstairs and see if the flapjacks are ready.

Anna turned off the computer, and they went downstairs to have breakfast.

Chapter 18

There was a slight stirring, a breeze, bringing relief to the long sun days on Neia. The days were longer than that of Earth. To the Neians, a parallel world of Earth, experiences of time had no relevance at all. It was if time stood still. One year on Neia was equivalent to 2,013.06 days Earth time.

Humidity was unheard of as temperatures would soar well into the 80's Fahrenheit of Earth. The Neian climate emitted electromagnetic radiation, as exposed by light particles, causing a fluorescent terrain. Lush forest plants were dense; as the early hours refreshed the planet as water fell every day quenching the plants and vegetation. A protective covering from the seven atmospheres thwarted intense heat from the 2 suns in the solar system. This helped the ecosystem immensely.

Harsh winters were never heard of in Neia, just the relief of the season of the sun. Neian bodies were of a higher vibration and the sun hadn't any effect on them at all. The season of the sun was nearly over, temperatures would be slightly cooler, and portals would open for other dimensions, except for that of Earth. The portal opened for 1 hour Earth time, every century or s0, the same for Neia. The way the energies will flow on July, 11, 2011, Earth time and Neia time, an hour before midnight, the point in time were exactly the same. Almost as if the Universe were coming from opposite ends to zero point.

This time lapse happened every 700 years in Neia, more than 100 years in Earth time. The waiting was the difficult part. If only Orisen found the formula earlier.

The balance of Neia continued, if they could not get Lorien bodily, all would be lost. As long as the Elders resonated together, there would be balance and harmony. It was within their lineage or DNA code that the planet kept steady, constant and unwavering.

Ever since Neia existed, the Elders existed. The Elders' energy was of a higher metabolism, which caused the atmospheres or aura in the sky to connect smoothly. There are seven vibrational atmospheres. The atmospheres communicate a level of information to each Elder. Neia has seven Elders, each one held the atmospheres along with their own DNA in the region they resonated with. Each Elder vibration carried a certain tone or code, and all of the tones together, reflected off different surfaces of the atmospheres resulting in the balance of the planet.

Ferian was the oldest of the Elders. In twenty years; Lorien would become the Elder of his region. He must get Lorien back. Ten years training would have to do. Time was running out for the portal to open during the Earth years of July 11, 2011, the next time it would open. The Seer had been working night and day with the Translators of Energy to regulate the mathematical formula.

They were indeed very lucky the envelope translated to Lorien when it did. It was a small window of time that helped with the holographic transfer There was an 8 second window to go through without harm. It was too bad that it wasn't feasible to grab Lorien and bring him back. Without the correct dosage of energy, and it only being a half hologram Lorien and Basquiere would have disintegrated. Ferian couldn't take a chance like that.

Basquiere had come from the planet Thetre. He volunteered to help on his way back skipping dimensions. He had hologramed from his space shuttle from another dimension. He couldn't appear on Earth from Neia, it wasn't possible at this time. The Translators of Energy had assured the Neians that he was not in any danger.

The contents of the envelope will help. Hopefully, Lorien put the envelope in a safe place. The others involved on Earth, have the right energy. They are different than us, some, part of our own lineage, yet their energy does resonate with ours, we are very fortunate!

It has been over 14 years, since Lorien had been pushed out of our world into the Earth existence.

In Earth years he will now be about 73 years old, when Lorien comes back to us, because of the codes, DNA and molecular structure; he will be 25 years old here. Oh my son, how I have missed you!

Ferian reminisced a few moments longer. July 11, 2011, will be exactly 14.9 years, we will try to bring him back, no... we must, Ferian thought. The .9 was very important in the mathematical equations, Orisen, one of the top Translators of Energy, had come up with the formula equation that works. This formula will bring our beloved Lorien back to us, and then ten years of training...will it be enough?

The Elders and the Council Members, along with the Seer, and the Translators of Energy met in the middle of Similjeun Mountains, the most sacred, secret place of the planet. There is a passage, halfway up the mountain, you cannot see by the naked eye. Only an Elder has the ability to see the insignia along the central base. Only an Elder knows the very sacred secret formula to translate into the mountain. It is within the code of their DNA. For two years, the Anoa had been trying to find out, but they are not aware that The Elders can see their every move, hear their conversations. An Elder has that ability. Any energy used to thwart the system brings a silent caution to The Elders' vibration and immediately sends out an extra shield of protection. Not even my beloved Meriasa knows. It is the vow each Elder takes, no one, no one must know, until another Elder is of age, then the secret is revealed to him.

Lorien will not know this information until the energy shift translates from Ferian to him. Then he will instantly know. He will become one of the Seven Living Libraries of the planet.

Chapter 19

Desmond swirled his piece of flapjack around the maple syrup in his plate.

It is happening again, last year was the first time he and Anna really connected, became friends. They had been through a lot. It was a real adventure. He had often wondered several times back at home if it was all true, did it really happen. The mention of the quest stones from Charles brought it back into perspective again.

Now they had Charles, Mr. Edis' grandson, looking for the book. Mr. Edis had lived in London. He had a wife whose family had moved to the States and then Mr. Edis moved here long ago. He has a sister in London, and he went to Saintes-Maries-de-la-Mer in France just recently. There is a connection somewhere...hmmm...but what?

"Desmond, you were a million miles away...what's up?" Anna asked.

Desmond came back to reality. "Just trying to put some pieces of the puzzle together, and just thinking about the quest stones and Mr. Edis."

Ellen Belk look up from her morning paper, after hearing Desmond say Mr. Edis.

"Remember, be ready for 2:40 this afternoon, it will take about 20 minutes to cross traffic in town, I'll drop you off to Mr. Edis' Antiquities Store and it will give you enough time for the meeting this afternoon. What project are you actually working on now Anna?"

"Top Secret Mom," Anna replied happily as she ate another bite of her flapjack.

"Hmmm," Ellen Belk laughed, "Just don't destroy anything this year, Anna and Desmond. She went back to reading another article in the paper.

"It's not that type of project, Mom! Okay if we ride our bikes down to Rose Cottage this morning? What time is it Desmond?" Anna couldn't see the hands on his watch.

"9:27." Desmond looked more energetic after hearing the words Rose Cottage. They didn't discuss what he and Anna would do after breakfast, but Rose Cottage would be top on his list...Desmond checked his jeans pocket to make sure he had his wallet.

Ellen Belk looked up from the paper, "It sounds like a great idea Anna, I have another errand to run before noon today so...hmm, be back for lunch, say, around 12:30, alright Anna, and Desmond?

Anna and Desmond were cleaning up their breakfast area, "Yup," they said simultaneously.

"Can we leave the dishes, or do you want us to do them now, Aunt Ellen?"

"Better do them now," Ellen replied, "You may not have time after lunch."

Anna frowned. "K," said Desmond.

Chapter 20

The day was absolutely perfect. How much more perfect could you get? Rose Cottage was a 15-minute bike ride from Anna's house. Desmond loved Rose Cottage. Funky shop, rocks, unusually rad souvenirs, camping supplies, root beer floats; one of his all time favorites, specialties, onion rings deep fried to perfection, or thick wedged French fries, gourmet coffee, pastries, trails out back with Airedale Point Gorge to the right, kayaking, water rafting the list was endless. On the trails, you would enter caverns that had stalagmites protruding from the roof 0f the caves, reflecting in the little brooks that ran through them. Desmond was in his element. He was going to study Geology when he went to college.

Desmond loved the Gorge. And after 10am kayaking and water rafting would be available.

"Do you want to go kayaking, Anna?" Desmond shouted out as Anna passed him.

"Dunno." She rode into a large parking area off the road and stopped. Grand Gorge View Observation Point was the place for tourists when they wanted to gaze out on part of the Airedale Point Gorge to take pictures. It was if the area was saying: "Fix your eyes on this..." Anna stood on the ground and looked at the view. She thought she spotted two eagles, but it was too far to tell. She turned to Desmond.

"I want to see Mrs. Perpecuwitz." Anna waited for Desmond to stop next to her. "Last week, before you came, I went to see her about some new words. She said something puzzling, and I wanted to ask her more about it." I didn't think about it until this morning, during breakfast."

Anna had a literary friend, Mrs. Perpecuwitz. She had made an herbal tea remedy for Anna, three years ago when she became very ill. Her recovery was almost instantaneous. By the end of the day, she felt so much better, and after a night's sleep, she was back to her old self again. It was hard to believe. Anna had been sick for one week and seemed to be getting worse. Mrs. Belk had run into Rose Cottage for a brochure of an upcoming event on the way home from the Doctor's visit with Anna, and Mrs. Perpecuwitz listened to the symptoms and made up a special herbal tea remedy. The remedy was spot on!

When Anna went in to thank her after her first day back to school from being so sick, Mrs. Perpecuwitz made a special Root Beer Float for Anna on the house for a complete recovery. There were not any customers at the moment, and Anna to her good fortune found out that Mrs. Perpecuwitz was a literary genius! Since that day, Anna would get some really great words passed to her, like spies do in the movies, on a folded piece of paper marked TOP SECRET and her assignment was to write a story using the words on the paper.

Anna and her Mom loved Mrs. Perpecuwitz. She was a strange lady. No one really knew where she was from, or if she had any family around, she seemed to have been there forever; at least that is what the locals said!

"So Anna, what was so puzzling last week?" Desmond asked.

"Mrs. Perpecuwitz said to be careful of the energy this coming week, especially around the old quarry." I'm not sure what she meant. "

"That is a little strange, but Mrs. Perpecuwitz is a little eccentric, isn't she? Desmond took bottled water out of his back pack and offered one to Anna.

"Thanks, Des." Anna took a sip and handed it back to Desmond. "And, she also gave me the words and phrases that brought up The Epic Catalog on the laptop. Could be just a coincidence"....then stopped herself and laughed.

"There are no coincidences!!!!" Anna and Desmond shouted at the same time, both laughing. "Just like the Shaman Guide said last year!" Anna reiterated.

"That is astonishing," commented Desmond. "Anna, this is starting to become like another adventure, almost what happened last year."

"Yeah, that was unbelievable. Sometimes I wondered if it really happened, Desmond, but then I look at the stone amulet I'm wearing, and I know it was for real. Do you still have yours?"

Desmond took out his stone amulet from under his t-shirt, "Yup, never take it off, unless I really have to."

"Me neither," said Anna. "Let's ride on; it will just be a few minutes before we get there."

Anna and Desmond had an adventurous summer last year. One that they had never experienced before; but that is another story, is it not?

Chapter 21

Rose Cottage was packed. A tour group passing along on the highway took a detour to get to the famous landmark before going on to their destination. They had just arrived 40 minutes before Anna and Desmond.

Mrs. Perpecuwitz looked up and smiled at Anna and Desmond from the counter, as they came in the door. You can never miss anyone coming in the door with the three sets of chimes ringing before a live audience, which bizarrely added to the charm that everyone loved...something about this area...something ethereal ... magical...

"Hello Anna!" Mrs. Perpecuwitz looked at Desmond, trying to recall his name..."and..."

"Desmond," said Desmond waving!

"Oh, how could I ever forget? Anna's cousin. So glad you are here for the month, is that correct?"

"Yes, Mrs. Perpecuwitz, actually I will be here for about a month and a half..."

"Very good, so great to see you both...I have loads of customers now, but I think their bus is leaving in an hour. Anna, you look like you would like to discuss something with me, so I will be available in about an hour."

"Ok, Mrs. Perpecuwitz, we'll go kayaking to the caverns," Anna replied.

"It's on me, Anna," said Desmond, "Mom said to share some of this with you." Desmond took out his visa card from his wallet and gave it to Carl who ran the card through.

"Thanks, man," Carl gave Desmond back his card along with a receipt and two tickets for the kayaks. Luckily no one in the tour group wanted a kayak.

"Thanks Desmond," Anna smiled. She loved to go down the small river to the caverns. The white water rafting was contained to the swiftly flowing river on the other side of the road.

Desmond and Anna went to the Kayak Shack; picked out the ones they wanted along with life preservers. It was a bright sunny day, the birds were singing, it was a day nature was at its best in.

When Anna and Desmond arrived at the Caverns, they found some of the tour group roaming around, taking photos of the stalagmites, some towering the roof of the caverns. Light came through small openings on the roof. When the sun reached slightly over half the sky, around 1:07, colors danced like rainbows from all directions in the cavern. The guide taking some of the tour group around just finished explaining this, and heard sighs and "Ohhhh, we'll be gone by then," etc. "Maybe we should stay a little while longer," said another. "Yes, we are just on our way home," another quipped. The Driver had different ideas.

"Excuse me folks, remember the train you need to catch at 6:58 pm. Everyone is booked for the Dinner Ride this evening before you get to your next destination in New York. I'm going to drive the bus there while you are on the train.

"Oh, yes, what fun," said a lady who was closer to the water. She then looked at other vacationers not from the tour group and said, "We've been traveling all week to several destinations. The Dinner Ride is near the end of our trip." Another traveler added, "After the ride, the Driver will pick us up at the station and bring us to a hotel booked in the area, and then in the morning, we drive back home to Upper State New York. A lot of ohhs and good lucks went around then everyone started to move on. The guide, who just noticed Anna and Desmond, waved while talking to the group. They waved back.

Anna looked at the group of people. They were an older crowd, but seemed fun and very energetic. "Let's go further down Anna," Desmond whispered.

After the fifth bend Desmond kayaked to the cavern shore, if you would call it that. Sunlight entered through openings on the roof causing luxurious grass to grow in small areas making it look inviting to stretch your legs and sit for a while. They both docked their kayaks and sat on a patch of grass. It would take the group about 15 to 20 minutes to get to this spot.

"So," said Anna, "let's talk about some of the occurrences from the last couple of days."

"Well, it seems when we need more, the book appears on the laptop," Desmond said.

"And there were the phrases that Mrs. Perpecuwitz gave me last week. Do you think she knows something about the book, Desmond?"

"I dunno, maybe. What strikes me funny is the fact that there is a lot of mystery here and the fact that Mr. Edis is somehow also involved...and his grandson Charles knows about the Quest Stones," Desmond was speculating.

"It's like we were chosen, that it was predestined. We were mentioned in the book," Anna looked around the caverns, the light and the reflection from the water and the stalagmites; illumination and radiance dancing on the water....it was very enchanting. "I like the fact that Charles is helping; the more people who help, the better the chances for us getting a hold of the book."

"Do you think we should tell Aunt Ellen, Anna? Maybe she knows someone at the school who would know where to get the book if we can't get it."

"Not yet Desmond," Anna turned her head. "Let's wait after the meeting with Mr. Edis later this afternoon."

"Hmmm, ok"...just then they heard voices from the far end of the other side of the cave.

"Let's continue on and go through Hanson's turnaround when we get out of the caverns. I want to go back to the Cottage, Desmond; maybe Mrs. Perpecuwitz is available now."

Chapter 22

Charles had gone to the pastry shop and back home again. The morning was beautiful; maybe he should take out his kayak and go down the river early. It was only 9:35.

Charles found his father in the kitchen area pouring a cup of coffee, "Would you like a cup of coffee Charles?"

"I'm not sure Dad, I was thinking of going kayaking down the river, soon. Grandfather wanted me to come in later today for a special meeting."

"Whatever is that father of mine up to these days, Charles?" Lawrence Edis smiled shaking his head as he sat down to have his breakfast. Charles handed him the bag of pastries.

"Thank you Charles." He took out one and placed it on a napkin next to his cereal. He handed the bag back to Charles.

"It seems to be a start of a mystery, Dad; at least that's how the situation is becoming. Two young teens, about 13 to 14 came into the Antiquities Shop the other day and inquired about a book that has appeared to be off the shelves for quite sometime. We looked for the book and Grandfather didn't have it in the store."

"Ah, your grandfather called me yesterday; he's back from his trip. He found something important for the Museum. What is the book, Charles?"

"It's called: The Epic Catalog, Dad."

"Hmm," said Lawrence Edis, sipping his coffee.

"It is curious, Dad especially some events that happened within the last couple of days."

Lawrence's cell phone rang. "Ah the cell phone, hmm, must be the Museum." He looked at the number to see who it was, "ahh...it can wait, what events, Charles?"

"Well, you know the old quarry on Perrine Lane?"

"Yes, I do Charles, It's been closed for about 20 years, is that the place you are referring to?"

"Yes, well, when I drove by it on my way to Sephia's Pastries this morning, my engine stopped."

"Wait a minute, this isn't one of those close encounter stories is it Charles?"

"No, Dad, nothing like that. It's just that the gate started to go hazy and there was some sort of energy thing going on and..."

The cell phone rang again. "Hmm, you may want to talk to your Grandfather about this, he is the science major in the family." The cell phone kept ringing.

"Dad, aren't you going to answer it?"

No Charles, I am not. We are still having a conversation, and I want to finish my breakfast and do some errands before I go in this afternoon to the museum. It can wait."

Lawrence broke apart the pastry, a delectable whiff took over his nostrils and he sighed.

Charles decided to have a cup of coffee and a pastry after that demonstration. He poured his coffee and refilled his father's cup.

Lawrence, looking very appreciative, continued, "Did you check the oil and fluids under the hood?"

"Yes, that's when I noticed the haze outside a sphere and a flash of light, it was a little peculiar, Dad, it looked like the energy was moving around through the gate, I even felt an electric shock when I touched the roses around the gate."

"Definitely a science question for your grandfather, did you say you were going there this afternoon, and how do you feel now, after that shock?"

"I'm ok, Dad, at first I was a little shaky, but I'm fine now."

"Definitely a paranormal experience, do you have any ideas what could have cause all that electricity to be at the gate? The weather's perfect today, and the newscaster didn't comment on a storm coming our way. It is curious."

"It was almost like a portal, a vortex or something to that effect. I saw images and an old man, and there was a storm brewing inside the property of the gate. He was trying to say something, but the air was full of electric charge. And as fast as it happened, it stopped. Everything was back to normal, as if nothing happened at all. My engine started up again. It was a little bizarre, Dad."

"Well Charles, in the past you have been known to have some wild adventures when Anthony was around, I think this is a case for my father to help you solve. It's out of my league."

"Yes, I intend to ask him later. Are there any more strawberries? I think I'll have a bit of granola before I go kayaking."

Chapter 23

Anna and Desmond took their time going back to the Cottage. John Bartley saw them make the steep climb toward the hill where the information booth was located; he worked there during the summer vacations. He was 3 years older than Anna, and lived three houses down from her.

"Hey, Anna,"

"Hi John," said Anna smiling

"And haaay, Des, man, how's it goin? Back, huh?"

"Hey John, good, yeah, this time I'm here for about a month & a half, just went kayaking..."

"Quite a crowd this morning," said John looking around the grounds, "about 43 people on the tour bus."

"Do you know when they're leaving? I wanted to see Mrs. Perpecuwitz about something," Anna asked.

John looked at his day planner scanning it for any extra activities scheduled. "Hmm, not quite sure Anna. I think I overheard the driver tell some of the group that the bus was leaving in about 45 minutes, but that was a little while ago. They should be, probably, I'd say, they got another 10 minutes to go."

"Thanks, John. Are you going to the Trails this year with Josh?" Josh was John's brother who was the guide for the tour group.

John was seventeen and Josh was sixteen years old. They had been planning to go to the Trails for a while. They bought a special set of walkie talkies for the trip and you could hear them communicating to each other throughout the grounds of Rose Cottage.

Rose Cottage, busy for this time of year was full to capacity when a large van of sightseers pulled in as Desmond and Anna walked through the entrance of the bakery. Mrs. Perpecuwitz had many employees in the summer. One of the employees was on the look out for Anna & Desmond.

"Hi Desmond and Anna," it was Calla C. That's how she introduced herself last year when Desmond bumped into her near the postcards. When he turned around, he was in love. Calla C was about the same age as Desmond and Anna. Her family spent the summer as residents at the campground. Calla C's parents were hired to work at the white water rafting station. They were both college professors from another state, but loved Rose Cottage and the surrounding area so much, they spent their summers there.

Mrs. Perpecuwitz gave Calla C odd jobs to do and gave her spending money, since she hung around most of the time. She would say: "I just love the energy of this place Mrs. Perpecuwitz, I just can't stay away!" She was eight years old going on thirty the first summer she came. Now she was almost thirteen.

"Mrs. Perpecuwitz is in the cellar, going over the stock, she said to go down there when you both come in." Calla's eyes lingered a little longer on Desmond. He sighed happily.

Thanks Calla C," said Anna. She grabbed Desmond's arm and pushed him in front of her.

Desmond gave Anna the look and turned to Calla as he was being pushed downstairs. "Thanks Calla, he said as he went through the doorway.

"You're welcome; see you both when you come back up," Calla said above the commotion of voices that just entered the Cottage.

Chapter 24

The Elders sat in a large semi circular room. Images were forming on the wall. The Seer, Guardia and the Translators of Energy were expected to give an announcement. Ferian spoke.

"My Esteemed Elders of the regions of Neia, time is drawing near. Guardia and Translators of Energy have important new developments for us."

At hearing their names, The Seer, and The Translators of Energy looked up from their work and acknowledged the Elders.

"We are all here," Ferian stated, "and yes, Ranier has indeed made an important discovery." At hearing his name, Ranier stood up and began to create a 3D interactive virtual hologram in the air in front of him.

"Esteemed Elders, We have tested and proven that certain formulas, when applied to the electrical field of the human Earth body, master spatial relationships creating the illusion of depth which is 3 dimensional. Since Earth inhabitants are within a 3 dimensional universe, we were able to measure the volume of energy in height, depth and width."

"What does this mean, Ranier? The portal in which Lorien will come through is still very magnetic, and motionless, it has caused an immense amount of static, very electrical static, for a human body to translate here, it would be for naught," the Elder Lestrian was concerned.

"Ahhh, Esteemed Elder, Lestrian, that is a very good observation, and we were trying to come up with a formula, in fact to the precise detail, until Orisen realized one point. Lorien does not have an Earth human body."

The Elders commented, "Indeed, we were looking in the wrong direction all these years. Ranier, where is Orisen?" Ferian inquired.

"He is in the Dimensional Room. We assembled this meeting with you to tell you that we think because Lorien has a Neian body; we know how to get him back unharmed. The last time you tried to speak to an earth inhabitant, Ferian, the weather around the vortex in which you astral projected was wild and fierce, did not the earth human feel the electric current?"

"Indeed he did Ranier, He was not able to hear my message, but hearing your words, have filled us with hope. The Earth dimension is very dense and intense and our molecular constitution is lighter and more fifth dimensional, can we use the portal in the area were the girl and boy dwell. Will it work?"

"It will work with the stones," Orisen, coming into the room, stated with actuality. There is a stone on earth which is comprised of cryptocrystalline; it is a form of silica. Silica is composed of very fine intergrowths of the mineral quartz and moganite."

"What does this mean, Orisen," asked the Elder Gradian.

Orisen began to work with the hologram, showing the Elders the structure of the stone they needed.

"Quartz and moganite are both silica minerals, but they differ in that quartz has a trigonal crystal structure and moganite is monoclinic. The chemical structure is based on the spatial arrangement of atoms and molecules and the patterns they make in certain types of energy and harsh amounts of heat. The energy we are dealing with collaborates with the atoms and molecules of this particular stone."

Orisen paused for a second, rearranging the hologram into a complex in-depth form. "The trigonal or more pointed crystal forms into groups and the monoclinic, a flatter structure, may be unequal in length, they form a rectangular prism, with a parallelogram at its base.

The hologram showed adjacent sides of unequal lengths and angles where they were slightly slanting, with two parallel sides, connecting in the middle.

"These stones have peculiar qualities. Many centuries ago, this stone was native to a dimension that many humans crossed over to and back from. They had no knowledge of this dimension, just that the land was more fertile, and the weather conditions were unlike anywhere else on Earth. The dimension has now been closed for about 3, 000 Earth years now, and the stone they brought back was a crystal-like carnelian."

"This form of chalcedony is common on Earth, but the two stones, in the form of carnelian, have this molecular structure with the quality that breaks down electrical energy, or transmutes it. We are not sure, where the two powerful carnelian-like stones come from but we have knowledge they are in the possession of the girl and boy who will help Lorien cross back into our dimension."

"Ferian stood up, thank you Orisen. We are in your dept..."

"It is important for the welfare of our planet, my friend, Ferian, that Lorien come back, you are quite welcome. We now will measure and define the amount of electromagnetic fields around other points of the Earth for Lorien's exit. If at some point he doesn't make it, there is a small window of time that can be worked with because of the .9 in the formula. We will let you know at a later date."

The images on the wall disappeared and the Elders took council and concentrated on the atmospheric pressure, helping to regulate and protect the flora and vegetation vital to the planet.

Chapter 25

Audrey Perpecuwitz was stacking boxes of supplies; a shipment was due to come in early in the afternoon. The Lights of the Riviera Party in three in half weeks was a big occasion every year. Boxes and storage material had to be moved to make room.

"Hello, Anna & Desmond, I'm making room for the shipment coming in later. Now, Anna, you wanted to ask me some questions, and we will not be disturbed or interrupted here. How can I help you, dear?"

Desmond walked toward a box of coffee filters, "Would you like us to help move some of the boxes from the counter area, Mrs. Perpecuwitz?"

"Oh, Yes! Thank you Desmond, and please place them on the shelves to the right."

"K, Mrs. P."

Anna picked up a small box of stationary, and then asked, "Mrs. Perpecuwitz, the last time I came in, you said to be careful of the energy near the quarry. What did you mean?"

Mrs. Perpecuwitz looked at the stairs and said softly. "Anna you have an idea of what this pertains to, don't you dear? You both do don't you?"

"Does it have to do with the last grouping of words, the story I got on the computer."

Mrs. Perpecuwitz sighed in relief, "Yes!" She put her box down. "Within the last number of months I kept having several dreams. I believe it was a contact from another dimension. The contact was from the planet Neia, a parallel dimension of Earth. The contact kept coming into my dreams. I am very familiar with this dimension. I am also very perceptive and intuitive; do you know what an intuitive is?"

"Yes, said Anna, My friend in school is one."

"I've read about that," said Desmond, I've even gone to see one with my Mother last year. It was at her friend's home."

"So you understand. Good. Well, the contact's name was Ferian; he is an Elder there or one of them...."

"There's more than one?" Anna asked.

"Yes, there are seven Anna, but we can talk about that another time. The Elder Ferian talked about two young people, who fit your descriptions, and when he mentioned your birthdays...I knew it was you Anna. The Elder said you and Desmond have the right energetic make up in your body. The dates you were born, coincide with the date when a very special portal opens, and remember the stones of that came to you last year?"

Desmond looked at Anna, surprised. "Yes," he said. Anna nodded in agreement.

"We don't have them anymore, Mrs. Perpecuwitz, at least not at the house. We brought them to the Antiquities Shop to Mr. Edis like you suggested. They're safe now," Anna placed another box on the shelf.

"The stones are going to be important. He gave me the phrases, so that you would not be frightened at first when the pages of the book appeared on your computer. Have you read the book? Do you know what to do?"

"That's just it, Mrs. Perpecuwitz; we think it's a hologram. It disappears and reappears, Desmond said.

"We're looking for a hard copy," Anna added, "we've been to the library, and The Antiquities Shop, and it wasn't at either of them. We met Charles, Mr. Edis' grandson, and he's helping to locate it also for us."

"Good" said Mrs. Perpecuwitz. "Well, the book is very important. There are some places I know I can inquire." She lowered her voice. "It is important that you tell no one, except for your Mom Anna. You must let her know at some point. That is what the elder said. Only the ones you can trust. The old quarry is where the portal will open. He said it is being stabilized and humans may feel somewhat of an electric shock when Neia projects their energy during certain phases this month and on July 11th."

Anna and Desmond understood and nodded their heads. "We have a meeting with Mr. Edis this afternoon"...Anna said.

"He is a good man. You can trust him. Alright Anna and Desmond, I have to go and check on the supplies upstairs and get the lights in order for Monday. You both will be coming with your Mom, Anna on Monday night?" Monday Night was the Big Splash Festival with a group of musicians who sounded like the Beach Boys. The whole place will be turned into a huge exotic beach. Every month in the summer displayed a special theme. Next Month was the Lights of the Riviera Festival in July.

"Yes, we are, we look forward to it every year!"

"It's a blast," said Desmond. "I'm glad I'm here every year in July and this year in June too, Mrs. P."

Mrs. Perpecuwitz laughed that delightful laugh she was known for. Then she became serious.

"Please, if at any time, Anna and Desmond, if you need anything, any type of help, anywhere, anytime of the day or night, please call me. " Mrs. Perpecuwitz looked on the counter near the shelf of supplies for a business card. She wrote her personal cell phone number on the back."

"Remember," She said, "I will help you both any time, any place, just call."

"Thank you Mrs. Perpecuwitz, we will," Anna said.

"Thank you very much," Desmond added.

They all went upstairs to their destinations.

Anna handed the business card to Desmond. "Desmond, I don't carry a wallet with me, and you do." Anna unlocked her bike. By the way, what time is it?"

Desmond looked at his watch. "Its 11:20, we have about an hour before lunch. Want to ride to the post office? I promised Mom I would mail some post cards during the month and a half…"

"Aunt Lenora is not even going to be home. She's on tour for the month!"

"Yeah, but Dad is," said Desmond.

"Uncle Will usually goes with Aunt Lenora…"

"He couldn't this year. The College has a huge expensive presentation beginning in July, and he's head of it. It's going on for the whole month and now they're preparing for it."

"...And in August, when Mom & Dad are both home, all three of us are going on vacation together."

"Okay," said Anna, "We have time. Did you buy some postcards?"

"Got 'em on the way out... Calla helped me pick them out while you were getting the sodas"

"Oh, brother...let's go," Anna was already on her bike."

"What...?" said Desmond as they rode to the post office.

Chapter 26

Lawrence Edis stopped at the local Deli for a sandwich to eat later in the day.

Preoccupied by running through a mental list of museum event schedules, Lawrence turned around without thinking and bumped into Ellen Belk.

His parcel fell into her deli basket.

"I am so terribly sorry, are you all right?"

"Oh, I'm fine," Ellen said smiling, "Here's your sandwich, I believe."

Lawrence took a good look at Ellen. He noticed no wedding ring on her finger, "I believe we've met before, haven't we?

"Yes we have, it was at the Library. I believe you gave a presentation on the Eighteenth Dynasty of Egypt on Akhenaten, the Armarna Period and Tutankhamen from the Museum" Ellen provided.

"And your class, made a miniature tomb and burial chamber, I remember," said Lawrence.

He went to adjust his glasses, "Mrs. ...?"

"Oh, it's Ellen, Ellen Belk, very nice to see you again, Mr. ...Edis? Its Mr. Edis, Charles's father, is it not?" Ellen just put it together.

"Do you know Charles?" Lawrence asked.

They both walked to the checkout line.

Ellen laughed. "It was a curious thing, my daughter, Anna, and my nephew Desmond went to The Antiquities Shop to buy a book, but it wasn't on the shelf." Charles very kindly drove them home the other day, because of the rain. "

Lawrence Edis suddenly connected the two young people Charles spoke of earlier.

"It was very nice to meet you again, Lawrence," Ellen had finished paying for her purchase, and was ready to leave.

"Wait," Lawrence was putting his change into his jeans. "The Museum is hosting a new exhibit of the Amber Collection from The Dominican Republic, and also of other parts of the world. I'm not part of the exhibit this time. It opens tomorrow evening, would, would you be my guest that evening? We are allowed to bring one guest, and, um, and I would like to invite you, Ellen."

"Oh, I would be delighted to go. What time should I be there?"

Can you meet me at the entrance at 6:45?

"Certainly, I can." Ellen arrived at her car.

"All right, meet you at 6:45, near the entrance tomorrow evening." Lawrence Edis turned around and dropped his car keys on the pavement.

Chapter 27

Anna brought in the mail when they arrived home. The Mail Carrier was just about to put the mail in their box when she peddled into the drive way. Her Mom was home and it was 12:25.

"Oh good, Anna and Desmond,   You're both home. You will just need plates and napkins for lunch. I picked up some grinders from the deli." Ellen opened the refrigerator humming to her self.

Anna looked at Desmond.   Desmond lifted his shoulders in response and lifted his eyebrows. She hadn't heard her mother hum since before her Dad died years ago.

Anna reminded her mom about the Splash Festival beginning Monday night at the Rose Cottage.

"Oh, yes ...what fun! By the way, I met Charles Edis' father today at the deli earlier. Such a nice man," Ellen pondered looking out the window at three swallowtail butterflies flitting by. "Hmm."

Anna and Desmond looked at each other smiling while eating their grinder.

"Anna, I am going to the Museum tomorrow evening for a new exhibit." Would you like Marisa or Lydia to come while I'm out?"

"It doesn't matter Mom, we'll probably be upstairs on the computers."

"All right then, I'll see which one is available. We're leaving in about 20 minutes for the Library and The Antiquities Shop, and now I have to see about a fax I hope came through and Ellen Belk went into the her computer room for a few minutes.

After lunch and the dishes were cleared away, Anna and Desmond went to get their backpacks. Anna said, "Mom usually doesn't go out by herself, I wonder if Alicia is going with her?"

Alicia was Ellen Belk's friend from school, and they sometimes went shopping or met for coffee, when Alicia needed a break from her three children. She had three boys, sixteen, twelve and nine. Her husband would call it a Boy's Night and they ordered pizza, had chips and sodas, etc., much to Alicia's dismay, but sometimes you had to overlook a few things.

Chapter 28

Mr. Edis, in his early 70's, was a man of incredible knowledge, stood near the counter when Anna & Desmond came in. He was tall, slim and very physically fit. He still retained all the grey vaguely out of place hair. He wore readers. He smiled and clapped his hands once rubbing them slightly when he saw Anna and Desmond.

"Hello Anna ...and ...Desmond, I believe."

"Yes sir," said Desmond smiling. "Hello!"

Anna smiling also said: "Hello Mr. Edis, we're here."

"And right you are my dear! Ahhh, here comes Charles now. Mr. Edis turned to his friend, Edward, and said: "Edward, Thank you so much for coming and covering the shop while I'm in this important meeting."

"Certainly Bart, what is the time frame?"

Mr. Edis looked at his watch. "Give us about an hour, Edward."

Edward, in his thirties was a very valued and trusted friend. He had been available and was very glad to help.

Edward Stiles and his partner Ronald Muir own the Café Umbria upstairs. Usually around 3pm the café had a lull of customers and Edward frequently had the extra time.

Bartholomew Edis had started the Antiquities Shop more the 40 years ago when he was in his late twenties studying archeology. His studies brought him to very intriguing and peculiar places all around the world. When he purchased the church building, he could not believe all the nooks and crannies hidden within the structure. He took out the pews, opened doorways, took down partitions and knocked out the wall near the parking lot and created a beautiful new room resembling some of the ambiance of the original structure.

This is where he decided to hold the meeting. As he opened the door, inviting his guests to enter, he quickly excused himself to get a folder he had forgotten in his office.

Anna and Desmond had never been in this room. As she looked around, taking in the beauty of the natural light, Anna thought that this was the most enchanted room she had ever seen. Orchids hung from one part of the balcony, the other, large murals of ancient historical paintings and ferns accenting off unusual hangers from the ceiling.

Charles and Desmond were talking about some of the paintings, but Anna was in a dream like state, drinking in the aura of the room.

"Isn't that right Anna?" Desmond asked from the other side of the room.

"Hmmm," said Anna dreamily.

Charles and Desmond laughed a little, ""She's not paying attention at all," Charles said with a smile. He continued, "This room will do it to you. It's quite extraordinary."

Anna, not aware of being the topic of discussion, had a vision as she stared at one of the murals. She saw two boys arguing, one pushing the slightly taller one. "I'm not going to do it, Lorien, and you cannot make me, I will not be second."

"Thereon, it is not like that at all, Mother and Father, have all ready decided. I had nothing to do with it."

Thereon, hurt, and disillusioned, sat down and started to cry. Lorien, feeling sorry for his brother, sat down beside him and wanted to comfort him, but did not quite know what to say. "Let us talk to the Elders again Thereon, we may both be able to take the transfer."

"It has already been decided, they chose you," Thereon was angry, Lorien stood up and just at that moment, Thereon stood up and pushed him. Lorien disappeared in broad daylight.

"Lorien, Lorien, where are you? Where did you go? I cannot see you….Lorien….."

The vision changed. Thereon was much older, talking to another being, taller than normal, he called him an Anoa.

"It is all going as planned," the Anoa said, "Lorien will be trapped in the Earth plane forever, if we can foil the plans of the Elders. Have you found the Sacred Place of the Elders yet?"

"No," replied Thereon, "They are very tricky; I seem to lose them at some point when I follow them."

"That is not acceptable," responded the Anoa. In order for us to gain, I mean for you to gain control then, we MUST find their Sacred Place, is this understood?"

Thereon began to feel uneasy, what have I got myself into, he thought. "Yes, it is understood,"

"Very well, we will meet again!" The Anoa stalked away.

Thereon sat on a boulder, with his head in his hands, he was frightened. The Anoa had never talked to him like this before. There were a few times that the Anoa had overstepped their boundaries, but now more than ever, they seemed to want to take control. As he thought about it, he realized they were in control all along, but did it slyly as he recalled many incidents he encountered with them in the past weeks. Thereon had no idea what to do. He was still young, twenty-four going on twenty-five very soon. "Lorien, what have I done?" And with this statement, alarmed he went in search of his father, a very wise Elder indeed.

Anna came back to reality. Everyone was looking at her. She suddenly became aware of this. Mr. Edis cleared his throat. "Hmmm, Anna, has something extraordinary just happen?" He put his folder on a near by table

"You looked as if you were in a trance."

"I'm not sure, Mr. Edis," Anna looked at Charles and Desmond. "I think I need to sit down for a moment."

"That, my dear, may be a very good idea." Mr. Edis showed her to the comfy chair area, guiding her to the one near the opened window. Birds were singing, melodiously to each other. It was a welcome peaceful feeling, compared to the anger and frightened feelings Anna encountered a few minutes before.

Charles gave Anna a bottle of water. Anna accepted it gratefully.

After Anna was settled for a few minutes, Mr. Edis spoke. "Anna, would you like to tell us what you just experienced and what may have brought it on?" Mr. Edis was very good at making people feel comfortable.

"I think I would, thank you," Anna began to relay what she saw and felt.

"And, it all started when I looked at this mural," Anna pointed to the mural in front of her.

"Ah, the Neian landscape," Mr. Edis said looking fondly at the mural.

"Neian?" Desmond had heard Mrs. Perpecuwitz use this word pertaining to the parallel planet. He didn't really connect it until now.

"Hmmm, yes," said Mr. Edis, nodding his head slightly, "continue, Anna."

Chapter 29

"When I first came into the room, I felt the beauty of it all. It made me feel safe and happy," Anna relayed.

Mr. Edis smiled, nodding.

Anna continued. It was a few minutes after, I saw the mural, I think it had to do with the book, 'The Epic Catalog,' I found myself looking deeper into the mural, and then the images came."

Desmond, mouth opened, listened intently. Charles had that quizzical look, like he had experienced something similar, in his earlier teens, on an escapade with his brother Anthony.

"I saw two people, Lorien and his brother, Thereon. They were sort of fighting, well at least Thereon wanted to. He was very angry about something that just happened. Lorien was trying to calm him down."

"It was so lucid, like I was there; I could feel the anger and fear. They were in a wooded area, it was very dense, and near a lake...with flowers along a path, the colors seemed brighter, and some I've never seen before..."

Charles became very alert, "I saw that...I mean near the old quarry, this morning....."

"Mrs. Perpecuwitz, mentioned the quarry this morning, Anna," Desmond said excitedly

Mr. Edis nodded his head and murmured, "Mrs. Perpecuwitz...hmmm"

"It must be all related." Anna turned to Mr. Edis, looking for a response.

"Indeed, but first Anna, is there any more?" Mr. Edis inquired.

Anna continued. "It was a very sunny day; I saw two suns, over the trees. When Lorien and Thereon stood up, Thereon pushed Lorien away from him; he didn't want to be consoled. Lorien disappeared, Thereon became frightened, he didn't know what had just happened or where Lorien went."

"Then, the images changed, Thereon was much older, I think it is now, in their time, I mean, I think he is about 25..." Anna looked at Mr. Edis; did he know anything about The Epic Catalog? Mrs. Perpecuwitz said we could trust him. Yes, she thought, we can trust him.

"Thereon, was talking to some being, I think I heard his thoughts also and he referred to the being as an Anoan. The Anoan seemed to be very crafty and he wasn't much taller than Thereon, he was about I think he was under six feet. He became very angry when Thereon couldn't find the Sacred Place of the Elders. He looked frustrated, and Thereon became really afraid of him. When the Anoa walked away, Thereon...I heard his thoughts again...he was thinking of going to talk to his father, the Elder Ferian...the images ended and I saw everyone looking at me!"

Mr. Edis sat on the side of his cushy chair; Desmond realized he was still standing, sat down on a chair next to Anna. Charles sat in front of Desmond.

"Well, let me tell everyone why I asked to see you today." Mr. Edis took a deep breath, looked at the Neian Mural and began; "It was 1947, my sister Abigail had just married. I am originally from England, hence the slight English dialect and accent. Abigail and her husband Walter found out that year that Abigail couldn't have children. For a year she had undergone tests, and still no results. One day, they were walking in a wooded glen area, and right in front of them, a young boy appeared before them on the path. It was a fairly wide path, they were following a rare butterfly, Walter was an Entomologist, and was trying to take a photograph of it, that's when the young boy appeared."

"He had strange clothes, very fair, almost translucent white hair; his body shimmered for a few moments. He looked confused, and said to them, have you seen my bro...and he appeared to have forgotten what he was going to say. He started to cry. Abigail and Walter Turner, looked for days for his parents, but no one knew anything about them or the boy they found. They went to the Council of Children to inquire if anyone knew if he were an orphan."

Abigail wrote to me and said they were adopting an older boy, around ten years old, I was on a dig in Turkey, I was 14 years old and allowed to go with my Uncle for the first time. I came for the signing of the adoption papers. Jeffery is my nephew.

"Grandfather, I get it now...Jeffery Turner...wrote The Epic Catalog!" Charles jumped up, ""How come you didn't tell father about it."

"I didn't really know his past until I went to see Abigail, Charles." Mr. Edis opened the file, in it was a book. Anna looked hopefully; she couldn't make out the cover.

When Jeffery, who became a doctor, went on holiday, or as you say here in America, a vacation. Strange occurrences began to happen. He began to keep a journal.

"When Charles contacted me about a book," Mr. Edis continued, "I was in England, visiting my sister, I asked her about it, if Jeffery ever wrote a book called: 'The Epic Catalog.' Abigail said he self-published, and then showed me his journal. The information in the journal was published, but just a few copies, which is why it was so hard for both of you to find it, Anna and Desmond. For some reason, he left his original journal with his mother for safe keeping."

"After a while, I sort of lost touch with Jeffery, except for holidays and family gatherings. I married and moved to the United States in my twenties. Jeffery married Rachel Carde and eventually moved to New York City 20 years ago. They never had children. I had a chance to read some of the content of the journal on the plane back home. It was the first time I knew about Jeffery's strange visions and dreams, when he met Rachel Carde and what had happened during the time of his vacation."

"Rachel died in 2007. She battled with cancer. Jeffery eventually came to terms with her death. It is curious; no one has seen or heard from him in 7 days. Abigail is worried about him. She knows who Jeffery really is, that he is not from our world. She also knows that this is the year he will be leaving us, not being sure exactly when. She can't reach him by his mobile either. We're not sure what has happened. Abigail knew he wouldn't leave without saying goodbye. We have filed a missing person's form and the authorities in New York City are working on his disappearance."

Anna felt dismayed and looked at Desmond's reaction. He appeared alarmed.

There was a knock on the door and Edward poked his head inside. "Bart, there is a telephone call for Anna?" It's her mother."

Oh, certainly, Edward, come in. Anna, would you like to be alone?"

"Oh no, Mr. Edis, I think my mom wants to know what time to pick us up."

Anna took the receiver from Edward. "Hi Mom, yes we are still in the meeting, I'm not sure, I'll ask"... Anna looked up, "Mr. Edis, my mother wants to know what time to pick us up."

Charles spoke up, "I can bring you home later, and I'm going home after the meeting."

"That sounds good, Charles," Mr. Edis added, "We still have to talk a bit more.

"Mom? Charles said he could drive us home after. No, he said he was going home after the meeting...okay, I will, I think it's going to be about another half hour to an hour. We will. Thank you, Mom, bye."

"Charles, my mom said to thank you for driving us home." Anna handed the telephone back to Edward.

"Edward, would another hour be alright with your schedule."

"It will be fine, Bart. I called in my niece earlier. She loves the extra hours."

Edward left the room and closed the door.

Mr. Edis handed Anna the journal. He also gave her a zippered leather bag to keep it in. "Anna, I am entrusting this journal into your hands; I trust you and Desmond will keep it safe for a while?"

Anna took the journal, opened it and looked at the hand written pages. "Yes, we will Mr. Edis." Anna closed the journal and placed it in the leather zippered case. She felt this was an important step, and would help her and Desmond to get Lorien back to the parallel world of Neia. Hopefully he will be found in time.

"Now," Mr. Edis walked over to the mural. He looked at the one where Anna had seen the visions. He drew in a deep breath and exhaled..."Where to begin..."

"When my wife and I had separated, it was 10 years after we had married; we had one child. Elizabeth couldn't take my type of lifestyle, she wanted more stability, and I didn't blame her. I was traveling at a moment's notice to everywhere and anywhere of archeological interest, when I came across the murals. They were the most fascinating thing I had ever seen. I met the artist. He was a visionist, and painted extraordinary things. I met him before he became famous; and I was able to purchase these five murals for this room at an affordable price."

He waved his hand over the large murals, Mr. Edis continued. "Elizabeth had died three years later; it was in a tragic automobile accident." Anna flinched, she knew about tragic car accidents. Mr. Edis was still looking at the murals. He turned around. "My son Lawrence came to live with me full time," Mr. Edis was smiling.

"Any way one day, many years later, a woman came to my shop. Her name was Audrey Perpecuwitz."

Anna and Desmond looked at each other, smiling, and then turned back to Mr. Edis, who was watching them.

"Yes, I know Audrey Perpecuwitz, in fact quite well. She was looking for a period piece, years ago when she noticed my murals. I remember her words, because quite frankly, I had never seen anyone recognize the murals as she did. "How curious," Audrey said as she pondered over them. "I have seen this exact place before, but I can't remember where." We discussed the period piece she wanted for her establishment, Rose Cottage. She was very knowledgeable about some of the areas I had traveled to, so...we had tea at the Café Umbria' discussing many topics of interest, when out of the blue she blurts out, "Neia!"

"I looked at her, very intrigue, and Audrey started to tell me of a 12ᵗʰ century manuscript with beautiful intricate colorful illustrations she was fortunate to examine during her earlier years of travel in Tibet. The manuscripts brought back some extraordinary memories and experiences from her childhood. Anyway, the manuscript told of a land living in harmony and balance with nature. It was a fertile region appearing to be more advance than some of the regions around the world at the time and it was said to be a magical place. There were other strange events and happenings around this vicinity. It was called Neia, by the natives who lived near the area where it was said to be located. We know it was an open portal for quite a length of time, 80-140 years in fact from earlier documents I had found on varied travels after talking with Audrey. The documents placed the portal around 10,000 years ago; before the Tibetans had recorded the manuscripts in the 12th century, just from the basis of information my team and I were able to uncover. They are from secret places; no one has ever heard of. Oh yes, they exist."

Mr. Edis paused for a moment looking at the murals. "My friend who painted the murals is in fact a descendant of Neia. His great, great grandparents were pure Neians, they came out of choice. It is said to help us advance into a world that will accept the changes to take place in the very near future. There are several here, in fact, whose ancestors had come through a portal that opened in Tibet this time, in the early 18th century.

The Tibetans have a record of the manuscript, which has been copied and well preserved from

4,000 years ago. The 12th century manuscript was a copy of the original. In fact, there are several well preserved and hidden in various parts of the world."

"So Grandfather, we must all be a part of this mystery?" May I tell you what happened to me earlier this morning?

Yes Charles, I am afraid we all have a part to play, and so does our good friend, Audrey Perpecuwitz. I will have to leave soon. There are some other details I need to discuss with her before I go away for a few days. "Please tell us Charles, what occurred this morning, your father telephoned me earlier and said you had an escapade..."

Charles frowned. "It wasn't anything like what happened with Anthony years ago, but it was peculiar, and I think it may have something to do with Anna and Desmond."

Charles relayed what happened at the old quarry; Anna was sitting on the edge of her seat and said, "Mrs. Perpecuwitz told us to be very careful around the old quarry, Charles. She said something about the energy there."

"She was right Anna; I got zapped a few times."

"Charles, I'll bet the older man was the Elder Anna and I saw in our dreams a few nights ago," Desmond blurted out with enthusiasm.

Mr. Edis looked at Anna and Desmond. Have you had contact with anyone else? We have about a half hour left.

Anna and Desmond informed Mr. Edis what they told Charles the day they came into the Antiquities shop.

"I think it's the same Elder who tried to contact me," Charles said encouragingly. "I didn't quite hear him; it was as if a violent storm was suddenly brewing..."

Mr. Edis added: "From what I understand, the Anoa can create storms using the electrical energy in both worlds....hmmm..." He looked at the mural, "How can they do that..." he murmured.

"Oh, Grandfather, Dad said you were the science major in the family."

"And right he was, Charles. Well I think we have some great leads to follow up on.... Charles?"

"Yes," said Charles, as he stood up and stretched.

"It's time to take Anna and Desmond home. I'd like you to read the journal with them... and; I am giving you a few days off. I will call Lucien in to cover for a few days; he owes me a favor anyway. Cover as much of the journal as you can, and when I get back, yes I am leaving again to go to New York City to help find Jeffery, then we will get together with Audrey Perpecuwitz to see if we can come up with more clues." Anna was glad; she liked spending time with Charles.

"Oh, and incidentally Anna," Mr. Edis rose from the arm of his chair and went to one of the murals, "the stones may have something to do with this mystery, look in the fourth mural."

In the fourth mural were two good sized orange looking stones, the carnelians.

"Whoa," said Desmond. Anna shook her head in surprise. "I didn't notice that before."

Mr. Edis left to pay a visit to Audrey Perpecuwitz, and then had a flight for New York City at 7:45 pm.

Chapter 30

Anna saw her mother sitting in her favorite chair in the living room going over the Chef's Magazine she checked out from the library. In fact there were several she had open on the coffee table.

Hi Mom, can Charles come over tonight, we're going to go over a book Mr. Edis lent us." Anna was holding the leather zippered case under her arm.

"Oh," said Ellen Belk, "Mr. Edis found your book! "Hmmm," as a matter of fact, Marisa wouldn't be able to come until 8:30 and Lydia is occupied this evening. I was going to call the evening off. What time is he coming?"

"I'm not sure; let me ask him Mom, he hasn't left yet."

Anna saw Desmond talking to Charles outside the Driver's window of his jeep

When Desmond looked up, he saw Anna standing in the doorway. Anna ran to the Driver's side, "Charles, Mom wants to know what time you are coming over tonight."

"Let's see, Dad has an engagement at six forty-five this evening. It's almost five now. How about seven o'clock?"

"Hmmm, Mom has to be at the Museum for around six forty-five, seven o'clock sounds good. Mom wants to know if you can stay until she gets back."

"Yes, I can, we have to read through as much of the journal as we can."

As Charles left, Desmond thought it was a pretty exciting and productive day. Strange about Anna having a vision like that and it was strange about the murals, and how Mr. Edis knows Mrs. Perpecuwitz. His telephone rang. "Hi Dad, yeah, I'm having a great time, are you away at the College now? WHAT? What happened? Is Mom alright.... Okay, Hi Mom, you ARE? WOW, YES Aunt Ellen is inside, okay, I'll get her."

Desmond walked inside the front door. "Aunt Ellen," he called, "Mom is on the telephone." He waited while Aunt Ellen talked to his parents. Anna gave him a quizzical look. Desmond held one finger up and mouthed "Wait!"

Anna sighed and whispered: "Okay."

Aunt Ellen gave Desmond back his telephone. He talked to his parents for a few minutes while Anna and her mom walked into the kitchen. "What happened, Mom?"

"Your Aunt Lenora is going to be on National Television tomorrow evening." It seems that when she went in to do a book signing at the Barnes & Noble of one of the cities she's touring, she bumped into an old friend who is a News Anchor on one of the local channels there. They are going to do a 30 minute segment during the evening news and it is syndicated. Isn't it exciting Anna? My little sister!" Ellen put her prepared dish for their dinner into the oven. She made eggplant parmesan, a new recipe she found in the Chef's Magazine.

Desmond was looking pleased when he came into the kitchen. He told Anna and Aunt Ellen all about his mother's plans for the rest of the week, and then her team was moving on to another state. After the College presentation, his Dad would join her like he always did. At the end of July this year, her book tour would be over and she would be free to enjoy the rest of the summer at the Great Lakes.

Anna was very happy for Desmond. She fantasized a little about what it would be like as a famous author! She came back to reality when Desmond whispered, "Anna, your not having another vision are you?"

Anna, semi blushing, turned around and said: "No," matter-of-factly, pushed Desmond slightly, smiled and started setting the table for dinner.

"What..." Desmond smiled back, "hmmm," shook his head, and reached for the napkins to place on the table.

Chapter 31

Charles Edis arrived at the Belk house ten minutes early. He was eager to know more about the journal. The eggplant parmesan was sitting on the counter cooling off before refrigeration. He looked longingly at it, as the aroma permeated through out the house.

Ellen Belk noticed his prolonged gaze at the eggplant dish, smiled and offered Charles a portion. "Well, I did just eat, and very little in fact, yes I would love some!"

She laughed as she put a generous portion on a plate and handed it to Charles. Desmond and Anna were doing the dishes. As Ellen left, Charles thanked her again, the eggplant parmesan was so, so wonderful, he thought. He devoured it as slowly as he could, savoring every bite.

After the dishes were washed and put away, Anna ran upstairs to get the leathered zippered case. They sat in the living room. The lighting was better actually in the den, but not as comfortable.

"Charles," asked Anna, "did you ever meet Jeffery Turner?"

"I did, a few times. Once when I was when I was very young, my father, Anthony and I took a vacation to visit Ireland, then to see my uncle Walt and Aunt Abigail in England. I think Jeffery was on vacation and came to meet us. Rachel was actually out of the country. We just called him Dr. Jeff. And a few times they would come to the States to visit my grandfather and we would meet up with them at his house."

Anna opened the journal and skimmed the first few chapters. "It looks as if the first chapters are what we've already read. I'll get some ice tea for us. Do you want to start reading, Charles" She handed him the leather bound Epic Catalog. The Journal itself was quite large; the writing was legible and easy to read.

"Yes, thank you, I'd like to get started and to be more acquainted with what you've already told me from the other day."

Desmond came into the living room with the laptops from upstairs. "Just incase the book comes back on the computer, it's kind of wild, how it comes in and out."

Anna placed the ice tea decanter on the table with three glasses on the coffee table. Desmond handed Anna her laptop. They fired them up and no book! Anna checked her e-mail, and eventually poured the ice tea into the glasses.

Charles looked up, laughing... "The lobster incident! Too funny!"

Anna and Desmond laughed. An exchange of dialogue flowed as Charles re-iterated incidents within the chapters, and an hour flew by. "Hmmm, interesting, Rachel is describing an experience she dreamed about, it sounds an awful lot like the old quarry."

Desmond whistled, "We're all in the story, Charles. We all have to do this together; I mean getting Jeffery back to Neia before it's too late."

Anna decided to get some more ice for the glasses of the ice tea. She heard Charles and Desmond laughing about something, and didn't quite catch the conversation.

"Whoa, Anna," yelled Desmond, "check this out!" There was an image in Anna's computer of...The Elder? Anna came running in with the ice.

"Look, it's one of the Elders, I think..." Anna examined the computer more closely, maybe not. "He looks like the others, but he's different"

The image became clearer. "This is incredible," Charles moved closer.

The image spoke. "I am known as The Seer, greetings from our world. I have been able to translate into the waves that communicate through the electrical element of your computer.

What you are seeing is a hologram, and what we have to relay is urgent. This hologram was sent in our world 14 hours ago. I will not see you. If your energy link...computer is on, then it will be received at the appropriate time it enters your earth realm. If it is not operating, then all will be lost."

"Lorien has been coming to me in visions. In these visions, he has been in a dark cavern. I believe it to be a place where there is a cave under the sea, for water was heard all around, but not in the cavern. I have also seen the Anoa's energy force which had come to him suddenly in a dream informing him that he will find hidden data which was incomplete during excavations a few years back when he and his wife Rachel were together during the last excavation. The Anoa have not made them selves known to him, but have tapped into the energy of his dream world, like a hologram, and created an illusion, forming an image of his deceased wife in his mind."

"The false consciousness has Lorien believing that he is hearing his deceased wife in a dream informing him of important artifacts that have washed up on the shore in the cave, and he will find tangible objects connecting information of an unknown preceding culture.

"Thereon, his brother had informed Ferian, The Elder and his father. Thereon is working quite well as a double agent here, since he has decided to help his brother."

"Once Lorien is in the cave, the Anoa plan to use the energy they had been able to manipulate, a small energy link to your planet, even though it is purely dimensional, it will still have an effect in your world, planet Earth. The energy will force the waters to flood the cave; it is not due to fill up for another 9 months."

"The Anoa are few. They have been trapped in our dimension for two and a half years. They have learned a few of our secrets, because of a willing source, who was Thereon at the time. We think we have an opportunity to send them back to their own world during the transition of Lorien's return. But, this is not the concern now."

"The Translators of Energy are working to infiltrate this illusion…. not… sure." The computer screen went blank, and then almost immediately, came back on. "……cave is, but the book……clue……in your debt."

The screen went blank again and the image did not come back

Charles was dumbfounded. "This is unbelievable, absolutely astonishing! I must call Grandfather right away!" Charles looked at Anna and Desmond and took his cell phone out of his pocket.

Desmond looked to be in a trance. Anna was about to comment when Desmond shouted:

"Saintes-Maries-de-la-Mer, or a region near there...it's in the book Charles, that's where Jeffery must of gone to!" Desmond pointed to the journal. "Um, where is it Anna?"

Anna nodded in agreement; she went to sit by Charles on the couch. Yes, he must have gone there, it fits the description in the journal, may I Charles?" Anna was pointing to the book.

"Yes, by all means, Anna, it will help when I talk to Grandfather."

Anna scanned the pages carefully. "Here it is, right after the Lobster incident!"

Charles looked over her shoulder: "You're right, Anna, there it is. Rachel is telling him over their dinner.

"We have the clue, Charles, and The Seer said it was urgent. Did your grandfather go to New York City yet?"

"We'll soon find out!" Charles dialed his grandfather's number. He listened, and then connected to his voicemail.

"Hello Grandfather, This is Charles. I'm at Anna and Desmond's house going over the journal. It's around 8:00 pm. Have you left for New York yet? Something strange has developed concerning the book, and we wanted to discuss it with you. Would you call me back as soon as you can? Thanks Grandfather. G'Bye."

"Well, this is beginning to be a bizarre and interesting night! A hologram on the computer," Charles ran his fingers through his hair.

"Isn't it bizarre?" Anna poured herself some additional ice tea and offered more to Charles and Desmond. She added; "first we find out that the book was a hologram on the computer...hmmm, how can that happen?"

"It must be from a book, not the journal," Desmond interjected.

"That seems logical," said Charles, "Aunt Abigail said he published a few copies."

"Wait a minute," Anna became excited, "when I looked up the copyright at the beginning, before Mom and I left to pick you up at the airport, Desmond, I saw, 'Copyright 1958.' I tried to print out what I read as I was getting ready to leave but I ran out of ink earlier. Mom bought some more the other day, remember, I tried to reprint it? The hologram has to be from a real book.

"Yeah, I do, Anna," Desmond turned to Charles, "that's when we figured out it must be a hologram, but how did the book in our world become a hologram in the Neia world?

No one knew the answer.

Charles picked up the journal and thumbed through it…..."Anna, Desmond, look,"   At the beginning pages of the book a copyright and publisher were displayed. "Jeff printed this in his own handwriting, and there is something else here, I can't really read it….it looks like he erased it."

Anna looked more closely. "I can't make it out either. Wait a minute, I think it says: "See appendix vii." Anna turned to Appendix vii at the back of the book. "There's nothing there, I don't see anything on the pages. She thumbed through the 17 pages. Wait, look, there is a sheet of paper taped to the last page of the appendix." Anna carefully pulled the attached paper from the appendix. "Hmm…the paper is blank, but I'm feeling something on it. She went to the pole lamp in the corner of the room and brought the paper up to the light and saw impressions.

"Let me see it." Desmond got up from his chair and put his laptop on the coffee table, Anna handed him the paper from the journal. He took it to the light under one of the lamps…hmmm, I think I see symbols, not sure if …let me get some paper and a pencil, and we can rub it.

Desmond found his backpack at the bottom of the stairs and came back with the necessary tools. He handed them to Anna. "You're really good at this Anna, you want to do it?"

"Sure!" Anna took the paper and pencil and started lightly rubbing the page of the book. "I've seen this before, I mean I think it's a secret language, I mean a cryptogram.

Τηε Χονστελλατιονσ Οφ Νεια

"Look Charles, there's something else." Anna rubbed some more.

Τηρεε κεψσ το φιτ ιντο τηε γατε

Ονε πιεχε οφ Νεια φαβριχ το πλαχε βετωεεν τηε στονεσ

Χοορδινατε τηε χοδεσ το τηε τιμε ερα

Ωηεν τηε σεχονδ συν ρισεσ ανδ τηε ονε συν δεσχενδσ

Ανδ τηε Επιχ Χαταλογ ρελεασεσ ιντο τηε σκψ

Ανδ τρανσλατεσ τηε ενεργψ φρομ ονε πλαχε το τηε οτηερ

Τηεν αλλ σηαλλ βε φυλφιλλεδ

"I think we are dealing with more than we bargained for here. It looks like there are symbols or a language...I'm not sure just exactly how to interpret it." Charles looked perplexed.

"I may I know of a way." Anna loved the language of words. "Desmond and I can work on it later with the computer. We can type a sentence; it doesn't have to resemble the symbols or language here in the journal..."

"Oh, I get it," interrupted Charles, you work with the fonts."

"We just go to each font that looks like a symbol or the language we see here and see if it is the correct one," said Desmond.

"And... if we can't find it we'll Google it!" Anna's eyes were shining. "This still doesn't answer the question about how the book became a hologram." Anna looked at the cryptic notes and scanned them for more information. "So the real question is the cryptic message.   Is it information that will help us?   Or are they just clues?"

"I think we should read more of the journal. Maybe we'll find information about the symbols," Charles was anxious to continue.

Chapter 32

As we boarded the plane, Rachel realized that our seating arrangements were not favorable. She was seated on the far right end of the plane. We had First Class tickets, but for some reason the whole area was full to capacity! It turned out that there was an International Convention in Europe and a few businesses and organizations had practically filled up the plane.

We looked in my seating vicinity....it was not encouraging at all, then to Rachel's...yes much better. We asked the Stewardess if there were any way we could sit together for the flight, and, yeees, I did a little name dropping to make the situation more beneficial to us.

Once she found out that the plane had the famous Rachel Carde on board, the Stewardess made the seating arrangements more suitable for us...I also gave her a twenty dollar bill. She was quite happy with the tip and brought us some coffee and each a piece of pie.

Rachel went over some of her notes that she needed to mail in the morning. I was reminiscing about the telephone call I had placed to Mother from the International Airport. I forgot about the time difference, and it was after 3 AM in London when she received my call.

Mother was thrilled to know that Rachel Carde was going to be our guest, and I could tell she had many questions concerning how I met her, but time was limited and she gave me an update on Father's condition.

Not sure what I should tell her, I mean about the dreams and other strange occurrences. I know Mother and Father are not my real parents, but will they believe this whole scenario. We may have to edit our story. Then I thought about Father and was anxious for his recovery. Rachel put the rest of her papers away and we decided to rest for a few hours. We both had a long and arduous day and tomorrow would seem infinite and apprehensive.

Our plane had landed, and we retrieved our luggage after 8:00 in the morning, London time. Rachel took a taxi to her friend's home on the outskirts of the city. She needed to make some calls relating to her next excavation in a small village near Saintes-Maries-de-la-Mer in France. Meanwhile, she had to sort out the rest of her notes and mail them by the end of the day. We agreed to meet at the Parkside Hospital in London by 2:30 pm.

I entered the Hospital and saw Mother waiting in the sitting area. She gave me another quick update of Father's condition. He was conscious and had a few fractures to one of his ribs, and a badly sprained arm among other irritations. "The doctor should be back with another x-ray," Abigail Turner looked a little worried. We walked quietly to Dr. Canfield's office.

"Jeff, so glad you're here. Take a look at this x-ray." Dr. Canfield handed me father's x-ray of his right arm."

I took the x-ray and put it on the light frame. "Yeees, it looks like a hairline fracture to the wrist Victor, see that line...right...about...there!"

"That's what I thought, just wanted to be sure. We have already set his wrist and have it in a cast, but as I was going over the x-rays just before you came in, I thought it may be more than a bad sprain. I noticed the hairline going across. It's hidden but if you turn the x-ray this way, it is very evident. Alright, here is the briefing on your Father. He is in quite a lot of pain. There are abrasions from the fall, a severe one around his right eye. One of his ribs has a fracture, and we have taken care of that, wrappings around his chest, you know, the usual scenario.

It may take 3 to six weeks to heal. We gave him a sedative last night to ease him of his discomfort...everything else can be filled in later. You can look at his chart in his room.

Victor put the x-ray in the file on his desk. "Come on old chap, his room is near the nurse's station. Mrs. Turner, after you," Victor opened the door and led us down the hall to Father's room, "Ah, here we are."

It was a beautiful summer morning, the sunlight and fresh air came through the opened window and curtains. Father was sitting up and he looked quite disheveled. Victor said earlier despite what had happened to him, he must have known the man upstairs quite well not to have sustained any permanent damage to his head.

Mother, was all smiles when Father looked up at us as we entered the room. He brightened up when he saw me.

"Jeffery, your vacation..."

"Nothing to worry about Father, I am so glad you're better, and it wasn't any worse." Mother was holding his good hand.

Father chuckled. "Now I have two Doctors, I feel like hell, but I'll get better. Now that you are here Jeff, I have to postpone my Lectures at Oxford and then at Cambridge. Could you make all the calls for me? I didn't want to burden your mother with all the University detail." Father looked at Mother who was frowning.

"Oh Walter, I already telephoned London University. I hadn't had the chance to tell you. The Entomology Department put your lectures ahead to the second quarter semesters in the autumn.

"Thank you, Abigail, thank you honey, and what about your schedule, what of your classes at Cambridge?"

"Not to worry, Walter, William Deveau is going to fill in for me."

Father had a bit of discomfort as he talked, he looked a little weak. He put his hand to the bandages near his eye. I think I'm feeling a little dizzy, Jeff."

"You will for a few days," I said as I checked his pulse. "Would you like something to drink, a little ginger soda, water or juice perhaps?"

Mother looked worried. "When did you eat last?"

"Maybe some orange juice, Jeff, thanks, hmmm, I think I ate around seven in the morning, although I am not sure. I feel slightly disoriented...."

"You had a concussion and it says here on your chart, you ate breakfast, and it looks like hardly anything, Father." I checked his head bandages, looked into his right and then left eyes. "I'd say, Father, that you may still have a concussion. I'll look in your closet here for a few more pillows." After the theatrics of the fluffing of the pillows, I eased them gently between the head board and his back and neck.

The morning Nurse came around, checked his chart and gave Father a pill for his pain. I knew her as part of the morning staff in the hospital.

"Good morning Gretchen, so glad you are the one attending Father!"

Good morning, Dr. Turner, Dr. Canfield said you had arrived a little while ago. Hello, Mrs. Turner. We are keeping close tabs on your husband's concussion, and his fractured rib.

Gretchen walked over to Father. Mr. Turner, do you still hear ringing in your ears?"

"A little," said Father.

"Any increased sensitivity to light……. sounds?"

No, it's about the same."

"Have you recovered your balance when you use the facilities?"

"Well I am a little dizzy, especially when I get up too quickly."

I waved a hand motion to Gretchen and Father, mouthing the word coffee, while she was going down the list with Father.

We could still hear the drilling as we walked down the hall

"It says here on your chart from the evening, that you hardly ate anything. Were you feeling nausea? Trouble slee…" We were out of ear shot now.

The Nurses station always had a fresh pot of coffee on, and I offered a cup to Mother, poured mine, spotted the fresh pastry, and put a generous amount in the payment cup.

"Mother, are you alright, you look drained."

"Yes I'm fine, and yes I am minutely tired, I am worried about your Father's injuries. The accident happened less than 24 hours ago. I am so glad it wasn't worse, Jeffery. When I received the call at Cambridge, The nurse on duty made it sound like he was not going to make it, he wasn't conscious and he had trouble breathing, I was beside myself."

Mother started to cry. "Jeffery, he's alive and that's all that matters for now!"

My heart went out to her. "Here," I handed Mother a clean handkerchief, "Father is going to be fine and I will help see to that. Don't worry," I hugged her gently.

As we sipped our coffees on our way back to Father's room, Mother turned to me. "Jeffery, did I hear you correctly, Rachel Carde, the archeologist, will be staying with us for a few days?"

179

"Well, yes, we met on the ship." I told Mother about the lobster incident. It was a relief to see her laugh. "There are some other odd events that brought us together."

We stepped inside Father's room and saw him dozing off. He spotted us, smiled wanly, and then drifted off to sleep. I looked at his chart to read Gretchen's notes. Not really any change.

Mother and I walked into the hallway and into the corner seating near a window, and I began to tell her in full detail what had happened since I had boarded the Queen Mary.

Chapter 33

Charles looked up from the journal. His cell phone was ringing. "Hello? Oh yes, Hello Grandfather!" Charles gave a thumb's up.

"Something strange happened a little while ago." Charles recounted the computer hologram and the message to his grandfather. He also added that they all thought Jeffery may have gone to Saintes-Maries-de-la-Mer in France.

"I will. Yes, we've been reading the journal. Let's see, it's about 8:45 here, no, I plan to stay for a little while longer." This made Anna smile. "Okay, Thanks Grandfather. Bye."

Charles shut his phone. "It seems that the authorities are still looking for him. Grandfather is at the police station in New York, and the detectives are going to check to see if Jeff booked a flight out to France. He's going to call me back as soon as he finds out.

"Do you think your grandfather will fly to Saintes-Maries-de-la-Mer, I mean if the detectives find out that your cousin is there?" Desmond looked at his watch. "I wonder if he'll be able to find a flight tonight on route to France."

"I think he will, Desmond. Grandfather wants to help; he just emulated that fact on the phone. He's read and skimmed most of the journal on the plane back to the states from his vacation, there is some history involving Grandfather that he is not telling us. In some areas, he was a little vague, especially when I talked to him earlier. Before I arrived here, he called my father. Since Dad wasn't home yet, Grandfather talked to me."

Anna suddenly remembered something, "Charles, did your dad go to the Museum tonight?" I think I remember seeing a pamphlet Mom took home from the library yesterday, about an Amber exhibition at the Museum?"

Yes, he did, he said he was meeting someone at 6:45, that's why I came a little early. We left at the same time.

"Anna," said Desmond, "Aunt Ellen said she was meeting someone at the Museum, and you thought it might be Alicia...."

Charles cocked his head to one side....The Museum....Alicia?"

Anna spoke up..."Alicia is Mom's teacher friend from school, even though it's the summer, they still go shopping and sometimes for coffee, if Alicia can get her husband to watch the kids.

"Mom said she met your dad at the Deli today."

"I wonder"...Charles absentmindedly replayed the conversation at the dinner table with his dad earlier.

Charles' cell phone rang again. He looked at the caller ID. It was his grandfather. "Hi Grandfather. He did...to England? You talked to Aunt Abigail? It's not going to help him now. Yes, I think so... Charles listened for about two minutes. Uh huh, that's interesting....so you think there may be something about the crystals in the book? I'm not sure, but we'll look. What time tonight? Okay, yes I will. Uh huh.....uh huh...sure, yes, I'll tell Dad, Bye Grandfather, and thanks!"

Anna and Desmond were looking at Charles in anticipation as he stood up and put his cell phone in his jeans pocket.

"Well it seems that Uncle Jeff *did* take a flight out of the country, but to England. Aunt Abigail said that he was looking for his journal of the Epic Catalog."

Anna looked down at the journal on her lap. "You mean this one?"

"Yes, but that wasn't all." Then Charles elaborated. "Jeff took a small box that contained strange crystals. Aunt Abigail told Grandfather the crystals are unique, and are rare to earth; no one has ever found any type of mineral and molecular structure similar to them before, not even remotely!"

Desmond thought of something. "I'll bet the cryptogram has something to do with it." He must realize that this is the year. I mean, the time for him to go back."

"Why do you think he took the crystals," Anna asked.

"Aunt Abigail said she would explain when grandfather got there. She also found that Jeff was a little distracted. He is planning to go to France tomorrow. Grandfather is flying out to England in about ½ hour from New York. He booked a flight from the Detective's office at the police station. He's on his way to the airport now. He thinks he knows where the village is that Jeffery is headed to; Aunt Abigail told him where it was and he is very familiar with that region of France."

Anna looked at the wall clock. "Let's see, it's almost 9:00 here, and how many hours is it Charles to England?"

It's roughly about 6 hours or so, depending on the air current. That would make it about, hmmm...3 o'clock in the morning in London."

Desmond looked intently at his watch. "Then you add 5 hours because of the time change, which would make it 8 o'clock in the morning in London."

"Grandfather has a flight booked for 9:35 to London. He may miss Jeff, by a few hours."

Anna looked worried. "Tomorrow may be too late. Mr. Edis has to get there before Jeffery walks into the cave."

Chapter 34

"Jeffery, have you written any of this down. You must keep a journal. My instincts tell me that the journal may be helpful to you in the future"

"You know Mother, it never crossed my mind, I hadn't really thought about writing it down. I think I'll go to Wilkinson & Son's Stationary and look for a journal of some sort and document the events as they occur."

"I think it is out of the ordinary how Rachel has had a few dreams concerning you Jeffery, almost paranormal, and the performance at the pier, how the man just disappeared. Your father & I have seen many strange things in our life time, but no stranger than when you appeared out of thin air."

I looked at her, with viable intention. You could hear the quiet in the background, if that is at all possible in a hospital.

She looked out the opened window. Two squirrels were chattering and scampering along the limbs of a nearby tree. Then Mother turned to me and spoke quietly.

"You had unusual clothing on. Colors we hadn't seen here, on our planet before. You looked so frightened. We saw you come through, along the walkway of the park. It was such a gorgeous day. The temperature was warm for early spring and beautiful flowers were starting to open. We were following a rare butterfly. Your father never saw one like it in the books and it had the most unusual colors. We thought we had lost our minds when it turned around. There were facial features Jeffery!" (After Mother's statement about a face, I sat right up with her full attention!)

"Your father thought he had caught it on film but the butterfly flew abruptly away down the walkway and disappeared as you came in. The photo was very blurry. I believe what we saw...Jeffery... was a real live fairy!"

"Your father being of practical mind, (I smiled at that statement), later said it was an atypical day, and maybe the sunlight & shadows of the trees or quickness of its movement along the walkway made us think we saw a face...but Jeffery, I know we saw a small face and it was a fairy of some sort."

"Jeffery, I am a teacher at Cambridge, and you know what a sensible mind I have, but with all the events of the day we found you, I had to broaden my mind to understand other existences."

"The butterfly or fairy, just for the benefit of doubt, was flying very fast when you appeared. We said to each other: "Did you just see that?

You didn't see us right away. You kept calling for someone, you seemed frightened and started to run, as if looking for someone, and ran right into your father. Looking up you asked: "Have you seen my bro...?" You looked around and seemed confused and had tears in your eyes. Your father put his sweater on you, because you started to shiver. We guessed you were about 10 years old. I asked you if we could help you find your parents, and then you asked where were you Jeffery, it didn't look familiar to you."

"You're in London," your father said.

"London? What is London? Where is the second sun?"

"Second Sun?" I asked

I took your hand, and said: "Let's go around the park and see if we can find someone you know."

"You looked at me Jeffery with such earnest eyes, and I could feel you trusted me. We walked for a few hours, but you didn't recognize anyone or anything, and your memory of who you were seemed to fade. Your father asked if you would like to come home with us and have something to eat and rest. You agreed, and have been with us ever since. We went through all the red tape and adoption proceedings. We both were ecstatic to finally have a son."

"The texture of your clothing shimmered and was styled very different from ours. I put your clothes in a box in the attic, when we bought you some new clothing. You also had a strange box with iridescent stones. We placed everything in a chest of all the things you had with you."

"The stones were the strangest. We had put them away because we didn't want anyone to find out that you may not have been from this world. You know I couldn't have a child, which is why we adopted you."

Mother looked around lowering her voice even more. "We kept this secret, if the information about you and what you brought with you fell into the wrong hands, you never know what others would do, and especially to you. We couldn't bear it, nor would we allow it. So, we hid everything in the attic. I will show it all to you later, Jeffery."

"Mother, I have been very fortunate to have bumped into you and father. I shudder to think what if it was anyone else."

I took mother's hands and said: Thank you for all your help and loving heart." Mother was getting teary eyed. "I know you have protected me, and I will do what ever I can to help Father get well."

We hugged each other and then the elevator opened down the hall. There stood Rachel Carde, about to step through the doors.

"Excuse me Mother, here's Rachel." We both stood up and I walked briskly down the hall to greet her.

Chapter 35

Desmond handed Anna the journal; it was her turn to read out loud. Hearing a key in the front door lock, everyone looked up and Ellen Belk walked through. "I have never seen blue or green amber, and it was unusual Lawrence!"

Hearing the name Lawrence, Charles got up and stretched. "Hi Dad, did you enjoy your evening?" "Charles! Yes, I enjoyed the exhibit without being a part of it this time!"

Ellen and Lawrence were beaming. "You should go to see the exhibit. It will be open for two more weeks."

"I may at some point. Dad"

I'm going to make coffee." Ellen went into the kitchen, and Lawrence followed her, finishing the conversation they had previously.

"The oldest Amber artifacts Ellen were predated 11,000 – 9000 BC..."

"Amazing, I thought the Knight's Set, Lawrence, was fascinating, especially....." The door swung close to the kitchen.

Anna and Desmond just looked at each other. Charles recouped, and sat back down on the couch. "Well, it has been an interesting night to say the least! Maybe we should continue reading tomorrow. I'm available for two to three days. Anna, can we try to figure out the cryptogram or codes in your computer now?"

Desmond retrieved Anna's laptop from the coffee table and handed it to her. He turned the overhead light on, and placed the cryptic words between them on an end table.

Anna looked up from her computer. "I'm going to put in a sentence like: 'The Epic Catalog has been a complete mystery.' Then I'll start with the fonts that seem out the ordinary."

"Wingdings is out of the ordinary," Desmond said as he started typing into his own laptop.

"Between Desmond and I, we should be able to find something...he's a good researcher, he doesn't give up easily."

Desmond looked at Anna briefly and smiled. She didn't see him, she concentrated on the glyphs. Anna hardly ever gave him a complement. In the past years, Anna called him a nuisance and always seemed irritated when he came over for a month in the summer. She never told him to his face, he had overheard a conversation a few years back, and Desmond felt embarrassed. But, last year changed all that. They started to bond and become friends. Desmond liked that feeling.

"Thanks, Anna."

Anna smiled with out looking up..."uh huh. This is not looking good, what are you getting, Desmond?"

"The Epic Catalog has been a complete mystery, hmm...here's a Simplified Arabic Fixed. No it still doesn't look anything like what's on the paper, Anna."

Charles flipped through the journal. "Do you think it was in some form of Gaelic, or, anything predating current language? Jeff may have discovered an older language whenever he attended digs with Rachel."

The kitchen door swung open, Lawrence Edis held it open for Ellen. She placed the tray of coffee, mugs and an apple strudel cake she baked earlier on the table. Everyone moved into the dining room.

"How did your book reading go, Anna and Desmond, did you find what you were looking for? I hope they didn't bore you Charles. Once Anna gets into the story mode...." Ellen sighed and smiled remembering past episodes. She poured coffee into the mugs.

Charles laughed, "Well Mrs. Belk, It is an interesting book. And it has particular meaning to me...it's my cousin's book, Jeffery Turner.

"You found Jeff's book, Charles?" Lawrence was inquisitive and intrigued.

"Grandfather brought back his journal from his travels. Aunt Abigail had it. Jeff had it published, and the problem is; where are the other books? We still can't find a copy, but it is almost word for word in the journal."

"I wonder..." Lawrence pondered; "The book may be rare, which explains why none were available." He then remembered the conversation at breakfast the other day, and thought how Charles relayed the incident at the quarry, and the two teens, looking for a book at The Antiquities Shop....Hmmm...

"Why the interest all of the sudden, Charles, and how did you find out about Jeff's book?

Ellen looked puzzled.

"I'm afraid, I was the one who started it all Mr. Edis," Anna replied.

"You? Ahhh, the two young teens," Lawrence Edis smiled looking at Anna and Desmond...

"Anna?" Ellen Belk looked a little concerned.

"Mom, it isn't what you think.....it all started with the last list of words Mrs. Perpecuwitz gave me. I used a word search in the computer, and The Epic Catalog, which is the name of the book, came up. We had to pick up Desmond from the airport that morning, so I tried to print it. Later when we came back home, I found that my ink cartridge needed changing, and Desmond's computer game was bringing up a lot of strange codes, which were the same codes in the book. Then we both had the same dream, and talked to an Elder......" Anna saw that her Mother and Lawrence Edis had eyebrows raised and coffee cups in mid air.

"Anna, would you like to tell us in full detail about the whole episode of the book?" Lawrence Edis accepted gratefully a piece of the cake from Ellen.

Anna and Desmond started from the beginning, the book on the computer, the dreams, the visit to the library, the quest at The Antiquities Shop, the trip to Rose Cottage to see Mrs. Perpecuwitz and then finally the meeting with Mr. Edis at the Antiquities Shop. Charles spoke of the quarry affair, how the three of them were mentioned in the book, Aunt Abigail's concern of the disappearance of Jeffery and Grandfather Edis on his way to France, after the hologram on the computer incident.

Silence....no one spoke for a few seconds. "I feel like I have just watched an incredible movie," stated Lawrence Edis.

It's unbelievable, but you say you have the journal?" Ellen Belk was shaking her head. "I don't know, Anna."

Anna retrieved it from the living room and handed her Mom the journal. "Mr. Edis gave it to us on loan to figure out the mystery. He's read most of the whole journal. Here are the cryptic notes we discovered as part of the appendix."

Ellen Belk flipped through the journal slowly, then handed it to Lawrence. She looked at the cryptic notes on the paper Anna handed to her.

"I'm completely baffled," said Ellen. "I'm not sure what to make of this whole ordeal, Anna."

Lawrence was preoccupied with the journal, murmuring... "This is quite fascinating."

"Mom, Mr. Edis knows Mrs. Perpecuwitz." Anna relayed the information of Mrs. Perpecuwitz's visit years ago to the Antiquities Shop and how she recognized the murals in the new addition."

"Anna, isn't the Big Splash Party on Monday night?"

"It is Mom."

"The next couple of days, I'll be busy, we have summer conferences at the school. I will have to talk to Mrs. Perpecuwitz on Monday."

Lawrence looked up from the journal, "I never knew about any of this, Charles."

"Grandfather knew very little also. He found out more from the journal, Dad."

"Lawrence, have you been to the monthly summer events at Rose Cottage in the past years?" Ellen handed him the cryptic notes.

"I have, Ellen. When is the next one?"

"Monday night, I am going to try to talk to Audrey Perpecuwitz then. Would you like to..."

Lawrence jumped right in..."Yes, I'd love to go with you Ellen. I would also like to know a little bit more about the murals."

Ellen turned to look at a picture on the wall trying to suppress her happiness.

Charles, an eyebrow raised, smiling, looked at Anna and Desmond from the quick reaction of his father for the invitation. All three were smiling. Lawrence noticed his son's reaction and smiled sheepishly.

The hallway clock chimed 11:00. Lawrence Edis cleared his throat and suddenly became aware of the lateness of the evening. "I didn't realize it was so late." He handed Anna back the journal and cryptic notes. Anna placed them in the zippered leather bag. "Charles, are you working tomorrow?"

"No, Grandfather gave me a couple days off, Dad. I'm to read the book with Anna and Desmond, and we need to figure out the cryptogram."

"I am on staff for the next few days. Ellen, may I come over again, say in two days, at around 7:00 pm. It will give me a chance to think about this, and maybe our children can tell us more of the journal."

"Oh, that will be fine, Lawrence."

"Good! Thank you very much for the coffee, and cake and attending the exhibit with me. In the meantime, I will try to get in touch with my father and see if he found Jeffery."

Chapter 36

The Seer met secretly with Ferian. It was early, before dawn. They drank kiuda; a tree bark tea like substance, it helped relaxed the body. The Seer and Ferian were in an atmospheric trance.

"The Anoa are getting braver, Ferian, little by little they are letting their true ambitions show through. Yet the Flyers have gone through the dimensions and saw the future of the Anoans here on our planet. Eventually they come into agreement within our culture. You have heard of their recent rendezvous near the Western Caridia Mountains?

"Yes, yes I have, Lestrian reported it several days ago. It has been almost three long years, Guardia. The Anoa are starting to get more comfortable here. How many are there, seven?"

"There are seven, although two of the Anoa have not been in agreement within the group, they have separated themselves from the others, Ferian. I will ask the Flyers if they would find out why. We are fortunate the Flyers are our friends. They are not indigenous to our dimension, yet they chose to come and help us."

"They are called The Faere in other dimensions. How they can transfer into different dimensions with out a portal..." Ferian slowly shook his head. "I wish it were that easy for Lorien. He has to translate back..." It is our genetic code, our bodies are of higher density than that of the three dimensional Earth, but the Faere, the Flyers, they can attribute their bodies when they astral travel. Even we, Guardia, could not do that. We can travel astrally, but never with our living bodies. The only way we can travel on Neia is through thought transference. We can only travel holographically in a trance or when we are asleep to other dimensions."

Guardia agreed, he was deep in thought, trying to contact a Flyer, and then he spoke. "Ferian, we are fortunate that the Anoa have not found out about Thereon's recent alliance to his brother."

"He has been very careful, Guardia, I have confidence that he will continue to do so. He knows now they can be dangerous. He has seen it for himself. It will be good for the planet when they finally leave. Has Orisen, been successful in the latest test?"

"The portal to the Anoan world was inaccessible... Wait! What is happening....?" The Seer was silent, watching, listening. Silence permeated the cavern for almost five minutes. "Ahhh, yes, thank you my friends! One of the Flyers had reported an Anoa coming back from a secret rendezvous; they have been working at stirring up the atmospheric energy near a portal of a base line planet. They are practicing a new method."

"Oh Guardia, they will never give up." Ferian sighed. "We must move them out of our dimension and back into their own. We are very grateful for the tiny Flyers. The Anoa do not know of their existence. They are invisible to them and most of our people." Ferian shifted his body slightly. "And Orisen, Guardia, what has he to tell us, has he reported his findings?"

"He is on the verge of a breakthrough. The Stones and Crystals will help during the translation. Orisen and Ranier discovered a flaw in the formula, it has been corrected. They have been successful in the recent tests."

"I am sure the Anoa will try to take control as Lorien begins to step through the portal. They will manipulate the atmosphere and energy around it. They really do not have a chance. Orisen and Ranier I think will outwit them."

"Can you foresee the Anoa's recent actions, Guardia?" Is Lorien still safe?"

"I have made the hologram and sent the message to the two children. The last astral trance, leads me to believe they have received it. They are more involved now. We can trust them. Bartholomew Edis is on his way to find Lorien. Time is a factor in their world. The Earth world has small objects that transfer sound waves, and they can hear each other and talk through them. It is different here, the earth dimension is not yet that advanced. So now, it is a race against time; I think Bartholomew Edis may still have a chance to find Lorien before he walks into the cavern."

"Good, I must report to the other Elders, Guardia. Thank you my friend."

The Seer acknowledged him, "Esteemed Elder." He stood and left through a hidden door, walking into the depths of the cavern, leading to his secret dwelling.

Ferian sat for a while, summoning the other elders and reporting the new developments telepathically through the seven atmospheres.

Chapter 37

Desmond slept soundly and suddenly awoke at 4:44 AM. Small flashes of light appeared around his outside window. The air was warm for the third week of June.

He threw the sheet cover off and walked noiselessly to the window. "Awfully big lightening bugs," he said softly. Then he looked more closely.

"I don't believe it" he whispered to himself, Fairies?" He remained hidden behind a curtain. One of the little light beings materialized through the screen. Desmond could see through it.

"We are known as Flyers or Faere" Desmond could hear the light being in his head. His bedroom door opened silently and Anna walked quietly into the room.

"Desmond," she whispered, "Is it another hologram?"

"I think so; I'm not really sure, I can hear him in my head."

"I can too," said Anna.

The little Flyer was a beautiful butterfly like creature with human features. "We are here to warn you. On the night of the translation of Lorien from your dimension to ours, the Anoa plan to create violent storms and unusual weather patterns to prevent him from coming through. It can be stopped with the use of both the Stones and the Crystals in Lorien's possession. The Crystals are very powerful. There are seven of them. They decode the energy of the seven atmospheric realms within our world and the seven star systems in our galaxy where the other world, Neia resides into your planetary galaxy of constellations, sun and energy"

"You must have in your possession the two large stones. Placing the stones at the opening of each of the sides of the portal will activate them. You will know they are activated when they start to release a bright orange color. Once they are activated, the cloth must lay between the Stones on the ground. The box must be opened seven seconds after the two large stones have been activated. Place the crystals in the exact formation you see in the sky through the portal onto the cloth. The energy or transmitter within the cloth will set in motion each crystal as you place them on the fabric. The Constellations of the Epic Catalog, from within our world, where all the constellations are formed, will make the transfer of Lorien through the open portal safe. We bid you farewell..."

They disappeared. Desmond turned on his small desk lamp. He faced Anna. "How did you know they were here, Anna?"

"I woke up suddenly at 4:44, and saw a flash of light outside my window, and then it came in, and went through my door. I followed it into the hallway and saw it go through your door."

"Me too, Anna, I woke up at the same exact time, and saw the flashes of light outside my window also."

"Let's write down what he said, so we won't forget it, Desmond!"

"K." Desmond retrieved pen and paper from the desk in the bedroom.

Chapter 38

Audrey Perpecuwitz's image stood on her patio outside her bedroom door. The crescent moon gave way to iridescent stars across the warmth of the earth below in mid June. Her mood tranquil as night visitors suddenly came into view.

"You have come back, my little friends, and why so soon? Audrey smiled.

One of the Flyers flew forward. They communicated telepathically. "We have visited the boy and girl. We have told them about the crystals."

"You have not told them anything else, L'elma?"

"No, only how to place them, as the portal opens."

Is there any danger?" The children will be safe?"

"There is always an element of danger. It has been reported that the Anoa will try the energy fields to discourage the translation."

Can it be done any other way? Does it have to be the children?"

"It can only be Dertia's descendants. They are of the bloodline of those who translated when the portal was opened in the earlier centuries of earth time. To help with the transition this world will undergo in the near future."

"And, L'elma, you know definitely they are descendants?"

"Yes, we have known and felt their vibration and it is higher than those who are of denser energy. Their modality is constant. They are of the ones who must help Lorien to pass through."

"What do you mean, of the ones?"

"We mean genetically. You know, Sephiria, you are also a descendant, but not of the same bloodline. Your mother's father was Neian."

"Audrey smiled, "Yes, if I were of the same energy, I would help, but you are sure, Anna and Desmond are related to one of Lorien's earlier ancestor's who came here in the eighteenth century?"

"The sister's ancestors were pure Neians. Dertia was also Lorien's Great, Great Aunt, from his mother's lineage. The codes in their DNA match. The children's mothers' carry it within their bloodline."

"How fortunate for Lorien, that they came when they did, L'elma. The translation would be of no avail if they didn't."

"They would have tried another way, Sephiria. This is the only option for now."

"L'elma, my name here is Audrey..."

"We know, we love your Neian name, we bid you farewell."

Audrey Perpecuwitz laughed, "Good bye my little friends. Give Meriasa my love. After a while the 5:30 alarm rang and Audrey Perpecuwitz woke up, refreshed and ready to take on the day.

Chapter 39

Some say it was an Angel, others say it was pure chance. No one really knows for sure. It was recorded as a mystery or a medical miracle if you will.

The year was 1968. Sephiria lay in bed with a fever, after a recent trauma. She was admitted to Hospital Saint Eloi in Montpellier, where she was finishing her vacation in the South of France. The murals in Tibet brought back some extraordinary visions or memories. But where did they come from and why?

After flying into France from Tibet, Sephiria had been in a near fatal car accident. She had partial memory loss, and was bleeding internally. The staff kept a close watch on her. It looked like she wasn't going to make it this time. They nearly lost her earlier when she came in, so much blood loss.

The Nurses on post that evening were quickly looking through the most recent blood donations on file, and the records did not come up with a single match. It was unlike any blood they had seen before; a very rare type. Time was crucial. Sephiria had taken a turn for the worse, she was in extreme critical condition. They contacted hospitals in the 50 mile radius, but to no avail.

It was around 3:33 AM; a younger middle aged woman burst though the doors and volunteered blood. It happened so fast. It was an unusual blood type and to find someone that quickly... They never found out who gave the blood. It was 4:34 AM when the nurse turned around to thank the donor, and record more information when the mysterious woman had vanished almost out of thin air. All the nurse could remember was the glow of light around the woman; she had a peaceful serene composure and was of an elegance you didn't naturally see in those days. When she touched Sephiria, the nurses on staff noticed an unusual light emanating to the injured body. It was beyond belief, yet it did happen.

Sephiria recovered quicker than normal. In fact it was amazingly quick. She was shocked that her body looked so young. She felt like she was 18 again. Sephiria thought in the back recesses of her mind that she was much older. Yet, because of the recent incident, a few memories came flooding back and left her with confusion. She felt more alive than in the past recent years. It was as if her life process had reversed... but that was crazy, she thought. After awhile Sephiria had a good look in the mirror... impossible, absolutely incredible... wasn't she close to 30, yet she looked 18 or 20... what happened... a dream, an awakening of some sort?

Did she wake up one morning in another's reality?

Days before, during the night when Sephiria was unconscious and fighting for her life, she had a very strange dream. An elderly man came to her; he was present, yet not there. The dream seemed lucid...so real. He comforted her with soothing words and Sephiria thought she felt his hand on her shoulder. The air smelled like perfumed flowers. He spoke to her with a gentle kind voice and told her that she would recover. She need not be afraid. They would be looking out for her well-being, and her mother would come and save her. She saw a vision of the woman who was her mother. She seemed familiar, but her head ached so much, she couldn't remember.

When Sephiria came out of intensive care and was able to go into a regular room, the nurse who witnessed the donor, told her of the strange woman who gave her blood the night of the accident. Did she know of anyone in this part of France who would donate blood to her?

Sephiria shook her head. She remembered very little because of her memory loss. As time went on, her full memory came back. The name Audrey appealed to her and after reading an article on Audrey Hepburn while recuperating, she decided to call herself Audrey.

It was during her vacation while in the hospital, and for the life of her, she couldn't remember from what, that she met Rolf Perpecuwitz. He traveled through the South of France periodically, on a business tour, and wasn't due to go back to his home in Northern France for another three weeks. He was a witness to the accident. A driver on the opposite side of the road swerved quickly to avoid a child who ran in front of him after a balloon. Unwittingly, with the afternoon sun in his eyes the driver drove into the oncoming car that Audrey was driving around the countryside in.

Rolf brought her flowers and visited her everyday for three weeks when he was free. He fell in love with her and she felt that romantic pull toward Rolf. It was eight years since he lost his wife to tuberculosis. It was a severe and unusual case. After his wife passed from this world, Rolf plunged himself into his work. France was not his country of birth, but he had lived here since college, married and resided there after his wife's death because of his established business. Rolf had just turned thirty-four in May.

After Audrey recovered her memory and was well enough to make the trip back to her home near Paris, they were married the following month. After two years, Rolf was transferred to The United States, and they lived there for eight blissful years.

Audrey Perpecuwitz had no regrets. Rolf died unexpectedly in 1978 to cancer. Audrey grieved for many months. Then when the property near the Gorge went for sale, she bought it and turned it into a major tourist attraction and founded Rose Cottage. Rolf loved roses.

Flashes of childhood memories would come and go. Audrey would remember strange places. She became used to the dreams and astral trances in her sleep of another world and time. Audrey never told Rolf, she felt he wouldn't understand. It was peculiar though; she never seemed to age much. No one really knew how old she was. Audrey wasn't sure herself.

Finally, during the year 1989, she had a visit from the woman who was her mother in a dream. Lanaia was tall and regal and she called Audrey her Sephiria.

Lanaia came many times, during Audrey's trance-like sleep. One evening, she asked Audrey to try to remember her birth and life as a child. Lanaia told her the story of how she met her father, Tory Jamison.

Lanaia was from a world close to Neia. Her beloved friend came from this parallel world, Earth. Tory Jamison was on expedition in the Himalayas, in the 1940's. His team had located a Yeti, and they were tracking it along the higher elevations. A violent storm, bringing snow and strong winds forced the team into a cave. As they ventured further in, they found an unusual tunnel and followed the corridor into a clearing full of light and warmth. They witnessed a land so beautiful, and tame, the expedition team had never realized they walked into another dimension. Animals, flora, and foliage, the likes of which they had never been seen before, all lived in harmony here. It was called: 'The Holding Place.'

No one in the expedition never really cared to go back to their own world. The team was reported to be lost in the mountain storm and the bodies were never recovered. What they saw was unbelievable. Could this be Shangri-La? Have they stumbled upon this sought after fictional place the world had read about in 1933, Lost Horizons?

Tory Jamison fell in love with Lanaia, and she with him. After a year, she bore a child and called her Sephiria. The dimension the team had stumbled upon was a holding transport area. You could not stay there for long, a month, three months at the most. Your body would have to be reenergized from the world or dimension you were from. Since Tory and the other team members could not go to the dimension Lanaia came from, their bodies not having the higher density they needed to live in that extraordinary place, they would live in the villages of the Himalayas for several months, and then make their way back to the cave, where the secret tunnel brought them to their Shangri-la, or The Holding Place to meet their friends from the other dimensions.

One day, when Sephiria turned 12, Lanaia let her stay with her father in the Himalayas. Their daughter was getting older and her blood and body had developed more density. Sephiria had trouble transporting back and forth into her mother's dimension. On her twelfth birthday, she couldn't transpose back.

On Sephiria's fourteenth birthday, a frequent group of travelers came to one of the villages in the Himalayan Mountains. Tory had an accident and was killed while driving a doctor to a nearby village for medical supplies. The doctor didn't survive either. A couple who visited every year from France let Sephiria stay with them while Tory was away for a week. The devastating news had finally reached the village and the couple seeing that the child's father had no relatives in the village, took her back to France with them and eventually adopted her.

Audrey had a wonderful life with the Parrence's, but since they were an older couple, in their 70's at the time of Sephiria's adoption and after well into their 90's, they left this earth when she was twenty-two. Yves and Eva Parrence both died within the year.

Lanaia was able to transpose to any parallel world when certain constellations of the dimensions would line up. However, when she came to Earth, she could only stay for about 45 minutes to one hour. After an hour, Lanaia's delicate body would become transparent, and she would lose herself in the ether. Once there, she would be able to regulate her cells, and arrange an aperture from where she came from. The constellations haven't lined up since she came and saved her daughter's life, not for another 28 years would they be in correct formation. It was difficult for her, not being able to see her daughter physically at will, and because Tory Jamison was of Earth, Sephiria's body held the denser energy. At the Holding Place, Lanaia could come at will, but Sephiria would have to meet her there.

Audrey tried to find the village and cave where she lived in the Himalayans with her father for the two years and without Yves and Eva it was hopeless to find. She only had her dreams when her mother came to visit, which she very much cherished.

Yet, Audrey was not unhappy. She loved her life, the people in her circle, the area she chose to live in. She loved it all.

Chapter 40

Jeffery Turner walked into La Chambre des Antiquités International in a small town near Saintes-Maries-de-la-Mer. Marcel Laurent was waiting for him near a turn of the century desk.

"Ah, my good friend Jeffery Turner, and how does this day find you... well, I hope?"

The two old friends shook hands as Marcel ushered Jeffery into a more private room.

"Marcel, so good of you to see me in such short notice. I'm well thank you, and you? You appear in good form." Jeffery took in his surroundings.

"Never felt better. I am sorry about Rachel, Jeffery. She was a wonderful woman."

"Thank you Marcel, yes, well I had to adjust being without her, it's been about four years now. I hadn't traveled much after her death, just to London to visit my mother now and then." Jeffery walked to a nearby window, gazing at a garden of flowers, "Hmmm," he appeared preoccupied about something. Suddenly he became alert. "Marcel, you know why I am here?"

"Ah yes. Well, right down to business is it? Marcel Laurent was jovial. And your flight, you had a good flight to France?"

Jeffery nodded, smiling, as he made himself comfortable in a nearby chair.

Marcel opened the door and called out from his private room. "Michel, I shall be with Monsieur Turner for quite awhile. We wish to remain private. No interruptions please!"

"Certainly, Marcel, I will see to it!" Michel turned back to his paper work.

"Jeffery, you came for the envelope? Years ago, you had promised me that you would one day tell me about your mysterious envelope." Marcel removed a potted plant from the window sill pushing a button beneath it. He carefully replaced the plant back on the sill. A unique Picasso slid to the side on the opposite wall revealing a safe.

"Do you remember Marcel the journal I had published?"

"Yes, it was in the late 1950's, about the time you left your practice in London, you were thinking of moving to the U...S of A."

"1958 to be exact," said Jeffery. "The envelope has something to do with the journal. Have you ever read it?"

"Yes, long ago when it was first published. I still have my copy in the library at my villa."

"And....?"

"And... what are you getting at...?"

"The envelope... the journal... you do know that it is all factual."

Marcel turned around, giving Jeffery his full attention. "But that is preposterous; do you mean it is all true, what you wrote?"

"Yes it is true Marcel and time is most crucial, especially this year..."

"What do you mean, this year? Marcel looked confused.

"Do you remember, in the journal, that I talked about another parallel world, a Neian world...?"

"I...ah...seem to recall you mentioning something in the book, I'm not really...sure... it has been a long time since I've read it, at least 30 years."

"I'm going back old chap this year; the portal will be opening in July, around the 11th, somewhere in America. I've done some research, but I'm still not sure where it will open. I may have an idea. I have a contact that may be able to help. The portal only opens in so many years, and this year, 2011, will be my last year here."

"You are old now, will it really matter?"

"Marcel, how old do I look?"

"You look a hell of a lot younger than you really are, and I happen to know you are as old as I am, but, I thought it was just a story." Marcel was flabbergasted, trying to think of the details in the journal.

"You know, I don't really feel old. I have aged, but not like people in this world. My body structure is not as dense. My DNA is different also. I have been told that when I go back, I will be a lot younger."

"Marcel said lightly: "Ho ho....maybe some of us could go with you, and then we would all be younger."

"It doesn't work that way, my friend," Jeffery smiled; then became poignant, "Your body structure is different. It's denser; I was told a body from this dimension wouldn't last." He fell silent for a moment. "I will miss everyone," Jeffery said sadly at last.

Well, you don't have much time left, it is already June 20th, and you have a little over three weeks."

"I know, but first I need to go to the caves Rachel had researched in the early years, there may have been something overlooked from long ago."

"How do you know, Jeffery? Have you heard of any new developments? I have not read anything about it in the periodicals. There has been nothing in the media, and can you spare the time?"

"It's more of a feeling, Marcel that something is missing. A few days ago I had a dream. I didn't actually see Rachel, but felt her talking to me in the reverie. She said I needed to go back to the caves; it was significant to the research, a missing connection."

Marcel plugged in his electric tea pot. "My friend be careful, dreams or not, remember the controversy, you do not want to stir up the past?"

"It's all over and done with, Marcel, don't worry, I'm just going to be there briefly, a day or so. It's the time of year that the tides are down, so there won't be a problem with that to say the least. I plan on going to see Raphael Gustauve to pick up my diving gear and..."

"Haven't you heard, Jeffery, Raphael has married and is on his honeymoon...?"

"Whhaat? You don't say, well, well, well," Jeffery emphasized with feeling. "What had gotten into him? When did the old codger get married, wasn't he a confirmed bachelor?"

"It was late spring, when he met Marielle. Swept him off his feet," Marcel chuckled, "Never seen anything like it. He is a changed man! He dotes on her..."

"Oh, I would love to see that, Raphael doting, well, well, my word!" Jeffery chortled, then said semi seriously. Well, it was bound to happen sooner or later."

"And later in his case," Marcel said with merriment.

"Ah, yes! And how old is Raphael now, Must be pushing seventy by now?"

"Seventy-three to be exact and he doesn't look a day over fifty-five, the scoundrel!"

"How old is his wife, Marielle?"

"Sixty-seven, and she looks like a model. They met when Raphael went to Provence to pick up some new gear for the shop. Not sure of all the details, but he was detained for quite a while. What should have taken a few days turned out to be a month or so. When he did finally come back, he was humming, and .....Get this Jeffery....smiling, and... saying hello to everyone ...isn't it a nice day....etc, etc... We all thought he was, as you English say: 'Off his trolley?' Then we met Marielle..."

"Unbelievable! Well, as I said before, everyone deserves to be happy."

"Oh yes, and is he ever!" The tea kettle started to whistle, and Marcel poured the steaming hot water into two mugs set with Earl Grey teabags in them.

"Will I find La Serine' Aquatique open during this extraordinary holiday and... I'm sure Leslie Parrant has written all about it?"

Oh she has, my friend, and what an article, 'Confirmed Bachelor to Wed....' Raphael took it all in good stride. It was a prized piece, read all over France." Leslie had retired, but wrote the article anyway and submitted it to her old newspaper. She still has clout! Marcel wiped his eyes after a good laugh. "This is one for the books! Ah, my friend, what times we all had!"

"Yes," murmured Jeffery reminiscing, "yes..."

Marcel shifted through some papers and folders in the safe. He came upon the envelope. "Ah, here it is!" He extracted it, and handed it to Jeffery.

"Marcel, do you have a cutting tool? Marcel handed him one and Jeffery unsealed the contents of the large envelope, revealing the keys, codes and fabric. "Thank you my good friend for keeping this safe for me all these years." Jeffery took out the piece of fabric. Marcel went over to look. Never had he seen anything like it. The same with the keys and the slip of paper in the envelope, it was unbelievable.

"C'est assez incroyable!!!" The contents of the envelope were glowing. Marcel could hardly believe it, and yet? He kept looking at Jeffery, then the contents of the envelope and back.

They talked about the journal and the past for quite a while, a few hours had past. Marcel opened the door to his private room and asked Michel to order lunch for them both.

The two old friends talked for another hour. It was well past one pm when Jeffery got into his rental car and drove to the La Serine' Aquatique on behalf of his underwater equipment for the next part of his journey.

Chapter 41

Charles was up and at the Belk's home by 10:30 the next morning. He smelled the remains of maple syrup, and what was it, French toast?

At times Charles missed his mother. She lived in New York City, but her job took her out to London a few times during the year. 'I wonder what she is doing now,' he reflected. His mother and father had divorced eight years ago. He was almost eleven at the time. When it came time to choose a college, Charles wanted to learn more about the antique business. He was also studying archeology. Eastern Rydner University offered exceptional courses with the benefit of being close to his grandfather who would give him employment and first hand experience. Charles had great admiration for his grandfather, Bartholomew Edis.

Lawrence was thrilled, and loved having Charles around more often. Eleanor was a social butterfly. Too social for Lawrence, who only wanted the simplistic life he led at the Museum.

Anna and Desmond entered the living room with their laptops bringing Charles out of his reverie. Charles had also brought his laptop computer and set it up on the coffee table.

Mrs. Belk made a quick appearance in the living room; she was on her way to the summer conferences at Rydner's Elementary School.

"I left lunch for everyone in the refrigerator. I won't be home until after 4:30 in the afternoon. The conference concludes around 3:30 and then we need to set up for the next day. Anna you know the number of the school, incase of an emergency. I won't have my cell phone; it will be in my purse locked in the office."

Anna was nodding. "Okay Mom, see you later." Desmond and Charles said goodbye and settled down near their computers.

Desmond stood up. "Hey, how about going into the dining room with the computers? There are more outlets in there and we may have to plug them in later."

"Sounds like a great idea, Desmond," said Charles. Everyone moved into the dining room with all their equipment.

"Charles, Mom left the coffeepot on just incase you wanted any coffee. It's not too old, only about an hour." Anna was up and ready to get Charles a coffee.

Desmond frowned, 'boy is she crushin,' he thought.

Charles loved coffee. "Sure, I'll take a cup. I brought some pastries..."

Desmond's eyes lit up. "From Sephia's Pastries?"

"Only the best in the whole wide world," said Charles quoting from the box as he pulled it from his backpack and placed it on the counter near the coffee pot.

Anna giggled. "Coffee for everyone! Hope you don't mind Charles, its decaf."

"Not a bit. So have you worked any more on the codes?"

Desmond took his choice of pastry from the box. "A little, we have a disc of fonts we were going to try out first thing."

Everyone reconvened into the dining room with cups of coffee, napkins and pastries.

Desmond plopped in the font's disk. Anna was on Google looking through font's information. Charles was bringing up fonts on a different search engine.

"This is tougher than I thought it would be." Desmond was in his research mode.

After an hour and a half, they all decide to take a break.

"Maybe we could find more information about the codes in Uncle Jeff's journal, said Charles hopefully."

After a few minutes, Desmond was already in front of his computer. He wanted to finish checking one more font site, and then he came upon a font he had overlooked. "I think I got it, I **think I got it!"**

Anna and Charles rushed to his side.

"The Epic Catalog has been a complete mystery," Desmond said as he typed the words again into the computer.

The Epic Catalog has been a complete mystery.
Τηε Επιχ Χαταλογ ηασ βεεν α χομπλετε μψστερψ.

"Anna do you have the paper from the journal?"

Anna went back to her computer and took the paper out of the journal. Everyone compared the words on Desmond's computer to the cryptogram on the paper.

"Look Desmond," Anna showed him the words: Epic Catalog. "They really look similar. I think you may have found the font Desmond!"

"It's about one pm. I'm going to see what Mom made for lunch, and then we can decipher the cryptogram." Anna found chicken salad sandwiches and a bowl of fresh green salad. Charles came in to help with the plates, napkins and utensils. Anna secretly smiled. She placed a sandwich on each plate, while Charles put a little salad on the side. Desmond was still trying to decipher the symbolic code.

He went through each letter of the alphabet; Anna placed a chicken salad sandwich on the side of his computer. Desmond absently mindedly ate as he deciphered each sentence.

After quite while, Desmond looked up and said: "Ok, here it is, it took longer than usual," he looked at the clock on the mantel.

"Yeah, about an hour and forty-five minutes to be exact," said Anna.

Desmond gave Anna the look.

"What have you come up with," Charles was anxious to know.

"Ok"....Desmond turned his laptop around so Anna and Charles could see it. Desmond showed them what was written on the screen.

Τηε Χονστελλατιονσ Οφ Νεια
The Constellations of Neia

Τηρεε κεψσ το φιτ ιντο τηε γατε
Three keys to fit into the gate

Ονε πιεχε οφ Νεια φαβριχ το πλαχε βετωεεν τηε στονεσ

One piece of Neia fabric to place between the stones

Χοορδινατε τηε χοδεσ το τηε τιμε ερα
Coordinate the codes to the time era

Ωηεν τηε σεχονδ συν ρισεσ ανδ τηε ονε συν δεσχενδσ
When the second sun rises and the one sun descends

Ανδ τηε Επιχ Χαταλογ ρελεασεσ ιντο τηε σκψ
And the Epic Catalog releases into the sky

Ανδ τρανσλατεσ τηε ενεργψ φρομ ονε πλαχε το τηε οτηερ
And translates the energy from one place to the other

Τηεν αλλ σηαλλ βε φυλφιλλεδ
Then all shall be fulfilled.

Charles read the words out loud.

"The Constellations of Neia, Three keys to fit into the gate, One piece of Neia fabric to place between the stones, Coordinate the codes to the time era, When the second sun rises and the one sun descends, And the Epic Catalog releases into the sky, And translates the energy from one place to the other, Then all shall be fulfilled. Hmmm... interesting. Can we find this in the book? Have we read about two suns?"

"This is cool, Anna!" Desmond was ready for another sandwich. He scanned the table and saw the empty platter. Any more sandwiches, Anna"

"I think there are two left in the fridge." Anna looked at Desmond's computer while he went to the refrigerator for another sandwich.

"Anyone want another sandwich?" asked Desmond peering over the refrigerator door?

Charles had two already, and with the morning pastry and coffee, felt full. Anna had enough, so Desmond took one sandwich, and grabbed the ice tea jug and went back to the table.

"We've figured out the cryptogram. We can work on it a little later. We should read more of the journal, to see if there are additional clues that we don't know about. Especially about the two suns," said Charles.

"Let's clean up the lunch dishes first," Anna stood up and Charles followed suit. Desmond stood up and helped while still chewing the remains of his sandwich.

After the dishes were washed, dried and put away, all three went into the living room, settling into comfy chairs to read more of the Epic Catalog.

It was Desmond's turn to read.

Chapter 42

Rachel Carde was a refreshing sight to see. I met her as she came toward us from the elevator. When we reached Mother, I introduced them to each other.

"It is such a pleasure to meet you Mrs. Turner. I am so sorry to hear about Mr. Turner's accident. I hope he makes a quick recovery from his injuries."

"Thank you Rachel, it is so nice to meet you also. His recovery will take some time. Walter still has a concussion, cuts and bruises and is in a quite amount of pain, he is also suffering from a fractured a rib."

"And Father broke his wrist. From what I read on the report, from the impact of the vehicle, he should have sustained several major injuries..." I looked at mother and said emotionally: "Father was lucky..."

"He was very lucky;" Mother said smiling through slight tears..."very, very lucky. I think I will go check on Walter, excuse me for a moment."

"Yes, of course," said Rachel sympathetically. I nodded and faintly smiled as mother went through the door to his father's room.

I let mother go into the room alone. I had the feeling she wanted a few moments to regain her composure.

Rachel turned to me and said: "Jeffery, you have a lovely mother."

"Thank you Rachel, yes I have two capital parents." I bucked up and elaborated. "I have been very fortunate; you know I was adopted, not sure if I told you on the ship."

"So much has happened, I'm not sure if you did." Rachel smiled trying to recollect, and suddenly remembered, "Oh, I left my luggage downstairs, I will need to collect them at the office on the main floor, later. The Director of the Hospital was kind enough to let me keep it there."

"Yes, certainly, Rachel,   I left mine in the storage room near the nurse's station on this floor. I hope you were able to accomplish what you needed to do, earlier."

"I did, and a lot more. The paperwork took very little time which allowed me to contact all the members of my team who will be assisting with the carbon dating of the cave and its authenticity. We need to be sure it's genuine. We have about two weeks before all the team members come together. My parents will be arriving in France in about ten days. They are in New York finishing up a book of some of their expeditions, especially on the mounds found in the United States and England."

"Yes, I've actually read about the Serpent Mound in... Utah?"

"Ohio," corrected Rachel, yes similar, but there are many such types all over The Americas and England"

"Like Glastonbury Tor in Somerset."

"Yes, exactly, my mother and father had been working and researching similar places for years. They finally had enough data compiled to put it into a journal, and then a book. It's all completed, and now they are finalizing the finishing touches.

The intercom could be heard in the background.

"Rachel, we didn't get to talk much about your next excavation on the ship. I was curious, how did the town find out about the sea caves? Isn't it in an isolated area?"

"Quite, and coincidently I have the article in my carry bag, from a New York Paper reporting from a French publication." "Hmmm," Rachel searched the bag. "Oh here it is..." Rachel read straight from the article.

"Four tourists from Italy made a recent discovery in the South of France. Almost a year ago, Southern France was hit by several violent storms stirring from the Mediterranean Sea. They experienced three tropical depressions with

hurricane like weather. One part of the coastline had so much erosion; parts of the landmass had fallen away. Residents had to contend with large amounts of debris, branches, extra sand to clean up, small boulders transported on shore from the sea, and undergrowth making it impossible to notice the small underwater cavern on a lower reef in the south eastern coastal area."

"When the four tourists went snorkeling north of the Saintes-Maries-de-la-Mer coastline, two of the divers decided to swim closer to an upper costal reef to photograph the habitant and coral. The sun playing on the water caused one of the divers to look closer and spotted something odd with the water level. Upon investigating it further, the diver motioned to her partner and swam through a submerged cavern discovering what looked to be an opening. The diver surfaced and jump to the ledge of the underwater cave. Upon viewing the walls, and noticing pottery lying around with other relics, the diver decided to go a little deeper and found what looked to be tombs in another cavern. The divers who wish to remain anonymous reported the finds to the French government."

"Since then, there have been several countries, including the United States who are authenticating the caves' validity. Among the archeologists are; Dr.'s Winston and Maria Carde, renowned for their work world wide will be accompanied by their daughter, Dr Rachel Carde later this month."

Rachel skimmed the rest of the article.   "And then it resumes on page A6... *'Our very own Jacques Bordeau, as well as his team from France will be examining and authenticating the culture, ancient text and hieroglyphs found on the interior walls and ledges. This has to be the find of the centaury! All artifacts will be reviewed and cataloged by the Muse'e d'Arche'ologie nationale in St Germain-en Laye, France. All artifacts and relics will remain in France."*

Jeffery cleared his throat and said jokingly, "Well Dr. Carde, you have quite an adventure ahead of you! I'm afraid I am going to be envious of what you are doing...Imagine that...a whole culture no one ever knew about. How old do you think it is, I mean, judging from the photographs?

"It's hard to tell, Jeffery, I haven't been to the caves yet, and the photographs are black and white, and not the best quality, our team will take color photographs. You know what seemed unusual Jeffery? In another article I've read, two unusual looking stones, orange in color, set in what looked to be an ancient Paleolithic alter, seemed very familiar. It was if I had seen them before. Any way no one is allowed to remove anything until all the teams get there. It is so thrilling!"

Desmond stopped reading, and excitingly said, "Anna, do you think those are the two stones Mr. Edis has in his safe at the shop?"

"We can look it up..."

"We might even find the earlier photographs, since Rachel said they were going to photograph them in color," interjected Charles. "It could be a link, if indeed they were the ones grandfather has in his safe."

Anna and Desmond agreed, and Desmond continued reading the chapter.

Mother came out of father's room and said he was awake, and wanted to meet the famous archeologist. I smiled, and out of the corner of my eye, caught Rachel blushing.

After I examined father, all for Rachel's benefit, we decided to let father rest for the night, it was well after six pm. I had hoped Rachel didn't catch father winking at me as he glanced Rachel's way. Father was joking with everyone even though he was in incredible pain. His concussion has narrowed down to a slight one and he seemed to be more alert. But, I'm afraid we had tired him out at last and it was time to go.

We collected our luggage, and Mother had father's station wagon since she knew we were coming directly from the plane. It had been a long day for all of us. Rachel planned to stay five days in London. Then she was off to Paris to meet with a representative at the Louvre, before going to Marseilles, where the rest of her crew decided to meet before moving on to the actual site.

We all talked long into the night and Mother was quite fascinated with the whole subject of archeology and asked Rachel if she would consider giving a talk about the expedition in Cambridge when she was done with her documentation.   Mother taught courses in Biological Sciences specializing in Plant Sciences, at Cambridge.   She also knew the Dean personally and was confident Rachel Carde would be widely received as an honorary guess speaker.

All the while Mother and Rachel conversed; I couldn't help thinking that the South of France is not that very far off from London...not far at all.

Chapter 43

Bartholomew Edis touched down in Montpellier, France at 2:55 pm. He received a text message in LaGuardia Airport before he boarded the plane in New York City from his sister Abigail with pertinent information. "Bart, don't come to London, Jeffery stopped by the house and left for the South of France. He intends to look up an old friend of his and Rachel's en route to the caves. This may buy you just a little time, love Abby."

Once in the air terminal, Bartholomew tried Jeffery's cell phone again. He wasn't picking up. The best thing he could do was drive the distance to the caves near Saintes-Maries-de-la-Mer. It was a race against time. As he went to inquire about a rental car, he suddenly remembered an old friend of his who lived in Montpellier. He thought to himself, "Why didn't I think of him before?"

He estimated it took an hour and fifteen minutes to drive to the caves without traffic, so Bartholomew "Bart" Edis decided to make a telephone call at the airport and reserve a small plane for a quicker ride. He telephoned his old friend Rene' "Flying Aces" Baigent who owned a sea plane taxi service business years ago. Upon hearing Bart's voice Rene' was very delighted, "Ahhh! mon tres bon ami, Bart!"

Their friendship began when Bart went on vacation in 1952 to Montpellier, France; he was around twenty-one then. Rene' was twenty three. Bart needed a quick ride to the island of Palma near the coast of Spain. He had some business at Bellver Castle. On their way, The Flying Aces Taxi Service, (Rene's name for his plane and company), nearly missed an unidentified flying object three times causing his navigation instruments to function erratically. The radio had blown a fuse, so all contact was lost.

Everyone on board the sea plane was quite shaken and by the time Rene's co-pilot noticed, The Flying Aces Taxi Service had flown so far off course, they were lost and ran out of fuel. Rene' found out later the plane landed on the Tyrrhenian Sea near Italy.

They had to wait for someone to notice them missing from their destination before a rescue team could be issued. Mobile phones were unheard of in 1952. Fog had drifted in. Rene' had to let the sea plane float on the Tyrrhenian Sea and almost collided into a large Freight Barge, who happened to notice the sea plane floating on the water with their navigational radios. Once on board the Barge, Rene' was able to contact the necessary avenues for a rescue at sea. This was the beginning to a lasting friendship with Rene' and Bart.

Bartholomew took a cab to the Flying Aces Taxi Air Service. Rene' Baigent was fueling a plane when he noticed the cab drive in. Upon arrival, Bart Edis exited the cab and took one look at the plane and laughed as he approached Rene'. It was a newer model, but still had the original insignia painted on the side. The original Flying Aces Taxi Service plane stood proud and tall in a museum especially for antiquated planes.

The two old friends hugged and slapped each other on the back. "Ahhh, you look the same Bart, and what is it with your hair, mon ami? The light sockets look, eh?"

"It is a little wild, can't seem to tame it, still smoking those cigars, hey Rene'?"

"Ahhh!!! Let's get your duffle bag on board." Rene' brought up the famous flight story again, which after many years was extremely exaggerated. Bart found himself wondering, what really did happen?

Rene's son, Jacques, who was studying to be a veterinarian, climbed on board. "Bonjour, Monsieur Edis, it is me, little pip squeak!! And now I am as tall as you!"

"Well I'll be ...Jacques! So good to see you..."

Rene' was a slight man, around 5'9" and his son of the same build, towered at 6'2". Jacques shook hands with Bart and then gave him a bear hug.

Rene' roared with laughter and, again elaborated the stories of Bart and their past adventures with little pip squeak, the famous name given to him by Bart.

Jacques, now 37, was the youngest of Rene's 3 children and a perpetual student, he had "seven degrees in heaven knows what," exclaimed Rene'. "When will you settle down, get married, ahhh!" He shook his head and laughed. "He does not like the girls; you know what I mean, Bart!"

Jacques laughed and said: Oh Popie, (his pet name for his father,) It is alright, eh? Bart and Rene' smiled at each other and Rene' lifted his eyebrows and hands in a gesture suggesting: What can I do, face. "And," Jacques continued, "Moma said "No more cigars!"

"Ahhhh!! It is not lit, Little Pip Squeak!!!" Rene' faked exasperation, took the cigar out of his mouth and put it in his pocket.

Jacques lifted his hands half in the air raising his eyebrows at Bart, and said, "J'essaie de mon mieux."

Rene' & Bart laughed reminiscing of past queries of his wife's insistence of keeping him healthy!

Rene loved all his children equally. He had three with "the Angel of his life, Marie." They had been "married for an eternity," Rene' had always emphasized, and both were still very much in love.

Rene' had two pilots flying the plane so he was free to sit in the back with Bart and Jacques. Bart was apprehensive as everyone buckled their seatbelts.

Jacques continued, "I stopped by the air terminal earlier and how do you say, hmmm.... mascot ... ah... a resident cat of the office terminal, to check on a stray kitten who six months ago adopted Popie."

"Ahhh, couldn't get rid of her, put her out side the gate, she kept sneaking back in." Rene' took his unlit cigar out of his pocket and put it into his mouth, tilting his head slightly.

"Giselle, the office manager said the little cat had been ill," continued Jacques, "so would I please come to check on her. I have just graduated a veterinarian, not uh how do you say....ah...practicing, but almost there. I found she is not ill at all but very pregnant and had four kittens a half an hour before you called. She is very small, but I presume she is over a year old." Jacques gave a little chuckle. "And, of course I had to stay when Popie said that you were coming. I also have a license for nursing. Popie filled me in about your nephew, Monsieur Bart..."

"Just call me Bart, Jacques..."

"Oh, oui, Bart, I may be able to assist if needed. We will reach the area very soon. A lot quicker than your famous flight years ago..."

Bart nodded and smiled with a little anxiety. He had time to contemplate, and was glad for the opportunity to cover more ground with Rene's plane in the air.

The flight en route near the coastline of Saintes-Maries-de-la-Mer came in view within 17 minutes. Bartholomew hoped he wouldn't be too late.

Chapter 44

The afternoon sun started to send its intense rays through the birch and maple tree leaves, Charles knew something was different in the back recesses of his mind. As Desmond read, he captivated his audience with his mesmerizing voice. Charles was right there, in the moment; as if he was part of the story...then, he blinked and put his hand subconsciously over his eyes trying to block out the sun.

Anna saw the sudden movement and jumped to alert, startling Desmond. She closed the living room blinds.

"Sorry about that Charles, I forgot the sun comes down on this side of the house. It must be around 5:00. Just then the clock on the mantle started to chime."

"Thanks Anna, Charles beamed at her, and Anna, turning towards the blinds blushing, said matter of factly, "Sure."

Desmond raised his eyes, and said, "Aunt Ellen isn't home yet?"

"She will be soon," Anna cocked her head towards the window in the dining room, "she probably stopped at the store before coming home."

Charles yawed nonchalantly. "The time went by really fast, and we did accomplished quite a bit today. Maybe we should skim around the rest of the book to see if there is anything else we should know about."

Desmond got up and went to his laptop and started typing in a search engine for articles about the orange colored stones. "I'm going to look in the computer to see if there is any information about the stones Rachel mentioned."

Charles snatched the journal off the couch and reread the part about the Italian divers. "I wonder, he murmured...hmmm."

Anna heard her mom's car door shut. She walked into the kitchen door with a bag of groceries from McKindle's Natural Grocer's. Ellen opened the refrigerator and took out a rectangle baking pan covered in tinfoil. She set her oven and timer for exactly a half hour.

Walking into the living room Ellen asked: "Hi, how did everyone's day go, any progress with your research?"

Everyone said hello and informed Ellen of decoding the code.

"May I see it?" Ellen was curious. She looked at the cryptogram, then the message. "This will be very significant. Have you any more information that will help understand the message?"

Charles spoke up, picking up the journal, shared what he thought about the stones.

"Anna and Desmond saw the murals in the new edition at grandfather's store. After reading the information about the diver's description of the area again, I think it may look a little bit like one of the mural."

"We should take a look at the mural again," said Anna.

Charles looked up. "Does anyone want to take a ride to The Antiquities Shop tomorrow?"

"It sounds good to me," said Desmond.

"Yeah, me too," Anna added.

Ellen Belk spoke up, "Charles, would you like to stay for supper?"

Anna hoped in anticipation.

"I would love to, Mrs. Belk, but I have to go to a friend's house and help him move to an apartment over his parent's garage. I told him this morning I would try be there by 6:00."

Desmond looked out of the corner of his eye at Anna's disappointed face. 'Yep,' he thought, 'definitely crushin!'

"That is quite alright, Charles, maybe another day!"

"Thank you Mrs. Belk, I would like that very much."

"Certainly," Ellen Belk smiled and went into the kitchen to put her bag of groceries away, amazed that Charles was so much like his father.

Charles collected his computer and packed it away. He turned to Anna. "Anna would you and Desmond mind if I took the journal home tonight, I'd like to see if there is anything more about the stones."

"Sure," they both said. "It is actually yours figuratively," said Anna.

"I know, but grandfather asked you to safe keep it, I think because you were the first one to discover it existed. "Ok, then, I will be back in the morning. What time is good to come?"

"Come for breakfast, we usually have breakfast around nine o'clock," Anna hoped...

"Will your mom mind?"

"No, Mom's good like that. She'll have something all ready for us before she leaves. She has to leave by 8:30 tomorrow for the last conference at the school. And tomorrow is Friday, so they'll get done in the early afternoon."

With the anticipation of a home cooked breakfast, Charles said goodbye and drove down the road.

"You were crushin on him today, weren't ya?" Desmond smiled.

"Was not!" Anna turned her head and blushed slightly.

"Its okay, Anna, I'm not saying it to be mean, I just noticed it a little, aaannd, I sort of feel that way with Calla C. at Rose Cottage."

"I think she is going out with Josh Bartley, you know one of the guide's at the caverns."

Desmond sighed, "Yeah, I kinda thought, but there is always "an open door for change....."

Anna laughed remembering that statement from a Shaman Guide last year.

Ellen Belk called Anna and Desmond into the kitchen to set the table for supper.

Chapter 45

The Seer sat very still in his home. Five of the Anoa had gathered in a secret meeting place. Guardia smiled.   The Flyers once again had informed him of their plans.

He sat in silence, watched and listened. The communication between the Anoa was very soft.

"Tegris, I am suspicious of Thereon. The last time we spoke to him, he was not as attentive in our gathering; he seemed uneasy, and quiet."

"It does not mean much, the time is coming soon when he will become an Elder, and he has much to think about, Jaetre..."

"But not for long, Tegris. Then you will take control and the rest of our people will come. Jaetre raised his voice slightly. "This will be our planet, and we will be in control."

"Silence," Tegris said lowering his voice to a whisper. "Do want them to hear you? They have spies, I am sure of it, although we cannot see them!"

The Seer chuckled to himself. If they only knew he mused.

"It has been almost three years we have been stuck here," Jaetre whispered. "Two of our group has broken apart from us. They will not heed to your plans. Will they go to the Neians?"

"I have had Kiam following them and secretly listening to their conversations. They will not go to the Neians; even though they do not agree with us to stay on this planet."

"All the more to go to the Neians," whispered Sergiian.

Tegris looked at the opening of the cave they met in. Kiam stood watch, saw his gaze and shook his head, Tegris then continued. "Artren had reported to me before they broke away. There has been more meteor activity and they have noticed unusual star formations in the sky. The two are afraid and feel this is a bad omen."

"What do you think, Tegris? I myself have noticed that my health is not what it should be. The stars seem to have gone awry. It is strange, and I have not felt as strong lately. I feel our health has diminished within the two and a half years of being on this planet," said Mernis.

"It has nothing to do with the stars; we have to become acclimated to this dimension. We must! The future of our people and race depend on it. This world is fertile; it has the type of atmospheres that is akin to our body types. We can use their atmospheres and manipulate them. Being here for almost three years has shown that we can survive." Tegris was adamant. "The Neians will be surprised when they see that we will use their portal for our own kind. We will manipulate the energy field to open into our dimension, so the others can come through."

Kiam made a signal to the group that a few Neians were coming over the crest of the mountain. He could see their lamps of fire. The sacred ceremonies must have ended early. The Anoan lamp fire was quickly extinguished. They left through the tunnel to the other side of the cave as not to be seen. Silently they went to their own dwelling places until they could meet again.

The Seer, Guardia, still in the trance contacted the Flyer, L'elma. He thanked him for the information about the Anoan meeting.

L'elma translated so he could see him directly and he came out of the trance. He radiated with pure brilliant light.

"Do not fear Guardia, our good friend, we know what will transpire and it will all come to naught what the Anoa are planning. We have traveled through many dimensions as of late, and in the dimension of the seventh sun, there is a planet fertile of the life forms as we know them. It is akin to the Anoa life sustenance and they will be able to live there in harmony with the peoples and the rest of Nature."

"L'elma, the Anoans have a sense perception that enables them to manipulate an energy current through electromagnetic fields that jumps into the Earth's atmosphere, and they can monitor only one type of weather activity if they so choose. This current also allows them to persuade thought diffusion. They can only suggest, but not control."

"As we so stated before, friend Guardia, we have seen all this and know what will transpire in the future, for we can travel through time. Do not fear. We have a higher energy and can diffuse all their actions. We know how imperative it is for you to get Lorien back. He is friend to us. We will never forget when he was a child how Lorien helped several of our kind. His ingenuity and gentle ways are what saved our friends who were caught in an atmospheric vortex, the current that first brought them here for the first time. It unbalanced their rhythm. Lorien expressed benevolence and helped heal them. We will never disregard his kindness."

"We are very grateful for your friendship, L'elma, You and of the other Flyers. What must we do to help the Anoa translate to the other planet? And how will the others know from their own dimension?

"You forget Guardia; we are of the source that can translate anywhere, in time and space. Our light bodies can travel through many dimensions at once. Once you have the information about the coordinates that I will bring to you and

Ferian, then you will be able to meet with the Anoan leader, I will make myself known to him. The other Flyers will help their people to make the translation directly to the dimension of the seventh sun. Orisen has tested the portal for Lorien to come through, that will succeed. The Portal to the planet of the seventh sun will be opened in the same area twelve days after Lorien gets back. Again, do not fear.

L'elma was greeted by his companion. "We bid you farewell, Guardia."

Farewell my friends. And thank you for this information and help.

Guardia stood, stretched and went in search of Ferian. They must be prepared, and meet with the Translators of Energy, he thought as he went through his secret tunnel to meet and inform his friend.

Chapter 46

Jeffrey Turner fully outfitted in his swim gear, dived into the water of the coastline just above Saintes-Maries-de-la-Mer. He felt this was important to Rachel. He had been there several times with her and other expeditioners, but it had been at least 17 years. The route came back so quickly. He knew the direction like the back of his hand. As he traveled through the first cave, he started to feel uneasy. Something wasn't right.

Rachel said the clue was in the very last cave. Jeffery swam to the second cave, through the third and into a corner tunnel to a secret cave. The water level was very low, and he pushed himself up on to the shelf. Water lapped to the sides of the cave below. On his head he wore a band with an attached flashlight. He took off his breathing apparatus to move more freely within the cave. Jeffery began to look for the water tight sealed box with the matches. The last crew put it..."Where is it?" he asked out loud. "It must be here, ah, here it is, I must have come in and turned around!"

Divers can become disoriented swimming in underwater cannels and tunnels. Anxiety can settle in if a diver discovers new and unknown territory, especially swimming through a small tunnel. Not so with Jeffery Turner. It was a very familiar route. He found the box and set it on the ledge.

A special large sealed box for under water contained lanterns, matches and other such paraphernalia. Jeffery lit the lanterns. For a man of 73, he was very physically fit. It was due to his genetics and DNA.

Jeffery shut off his head gear, and took the lanterns and placed them in strategic places and looked around.

"Rachel, what were you talking about? I don't see what you were referring to," Jeffery said out loud.

The water level rose a quarter of an inch, then an inch, slowly it was rising. Jeffery hadn't noticed, he was too intent looking for the clues in Rachel's research.

"Wait a minute...what is this? He looked up at the ceiling of the cave and saw a thin beam of light reflecting from the left to the right. Jeffery couldn't reach it from the angle he stood from so he stepped over to the other side of the shelf. The water was covering his flippers now. His breathing apparatus, started to move with the flow of the water falling from the shelf and sinking slowly in to the pool of water. Too preoccupied with the dancing light, Jeffery still hadn't noticed the water level rising.

The light seemed to travel down and shimmered in front of him. "Lorien," said the light. "You are in danger, it is a trap set up by the Anoa. Look at your feet."

The light became vivid, and an image appeared. It was a Flyer. Jeffery stood there with his mouth opened.

"It's you, one of the Flyers?" Jeffery then came to his senses, and looked down at his flippers. The water level, it was rising. He went to the other side of the shelf and looked for his tank of oxygen and breathing apparatus, it was gone.

"My equipment, it must have sunk with the rising water. What is going on? The water level should not be rising, and it's too early in the year for that. I don't really understand what is going on here. I have met you before, haven't I, a very long time ago? Are you sent from the Seer?"

"We came of our own accord. And yes Lorien, you had helped us in your own world, Neia, where you are really from. We are repaying the kindness from many years ago. Do not fear, Lorien, help is on its way." The flyer turned back into a flash of light and disappeared from the cave."

The water level continued to rise...

Chapter 47

Charles had a fitful sleep. He dreamt of a violent storm at the old quarry. In the dream, or nightmare as he recalled it later, he was standing at the gate of the quarry. The night sky had ominous clouds; he could hear violent claps of thunder and lightening, without rain. After some of the adventures he had with Anthony, he was use to anything, but Charles was frightened, the nightmare seemed so real, very lucid. He could see the old man again, shouting and holding up three fingers.

Charles was at the other side of the gate. "What?" He yelled, "I can't hear you." The motions were familiar of the other day at the quarry, except for the raging weather. The storm was getting worse. Then it started to rain. Pellets of water came in frenzy.

The old man stood firm. He was not affected by the storm. It was as if he wasn't there. He could hear the wind wailing, the old man shouting, holding up three fingers. Charles was getting blasted by the wind and rain, he could hardly breathe, and the tension of the electric charge in the atmosphere was getting thick. He grabbed hold of the gate and was shocked by the electricity in the air and around the metal of the gate. The old man kept yelling....

Charles woke up in a sweat..."KEYS!!!" rang in his ears. He felt traumatized, chilled and shaken. It was a warm June night.

Looking at his clock, Charles noted the time, 3:33 am. After a few minutes, he collected himself and said out loud, "I should write this down." He felt he had a heighten sense of awareness.

Charles reached for the light on his nightstand beside his bed and switched it on. He decided to look for a pen and paper, so he left the comfort of his bed. Charles found a pencil, but no paper was to be found. Then he remembered the receipt from the bakery he threw on his desk after emptying his jean pockets before he went to sleep. Charles found it under the journal.

Charles repeated the words out loud as he wrote. "Keys, 3:33, episode at gate." He was running out of space, "old man, storm..." Charles placed the paper in the journal for safe keeping. He knew it was significant and may be a clue. Satisfied, and feeling better, he yawned, turned off the light and lay back down until it was time to get up.

The sun peeped through the early morning windows. Charles awoke to the birds chirping and the air with the scent of mint lingering in the room.

Theos, his Abyssinian cat, had possibly rolled in the mint, earlier. Dad must be up. Charles heard the cuckoo clock in the hallway. One cuckoo, he looked at his alarm clock, 6:30 he said to himself. Hmmm, do I get up now or do I sleep until 8:00, he thought.

Charles immediately recovered. "The dream," He said out loud. He threw his sheet cover off and jumped out of bed. Theos meowed disapprovingly. He was dreaming of stalking a mouse and now he was awake without any satisfaction of catching it! Theos purred as Charles sat back down on the bed with the journal. He flipped through the pages and became interested as he saw the word stones.

Charles began to read out loud to Theos: "Rachel and I were married in 1952. I had resigned from my practice in London and was employed by the company Rachel and her team worked for. I was the medical doctor on staff when the group went on digs and expeditions. They happened to be in need of another physician as the previous one had retired. Rachel had kept her professional name, which was quite alright with me."

Theos rested his head on Charles' lap, turn his body and looked up at him. "Meop," meow, meooop..."

"Too early for breakfast, Theos," said Charles.

"Meorrrrrrr..." Theos turned around, and gave Charles one of his stares. He jumped off the bed and pranced out the door of the bedroom hoping to get better results from Charles' father.

Charles, use to Theo's antics, continued reading...

"It was one particular night, when we were having our tea in our apartment, (we were on vacation) that we noticed as we viewed the television that several of the artifacts from the location near the Saintes-Maries-de-la-Mer caves were missing from a museum in Paris. Two in particular were the large orange brown glowing stones. It was if they disappeared over night. It appeared there weren't any forced entries or locks tampered with. It left the authorities stumped. Further investigations were scheduled."

Charles flipped through the pages and read: "I was told by The Seer, when the time came to translate, instructions would be given by The Flyers, the course of action to be taken but not given to me but to the two who were chosen in the future. There would be several there, but only two whose energy of the same type could actually open The Epic Catalog."

This statement confused Charles, wasn't the journal called The Epic Catalog? There is more to it than he thought. Still, it's another clue. Hmm.

Charles flipped back, "Rachel had another dream of a violent storm at some facility."

Charles said the next sentence slowly.

"A young man stood outside a gate, shouting at someone on the other side. Lightening and torrents of rain came in such force with the rushing wind…" He stopped reading and looked at his notes recorded during the night; Charles' heart started beating wildly for a few seconds and then subsided. "It's not just a coincidence!"

Chapter 48

The plane descended on a small runway five miles from the shore. In the distance, wild white horses roamed freely on the Reserve Nationale De Camargue. Vivid memories were brought to mind as Bartholomew Edis envisioned his honeymoon around fifty years ago when he married Elizabeth Harding. She had been in design and was lining up a series of displays for a cultural gallery. The photographer had some winning photographs of the wild horses of Camargue in action. The designs and images were absolutely stunning. Elizabeth was the head of the project. She was twenty-three.

Bart made a stop in Marseilles during one of his travels with Rene' Baigent. He needed to send a wire to London, England and when he came out of the post office, he accidently bumped into Elizabeth Harding, who was carrying large rolls of paper, a portfolio and a cup of coffee. Bart chuckled as he thought of the coffee falling onto his white shirt and jacket. "Ahhh," he sighed, the memories of his honeymoon over took his thoughts for a moment.

Jacques was carrying on a conversation with Bart. Laughter could be heard in the background. Inadvertently, Bart would say softly, "hmm, ah yes, uh huh......, oh, Eliza..."

"Are you listening to me, *Mon ami*? Your thoughts are not with us," said Jacques with his intermittent English.

Bart lost in the 1950's, looked around, and noticed Jacques making a comical face intently at him said, "What was that little pip squeak?" Startled into reality Bart reiterated. "Oh sorry Jacques, I was a million miles away, I wasn't paying attention."

Jacques & Rene' looked at each other and laughed. "We had figured that out when I asked you after a while, how you do you say, ah, a whacky question…?"

"What was the question?" Bart looked amused.

"Ahhhh," Rene' shook his head laughing, "You do not want to know," and looked at Jacques, they both bursted out laughing.

Bart, used to their antics just grinned and folded his arms.

The sea plane came to a full stop and it was time for everyone to grab their gear and climbed out of the plane.

Rene' went to the dock and talked to one of his friends. Within 15 minutes he came back with the keys to a small sailing yacht. It was a Colvic Watson 34'6" Motor Sail. Jacques looked pleased. "My father, he has good connections!" They all climbed aboard. We must put on our attire, um, wet suits..." Bart nodded. "Oui?" said Jacques.

"Oui," said Bart, smiling and started to put on his swimsuit.

"Yes! Well!" Jacques took over at this point. He was a scuba diving instructor in his early twenties. "We must be ready to dive in once we are there." Popie, you will stay with the boat?" Rene' nodded smiling doing a hand salute, Oui!"

Bart took out his scuba diving equipment from his duffle bag. It took a few minutes for everyone to dress, as each were outfitted with face masks, snorkels, oxygen tanks, wetsuits, fins, etc. Even Rene' had his equipment on and in operational order just in case of an emergency. Jacques went to look at the radio system in the navigation controls of the dashboard area.

"Bart," Jacques continued with his face mask on the top of his head, "we will have full radio contact. I have been to the caves oh, about eight years ago. Purely ah, recreate...recre-a-tion-al? Yes? Recreational, it is not too far, now, we should approach the inlet.

"We should be there in about 10 minutes. Rene' said complimentary

"We will have about an hour per tank. I am glad you have two tanks also, Bart." Jacques handed him a full face mask. "You will not need your own mask; this one has a three way radio mechanism. It works well under water." He gave Bart a clip earphone and a watch like instrument. When you talk into the face mask, you will hear yourself in the earphone, and you will hear us also. The watch sends a signal frequency to your earphone. It was what I could get at last minute. This equipment was used for an underwater documentary for the, ah, jellyfish behavior and coral near Nice. It was put on by, um, Planet Animal? Anyway the radios have the same frequency as the dash intercom system in the boat." Jacques looked at Rene', "Popie, what setting?"

"18 Jacques, set it to channel 18." They synchronized their watch instruments to channel 18.

They were in the harbor now. Rene' pulled up to a boat anchored in the water, not far from the underwater caves.

"Regardez...la'-bas!" Bright iridescent light kept playing on the water. "What is that?" Jacques looked through his binoculars. He handed them to Bart.

"It looks like flashes of light. I can't see where it is coming from, Bart handed the binoculars to Rene'.

"I have my suspicions," Rene' murmured peering through the binoculars.

Looking at the other boat, Jacques spoke, "This must be your nephew's boat?" He is down in the caves already. We did not catch him in time."

Bart put his full face mask on, and connected an oxygen tank to it. "Let's go then."

"Oui," Jacques, with face mask and oxygen apparatus in place fell backward into the water. Bart followed, and Rene' saw the dancing lights near the caves disappeared.

After a few minutes, Jacques found the opening of the underwater caves; he turned and waved to Bart. Both had their hand lights on. Jacques had obtained two wrist/arm motion SOLA dive 1200 lights. His friend's mother owned a scuba diving apparatus store, and she was glad to lend him the essential supplies for the day. The last two weeks in May, Jacques had been house sitting her two dogs while she went on vacation, as a favor. Mariella insisted on letting him borrow the equipment for an excursion with a few friends for his vacation. He was going to return them after going to the hanger to check on the pregnant cat, but after meeting Bart, decided to keep them with him instead. 'How fortunate,' Jacques thought 'that I still have the equipment on hand.'

The first cave they entered had almost filled up with water. "The water level should not be this high at this time of the year," said Jacques. Bart looked at Jacques and nodded. They both swam on to the next cave, and rose to the surface of the water. This cave was a little higher, and the water had not reached the mouth of the cave yet.

Bart swam back down into the water, Jacques followed him. After half hour, Rene's voice came through the radio system. "How are you both doing down there? There is a storm brewing not far off. It will probably hit us in about 15 to 20 minutes, over."

"We are approaching the third cave, but I do not see Jeffery, thanks, Popie, over." Jacques was already at the surface of the water level of the third cave. The cave ceiling was a foot higher and the water level to his shoulders.

Bart swam in and out of the surface, searching for feet with fins, a body, anything. "I don't see him. He must be here somewhere."

"Look down on the floor, Bart; let's shine the light on the floor surface. Jacques light went out. "Je ne le crois pas!"

"What is happening down there?" Rene asked.

"My light, it has gone out!" Jacques looked around the surface of the cave, then saw a faint light, He set his attention at the north wall of the cave, "Bart, Bart, Shut off your light for a moment, please! "Look!"

Bart closed his arm light. "Look, Bart to the north!" Jacques submerged back under water, "You can see it better underwater…"

"Well I'll be damn!"

"What, What!" said Rene' emphatically.

"Rene', we see a faint light at the northern part of the wall. Jacques is already there, wait where did he go? Jacques…"

"I am entering a smaller tunnel; I did not know it was here…"

Bart swam toward the faint light, and then he saw it, a secret tunnel.

After a few minutes, Bart heard Jacques voice. "I am in another cave, Bart. There is not much of an opening at the top of the cave."

"Do you see Jeff?"

I am looking mon ami, "I think I see him, I do not have a light, Bart, but I see a lantern right near the ceiling of the cave. The others have burned out and are floating in the water."

It took a few minutes, Bart had his light back on and he saw something shining on the floor's surface. "I see an oxygen tank on the floor of the tunnel, with a face mask, Jacques. I'm picking them up, I'm coming…"

"I think I see him, he is unconscious I think." Then there was silence for a moment. "Quick, come quick, Bart! He still has a slight pulse!"

Bart's light came into view; he swam up along side of Jacques.

"We must put my face mask and tank on him. He is still breathing, but barely. I am afraid he has taken in a lot of water. Can you hold him up?"

"Yes, I'm coming to his other side, Jacques."

Jacques took off his facemask and oxygen tank while wading in water, there was only shoulder length room and the water was steadily rising. Bart holding Jeff up with Jacques made the exchange of oxygen tanks and face masks. Jacques quickly slipped on Jeffery's equipment, while Bart held him up. Once Jacques had finished, he held Jeffery up while Bart slipped Jacques gear on Jeffery."

Jacques gave the thumbs up sign, pointed to his mask. Jeffery still had air in his tank, just enough to make it back to the boat. Bart could see the bubbles escaping into the water.

"Now go, Bart, you lead with the light, I will take Jeffery." Bart couldn't hear him, Jeffery's facemask had a different radio signal, but he could see the hand signals Jacques frantically made. Jacques pointed to his dead arm light and made movement for Bart to go in the lead.

The water started to rush in with a violent force. "Whoa," exclaimed Bart. "Rene'," he spoke into his facemask.

"I am here Bart, the storm is here, and you must come quickly!"

"We're coming Rene', it seems that the water is rushing in with force down here, we're swimming against the power of the water. It's as if the sea won't let us go!"

"You must! You must my friend, swim with all your strength." Claps of thunder could be heard, and then there was dead silence. The radio connection was severed.

Chapter 49

Charles arrived at the Belk's house just at 9:00 in the morning and rang the front bell. Earlier at home, his dad had been up and left for work by the time he made it downstairs at 8:30.

He saw his father's note. "Charles went to the museum early today. Morning staff meeting I forgot about... will be home around 4:30. Let's order pizza. Oh... we will be going to the Belk's tonight to discuss the journal. Ellen said 7pm. See you at 5pm, Dad."

Charles left a note for his father, just in case he came home early. He opted not to telephone him if he was in a meeting.

Anna answered the door. "Hi Charles, come in."

Desmond came downstairs, hair not combed, shirt half tucked in. "Mornin... Charles," Desmond said groggily. He just got up and threw his clothes on when he heard Anna yelling from downstairs that Charles just drove in the driveway. He had not slept well during the night.

"Good morning Desmond, and good morning Anna," said Charles.

Charles was cheerful. He could smell the aroma of breakfast lingering...it kind of reminded him...what did it remind him of? Something about sugar plums dancing around in the back recesses of his mind. Shaking that hysteria away, Anna led him through the dining room into the kitchen.

"Mom made loads of blueberry pancakes for breakfast, she just left about 20 minutes ago and there is a fresh pot of decaf brewing."

Desmond trailed behind and suddenly became alert when he heard blueberry pancakes and Charles beamed with astonishing happiness!

"Oh, I have the journal, and during breakfast, I need to tell you about a dream I had during the night, and some other data I found in the journal, I bookmarked them. Anna, have you and Desmond had anything unusual happen?"

"What about the Flyer contact the other night, Desmond? Anna tried to remember if they discussed it with Charles the other day.

"What Flyer contact?" Charles helped himself to a generous cup of coffee and sat down at the kitchen table. Anna uncovered the blueberry pancake dish from the oven.

"Well," said Anna, "They appeared at 4:44 in the morning."

"Strange," murmured Charles eyeing the pancakes as Anna placed them on the kitchen table.

Desmond peered into the refrigerator, pushing containers out of the way until he spotted the orange juice. He liked the kind with all the pulp inside. "Not yesterday, but the day before," Desmond added. He poured a large glass of orange juice and sat next to the pancakes. Anna placed a dish of bacon on the table along side the maple syrup and also sat down at the table.

The aroma set them all in motion. As they ate, Anna and Desmond filled Charles in with the details of the Flyers, how they resembled Fairies how they were able to communicate telepathically, and how to assemble the orange stones.

Charles' attention strayed away from his bite of pancakes. "There is an interesting story attached to the stones, if they are the same ones we have in safekeeping. He paraphrased what he read in the journal, about the theft of a few artifacts, and the stones being part of the burglary..."Anna, how **did** you get a hold of the stones?"

Desmond blurted out, "Shaman," in between a swallow of orange juice.

Charles looked at him inquisitively.

"Last year," Desmond continued, "we met a Shaman at Rose Cottage. He's one of Mrs.

Perpecuwitz's friends. We went on a journey with him to the jungles of Peru, or Andes. Was it the Andes Mountain?"

Anna gave an account of the location, "It was the Andes Mountains along the Peruvian coastlines.

"Oh, I get that part confused sometimes. Well...deep inside the jungle was a hidden cave..."

"We didn't actually go to Peru by plane, Anna explained, "it was sort of a mystical journey."

"It sure seemed real to me, Anna, after that fall off the cliff...," interrupted Desmond.

"It's sort of a long story," and Anna and Desmond explained their journeys to Peru last year. "I think it was a portal that took us to a place in time and space on Earth, and it was in the caverns at Rose Cottage," finished Anna.

I wonder, thought Charles, and then let it go. Savoring every bite, he told Anna and Desmond about the dream that occurred in the night. "It is really strange how Rachel had a dream of me having a dream. But the first time, which we read in the journal a few nights ago, Rachel, had dreamed of my episode at the old quarry, where I saw a vision of the old man. I have an inkling of what the three fingers mean, KEYS," Charles said with emphasis!

Anna pushed her plate away. "May I look at the journal Charles?"

Charles took the journal out of his backpack, and placed it in her hands. He accidentally unwittingly brushed his hand on Anna's fingers, and she felt a slight tingle in her hands.

Desmond happen to catch the whole episode as he looked up and reached for the maple syrup, he just turned away and concentrated on his bite of pancake.

We'll clear away the dishes if you read us the places you bookmarked, Charles," said Anna as she stood up. She gave Desmond the look. "What?" said Desmond as he got up to help her.

Charles began to read out loud: "Rachel and I were married in 1952. I had resigned my practice in London and was employed by the company Rachel and her team worked for. I was the medical doctor on staff when the group went on digs and expeditions. They happened to be in need of another physician as the previous one had retired. Rachel had kept her professional name, which was quite alright with me."

Charles flipped to the next bookmarked page.

"It was one particular night, when we were having our tea in our apartment, (we were on vacation) that we noticed as we viewed the television that several of the artifacts from near the Saintes-Maries-de-la-Mer caves were missing from a museum in Paris. Two in particular were the large orange brown glowing stones. It was if they disappeared over night. It appeared there weren't any forced entries or locks tampered with. It left the authorities stumped. Further investigations were scheduled."

"And as I read further along in the journal I found that the stones were never recovered, they may be the same stones at the Antiquities Shop.

Charles flipped through the pages and read: "I was told by The Seer, when the time came to translate, instructions would be given by The Flyers, the course of action to be taken but not given to me but to the two who were chosen in the future. There would be several there, but only two whose energy of the same type could actually open The Epic Catalog."

Charles cleared his throat and reread the last sentence. "The reference to the two must mean the two of you…"

"It may be." Desmond sat down with a cup of de-caf coffee.

"I think it is," Anna said thoughtfully.

"This next statement confused me at first," Charles went on, "… but only two whose energy of the same type could actually **open The Epic Catalog.**"

Anna said, "The journal is titled The Epic Catalog, but what if it is a reference for something else?

"What if it is entirely something different?" Desmond cut in, "I seem to remember something from the other night, you know, Anna, when we met the Flyers! Desmond stood up and ran upstairs to get his notes. "Be right back!"

"Do you mind if I have another coffee, Anna?" Charles looked at the coffee pot. It looked like one more cup was in the carafe.

"Mom only let's Desmond & I have one mug if we want it in the morning, so you're welcome to the rest." Anna took out more cream from the refrigerator.

Desmond came into the kitchen as Charles rinsed out the empty coffee carafe.

"Here are our notes. We were able to write down the actual message word for word. I wouldn't remember it now. Anna would, she's a whiz at that stuff."

Anna smiled. "I do have the ability to remember at verbatim, I always did."

Desmond read the message: "We are here to warn you. On the night of the translation of Lorien from your dimension to ours, the Anoa will be planning violent storms and unusual weather patterns to prevent him from coming through. It can be stopped with the use of both the Stones and the Crystals in Lorien's possession. The Crystals are very powerful. There are seven of them. They decode the energy of the seven atmospheric realms within our world and the seven star systems in our galaxy where our world, Neia resides and into your planetary galaxy of constellations, sun and energy. "

"You must have in your possession the two large stones. Placing the stones at the opening of each of the sides of the portal will activate them. You will know they are activated when they start to release a bright orange color. Once they are activated, the cloth must lay between the Stones on the ground. The box must be opened seven seconds after the two large stones have been activated. Place the crystals in the exact formation you see in the sky through the portal onto the cloth. The energy or transmitter within the cloth will set in motion each crystal as you place them on the fabric. The Constellations of the Epic Catalog, from within our world, where all the constellations are formed, will make the transfer of Lorien through the open portal safe." Desmond looked up from the notepad. "There it is again, a reference to the Epic Catalog here also."

"May I see the notepad, Desmond," Charles asked. He reread the last sentence out loud. He emphasized, "The Constellations of the Epic Catalog." He went back to the journal, "but only two whose energy of the same type could actually open The Epic Catalog."

Anna interjected, "Epic means something really large, and extraordinary, and catalog means a record or directory of some sort."

"But that is our definitions for Epic Catalog; the words may have another meaning in the parallel world," Charles added.

"What if the words have something to do with the seven atmospheres, and the crystals opening up the portal?" Desmond looked back at the notes. "It says here that our galaxy connects to the atmospheric realms in the seven star systems through the energy of the seven crystals and decodes them."

Anna jumped up. "I know what it is. It is the activation of our world to the parallel world, Neia together forming what they meant as an Epic Catalog. Both galaxies creating an ummm...link or connection of some sort, a wave of energy that opens the portal every so often. The crystals have a memory, a catalog of data that transmits information to the Neian galaxy. It opens a record of one world to the other..." Anna became silent; she seemed to be regrouping her thoughts. "It records the data so that it could transmit a code so that Jeffery could enter the threshold safely."

"Astonishing, it's starting to make sense." Charles looked back and forth from the notes to the journal.

The dining room clock chimed 12:00. "I think we should go and look at the mural at The Antiquities Shop, Charles said. "We may find some more clues there."

Desmond and Anna both agreed. They left a note for her mom, took the journal and the notes and left in search of more answers.

Chapter 50

Tegris summoned the four most important to his plan. Kiam, Sergiian, Mernis and Jaetre were just coming along the bend. They were in the Western Caridia Mountains, Three and a half days away from their dwellings. The group had traveled many miles to conduct the energy work to stop Lorien from coming out of the underwater cave in France. Some were uneasy, never before had they intentionally harmed anyone, but their civilization depended on it. For their plan to work, Thereon needed to be the next elder. Tegris hoped it wasn't too late.

No words were needed. They were in a low mind trance, concentrating on the outcome of their quest. Kiam indicated that they were not followed. In single file they walked through the dense bush and into a path covered in thick floral scented vines. It was an ancient corridor, not used in about 200 years. Tegris knew they would be safe to conduct the energy work at this time. The current they needed to transfer into was indeed stronger in the Caridia Mountain atmosphere. Almost nearing the threshold, the mood was pensive and solemn. Everyone was on high alert; the connection to the higher energy proved successful during a recent experiment. Tegris timed the arrival perfectly; in thirty minutes an atmospheric electrical portal would open for ten minutes. It was not a gateway where a person could walk through, but an energy band of solar flares as you might call it. The energy the Anoans would transfer with the solar flares would disrupt the frequency waves carried to the Earth dimension, the disturbance would last around two to three hours because of the ten minute time continuum in Neia to Earth time.

Twelve planetary systems were regulated by two dwarf suns in the middle of the galaxy. Anoa was the fifth planet from the two suns. The planet Saia closet to the two suns erupted causing debris to spiral off course. Anoa was hit with such impact and force that one fourth of the planet was utterly destroyed. The planet had already suffered small withdrawals of atmospheric gases caused by solar flare storms from one of the suns two years before. Carbon dioxide and nitrate oxide helped keep the planet's energy balance hundreds of miles in the upper atmosphere, and now there was a leak in the magnetic fields and it was affecting the planet.

It may well have been healed with the correct apparatus and knowledge of scientific data. The Anoans had the ability to heal their planet, if they could right the magnetic fields, atmospheric gases, and monitor the solar disruptions. It was a healing that would take time.

They were used to the two suns in their solar system, their body type tolerated it. That is why they could endure the two suns on Neia.

Two and a half years ago, when a group of seven Anoans were on their way to a formal procedure to help heal their planet's electrical flow of the atmospheric, elemental, and magnetic imbalances, they inadvertently stepped through a portal that brought them to the planet Neia. With the seven Anoan specialists gone, there wasn't much chance for their planet to heal.

It was difficult for each of the seven not to be in contact with their people. Thought transference could not penetrate through the waves of energy from Neia to Anoa. Something was blocking it, Tegris had known the radiation build up in the atmosphere depleted the flow of divergent elements vital for contact. It reacted by creating density on their planet. So now they would have to wait, twelve days after the opening to Earth on July 11th for their people to come. They have waited 2 ½ years, they could wait a few more weeks, earth time.

The five travelers stopped near a small stream. Tegris waited.

Jaetre took out five tubular objects from a unique case; the alloys in the metal shimmered with fibers of colors not familiar to Neia or Earth. He handed each one their instrument. Two were left in the case. The openings were small near the rim and were a half an arm's length in size. The instruments were known as Frequency Changers, but here on Neia, they could cause disturbances in weather patterns with the use of water in particular currents of energy, especially on Earth.

Tegris stepped into the water, and steadily blew into the Frequency Changer. Sergiian was next; he stood two arm lengths away in the stream. Mernis took his place two arms' length from Sergiian in circular motion. Kiam stood 1 ½ arms' length from Mernis. Jaetre stood in between Kiam and Tegris. A semi-circular star pattern was formed. After Tegris had finished, he nodded, then started again, each one followed in the circle until the soft sounds were heard as one resonate note. The vortex of the atmosphere opening had the impression of heat rising from pavement on a hot summer's day

They had practiced the thought energy extensively before this day had arrived. Today the energy would precede the notes within the electrical current of the turbulence that would form in the planet Earth's atmosphere. They had the coordinates to the exact location. Sergiian was able to astral project and travel before the weather activation to the Earth dimension. The others were able to tune into a thought trance as one. Sergiian provided his sight that made it possible for everyone to see the location. They were at the South of France figuratively, in their minds looking through an opened channel. With the use of the Frequency Changers, their thoughts projected the violent turbulent weather that lasted about three hours. They did not want to harm anyone else of Earth, just to flood the underwater caves where Lorien was.

A long boat seemed settled in the distance. A man was lying on the deck with an odd suit on. He appeared harmless. The Anoans had no idea a rescue team was underway for Lorien. Another small boat was anchored near the caves, they were confidant it was Lorien's boat. The group just facilitated the turbulence concentrating mostly near the underwater caves. The long boat in the distance seemed safe enough with the backlash of some of the weather.

Convinced the caves were full of sea water, the extreme weather forced powerful surges of water into the caves, to thwart any movement of escape.

After 2 ½ hours, three swimmers rode up to the long boat riding with a pod of dolphins, Tegris discovered that Lorien was still alive, after his facemask was removed, he was stunned. It was a failed mission on their part. There was no mistake about one of the people; Lorien looked like Thereon in advanced years.

Sergiian motioned to withdraw, since the window was closing, and the opportunity was lost for now.

The Flyers left the Caridia Mountains after the five Anoans started back on the long trek to their homes. L'elma, who was in contact with The Seer before the Anoans started out to the Caridia Mountains, met with the other flyers assigned to the South of France. All transposed through the dimensions of Earth to Neia, converging near the cave of The Seer's dwelling where news of the Anoan ploy that had failed was communicated. Much rejoicing was held by the Neians after the conference!

Chapter 51

All three stood in awe. The murals were much bigger in size than Anna & Desmond remembered.

Charles went to take a step back. "It's different than what I remembered from the other day. I'm sure of it!"

"What do you mean Charles?" Anna thought it was a little different herself, but had only seen it once before.

"The two people in it," Desmond interrupted.

"That's just it. It is odd. I don't ever remember two people being in the mural before." Charles identified others changes within the mural. "It has changed."

"There weren't any people in it, I'm certain of it also." Anna went closer and touched it. She felt a faint tingling of ...electricity?   Can't be, she thought, static, maybe? No it's different...almost alive.

Anna was too quiet; Desmond stepped forward along side of her. "Touch the mural, Desmond." He extended his arm and touched it.

"Charles, the mural... it's causing a tingling sensation!" Desmond became excited. "Do you remember it feeling like this before?"

"No, even though I have touched the mural before, I hadn't felt any tingling. This is extraordinary. Can you hear the humming? I wonder...." Charles stepped away. Then further back. "Anna and Desmond, step back, at least to the couch." Charles saw movement near a... gate? Could it be the old quarry?

They all stood back, and to their amazement saw an outline of the old quarry gate. Throughout the length of the gate trailed wild roses, and inside beyond, an unusual star system was pictured across the evening sky and... was there a shooting star that just went by?

They all stood there as if in a trance. The mural started to take form, in the way as a vision. The two orange/brown colored stones were given each to Anna and Desmond, who were the two people identified now in the mural. They each placed the stones on the ground to the left and right of the entrance of the gate. As the stones became larger, three-dimensional images of light interference patterns opened the gateway to the cosmos.

The stars on the other side were moving. Anna was given a box by an older man, who happened to be accompanied by an elegant elderly woman. Seven crystals were placed by Anna on a piece of illuminated fabric as Desmond handed them to her one by one. Each stone glowed in hues of color as they were placed in concise order as requested by the Flyers. Inside the quarry gate, another world started to take shape; there was a community of people dressed in unfamiliar clothing moving around waiting for someone. The colors were extraordinary.

Anna recognized two of the people, the Elder and the Seer. The Seer looked directly at her and said, "Yes Anna, this is a crucial time for us. It is time for Lorien to come through. We are in your debt for all your help, you and your cousin, Desmond and all the others who made this translation possible. We thank you all." Anna smiled and said: "You're welcome, we were glad to help." The Elder and Seer nodded.

The stones had finished coordinating the data, and they emitted a soft orange glow. The stars of Neia, beyond the gate became aligned with the stars system of the Earth. It was intense. In one minute the electric charge would be subdued when the glowing light turned white and it would be safe to enter Neia. A storm was brewing in the eastern sky

Jeffrey Turner, who now is known as Lorien, hugged the elegant elderly women, Abigail, his adopted mother and took Anna's hand. "Thank you Anna and Desmond for your perseverance and not giving up." He shook Desmond's hand, and hugged his Uncle Bart. He turned to step through the gate.

The vision suddenly vanished. Charles did a double take. All three stood there for about 5 seconds, Anna went up and touched the mural, Charles and Desmond did as well. No feeling, or tingling sensations. The two people in the mural vanished and it looked as it did a few days ago when they met Mr. Edis.

"Well, what did you both make of this, Anna and Desmond? Did we witness something mystical?"

"It definitely was for me Charles," said Desmond. He took a few steps back to study the stones in the mural. He took a sheet of paper out of his back pocket, and examined it. He walked over to the mural and examined it again.

"Yup, I'd say these are the stones from the museum in Paris, Desmond handed the paper over to Charles.

"They do look similar," Charles handed the paper to Anna. "What do you think Anna?"

Anna looked at the mural more intently then studied the paper. "I think they are. See the dark line formation, right here on the left side of this stone? Anna showed the paper to Charles and Desmond. They both saw the same marking in the exact place on the rocks in the Mural.

"Charles, may we see the stones now? Desmond was still curious as to how the stones became missing from the Paris Museum and into the cave of the Andes. And how did the Shaman last year know that they were the ones that were needed now? Could he foresee the future?

All these thoughts going through Desmond's head, as he stood staring at the mural. Charles' mobile phone started to ring, startling Desmond out of his reverie.

Charles answered on the third ring. "Anthony…."

Chapter 52

Rene' Baigent had "batten down the hatches" and prepared the sailing vessel for the storm. There was a lot to do for one person, but 45 minutes ago, it was a beautiful and pleasant day. Rene' had been fantasizing about retiring on a yacht such as this, as he lay back in his wet suit stretching out in the sun. The small yacht made smooth sailing, and now was anchored down, "Ahhh" what a delight," he said to no one in particular, looking up at the puffy white clouds in his view. Rene' took in his surroundings. It was a comfortable warm day, and seemed almost surreal as he visualized catching the prized fish he would show off, and thinking, what a life.

He took his stogie out of his pocket and was about to light it when he looked out into the distance. Dark ominous clouds, the blackest of black had outlined the horizon looking formidable. Rene' quickly radioed out for weather information and was cut off while contacting the Maritime Security Regime; he hoped they heard his message. He quickly went on the band radio to warn Bart and after the thunder and lightening exhibition; the connection was severed.

Rene' had an inner strength and vitality. To look at him, you would not place him at the age of 73;

he had a lot of life still left. He wasn't really scared of anything, not even death. Throughout his years he had many close calls, but fate seemed to be always on his side. You might say he was lucky. But today, at this moment, Rene' felt real fear. He was worried about Jacques, and his friend Bart. The storm blew up to be almost a tropical depression. The weather for the day was supposed to be pleasant, sunny and in the high 70's. Where could this have come from?

"Still no sign of Jacques and Bart," René muttered. All radio contact was dead. He was alert and ready for any type of movement in the treacherous water that resembled the divers.

Bart & Jacques clung to the sides of the caves, clasping on to protruding rocks as they made their way through the tunnels. They were out of the second cave. It took a long time, but going slowly was the only possible way. One slip and you would be hurtled away. "

What a man, Jacques turned out to be, Bart reflected. Quite different from the "Little Pip Squeak" from long ago, over 25 years ago, but now he had to concentrate. Bart almost lost his footing as the water seemed to gush through him, he was glad of the overhanging of rocks lining the wall of the cave.

Jacques carried Jeff with an elegance and powerful grip at the same time. He half slung him over his shoulder while Bart tied him to Jacques' torso but the violence of the water and debris would have caused anyone else to flounder. Not Jacques, he would be deemed a hero after this experience... if they got out alive, Bart observed. After this tunnel they would reach the first and last cave. It was the longest one, and also wider.

Sand gushed up from the ocean's floor. Small rock particles were propelling through the water. Bart turned slightly around to see the progression of Jacques and Jeff. Jacques made the thumbs up sign with his right hand. Bart nodded and turned around. A small rock flew into his face mask. The impact was slight but with enough force to cause a crack in the glass. Bart was afraid water would seep in, but it appeared to be all right at the moment.

Blasts of water continued to come into the tunnel. Jacques almost lost his hold, but managed to get a good grip on one of the protruding rocks. They were almost there, almost to the first cave, just one more corner to go. Another small rock hit the side of Bart's facemask again. Water started to seep in. A crack would cause a leak in oxygen through his facemask. He would be struggling for air if they didn't reach the boat soon.

Jacques observed Bart's body language, something was wrong. With the weight of Jeff on his body, Jacques would not be able to swim any faster. Bart was moving a little slower and his movements looked funny. Holding Jeffery over one side of his body with all the scuba equipment was strenuous; Jacques knew he would run out of oxygen soon. He might just make it if they kept to the pace, but now he wasn't sure. They were around the corner and into the cave now.

Jacques caught up with Bart and tapped him on the shoulder, as soon as he turned around, Jacques saw Bart's facemask, it had a crack on the left side and water was seeping in. Bart was coughing, and trying to breathe slowly. The water was gushing into the cave in full force. The rope was loosening and Jacques almost lost Jeffery, he tried to tighten the knot with one hand.

The water appeared calmer for a moment. Had the storm subsided? Jacques tapped Bart's arm and motioned toward the calmer water, and they both swam in that direction to the mouth of the underwater cave. That's when they saw the dolphins. They were twirling around in the water causing a vortex of calm. Jacques looked in wonder and felt the dolphins were here to rescue them.

One dolphin kept nudging Bart's hand and could hear the dolphin's voice in his head. "Hold on friend, we will take you to safety." Bart had swum with the dolphins on an expedition in the 70's near Maui, Hawaii. To him, it was one of the most moving experiences he ever had. Bart trusted his instinct. He nodded and held on to the dolphin's body. Jacques held on the dolphin nearest him. They swam out of the cave area and to the surface of the sea. But it wasn't the surface of the original sea they dove into. It was... where was it? Where were they?

The dolphins brought them to a tranquil place, a deserted island of calm and beauty. They were in some vortex; Jacques heard a dolphin telepathically. "Your friend will live; you must work on him quickly. We were sent by the Flyers. There is a pool of rejuvenating water 100 feet into the foliage. You will find a cup from a coconut there. Bring some water to your friends. You must all drink from the pool. It will revive everyone and give strength to continue on your journey back to the ship. Go now, help your friends." Jacques took advantage of the situation. He hauled off his facemask and untied Jeff from his body. Bart appeared in the distance with the dolphins. He had to put all his effort to bring Jeffery around. Jacques undid Jeff's facemask and equipment, checked his vital signs and started to resuscitate him back to life. He was almost blue. After a few minutes, Jeffery coughed up water and started to come around. Jacques studied Jeff for a few seconds, and propped him up a nearby tree. Jeff opened his eyes. Jacques spoke to him and then left through the foliage to the pool of reviving water.

The dolphins brought Bart as close to the shore as they could. Bart waded in and unhitched his mask and fell to his knees on the sand, gasping for air. When he felt he could breathe normally, he looked for Jacques and Jeffery. He saw a figure bent over with his face in his hands. Then the figure looked up, it was Jeffery, but where was Jacques?

As Bart approached, he saw the fatigue in Jeff's face. His eyes were opened and his movements were slow and irregular. Jeffery was trembling. Bart sat next to Jeff, took his hands and said, "Jeff, Jeffery!" Jeff slowly turned his head to the voice, Bart continued, "Am I glad to see you!"

Jeffery recognized the voice, was confused, it can't be he thought. "Uncle Bart," Jeff said feebly. Just then Jacques appeared with two coconut halved shells full of water.

"Drink this Jeffery, it will revive you. You too Bart, this is what the Dolphins told me to bring. When you are done, I will bring the coconut cups back to the pool and take a full cup myself."

They drank in silence. Slowly, Bart and Jeffrey's senses became more acute, and they could feel the life force come back into their very being. Jacques retrieved the cups, excused himself and walked through the foliage back to the pool. He drank one cupful and could not remember tasting anything so delicious. He began to feel revived and refreshed, and let his gaze linger, to remember the beauty of the place. "Thank you my dolphin friends, we are forever in your debt," he murmured. Jacques had never communicated with dolphins before. He had some communication with the animals where he interned at the animal clinic. Picking up some urgency from the dolphins, he quickly put the cups back in the original place where he found them and made his way back to Bart and Jeffery.

"To tell you the truth, Uncle Bart, I was feeling right knackered."

Jacques came into view. "I am Jacques Baigent." He shook Jeffery's hand.

"Jeffery Turner, you were my rescuer..." Jacques nodded. Jeffery had stood up looking like he had just won the marathon. Bart was feeling pretty darn good himself.

"How did we get here?" Jeff asked. The last thing I remembered was diving in and out of the water looking for my tanks when I slipped and hit my head on a protruding rock.

"We will explain it all later, *Mon Ami*, but now, we must get ready to go back into the waters. I am hearing the dolphin's urgency to hurry. We must, put on our tanks and masks. Jeffery had a first aid kit tied to his belt and Bart taped the crack in his mask. The repair would buy him a little time. They waded out to the waiting dolphins; each getting a good grip on one as they were brought back into the sea.

It didn't take long to enter the vortex. It was a swirly orange color, and then it was gone as the last dolphin came through. Jeffery almost lost his hold as he came through, but held on tightly as he hit the raging waters.

It took a while to get to the ship; Bart's mask was slowly filling up with water again. At last they came in sight of the ship.

 Rene' saw something in the distance. He couldn't quite make it out with the rain and wind coming in full force. Then he saw them, the dolphins were coming in with extreme speed. "Well I'll be! It is them!" Rene' yelled, "Jacques, Bart…Bart, over here!" The dolphins brought their passengers to the vessel and Rene reached over board and took hold of Bart, who was first, and pulled him out of the water. He saw Jacques and Jeffery come to the surface the same way. Seeing the water in Bart's face mask, Rene' reached over and pulled it off. Bart gasped for air, heaved and struggled for breath for a few moments. Rene' then grabbed hold of Jeff as Jacques held on to the side of the boat and pulled him in. Jacques waited for Rene' to pull himself out of the water.

The dolphins waited a few moments as Jacques turned around to the sea and waved gratitude of thanks. The dolphins sent their message telepathically and disappeared.

Jacques hugged his father. "It is so good to see you Popie, but quick, get us out of here!" Bart breathing more normally was held and guided by René down stairs also. Jacque and Jeffery ran down into the cabin and out of the storm. Rene' went into the control room and fired up the engines. The sun came out and all was calm again. Rene', bewildered wanted to "Get the heck out of here," just in case any other bad weather would materialize. It was a powerful engine and he flew back to the harbor where they started from.

Chapter **53**

"Anthony, hello, are you coming home? No, I'm at the Antiquities Shop. Hmmmm, I'm not sure, Dad's at the Museum. Well, he may be in a meeting and probably left his cell phone at his desk. You got a call from Grandfather? Oh, uh huh, yes, but there is a lot more to it…." Charles listened for about three to four minutes. "Thanks Anthony, have a great time and see you when you get back! "

"Grandfather is on his way back to England, and great news, they have Uncle Jeffery!" Charles felt elated. "He called Anthony's number by mistake and asked him to relay the message. Oh, I'm sorry; Anthony is my older brother, well anyway, the rescue for Uncle Jeff was sketchy at first, but went well in the end. He said some other people are coming back with them. They should be in the States in about five or six days."

"Hmm, let's see…what else…oh yes, Anthony went to Brazil after his classes in May. A group of professors and students went to help conduct a survey of the pink river dolphins in the Amazon River. He went there from France, taking an independent study group where he teaches, for a few months after last term."

"Aaannd.....Anthony was interviewed as part of The World Wildlife Fund Survey Team to help save the habitants of the Amazon River in Brazil about ten days ago. He said the article will appear in the July issue of the magazine."

"So, anyway, he's in France now, and traveling with the Fat Tire Bike Tours and something to do with a Paris Pass. Anthony was talking so fast, I didn't quite get it all. He went with his friend Theo from France.....not sure when he's coming back, the connection started to break up."

"Man, I'll bet that's real cool, I've been to Paris with my parents," said Desmond. A Paris Pass I think saves you a percentage on some of the places included in the tours, and you get in some places for free. I think that's what mom & dad got when we were on bikes last year."

"Anthony was having a great time, he sounded happy. He's been under a lot of stress; this year was tough, with the transition to a new culture and country. It was his first year teaching in France he has a doctorate in Ecology and Evolutionary Biology. He was affiliated with Cornell University in Ithaca, New York."

Anna wondered what a pink dolphin would look like. "I'm going to look up pink dolphins on the computer, later; I can't imagine how one would look."

"Me neither," said Charles smiling at Anna causing her to semi bluish. "All right then, let's go and check out the stones grandfather has in his safe keeping!"

Desmond's stomach began to growl. He looked longingly at the Café Umbria and thought of all the delectable's he found there last time they were at The Antiquities Shop. As they past the shop en route to Mr. Edis' office suite, Charles noticed the gaze and commented. "We can stop there after, Desmond if you like." Desmond beamed with satisfaction.

Lucien met them as he came out of the Café Umbria. "Oh Charles, so glad you're here! Bart left you a telegram about ten minutes ago; I was just on my way to the office to telephone you again, because your line was busy earlier. What a coincidence!" Charles shook Lucien's hand with a strong friendly grip.

"Thanks Lucien, it's great to see you! I was on the line earlier with Anthony.

"Ah, yes," Lucien nodded.

"How is Marcus" We haven't seen him in here for quite a while," Charles asked.

"Marcus, I think is traveling abroad now and I am thinking he actually met up with your brother in Paris!"

"What are the odds of that?" Charles chuckled; knowing that was a probable possibility. Anthony and Marcus were inseparable growing up. It was as if they were twins having similar tastes in everything.

When Lucien and his family moved to Charles' street in the late 1980's from France, they were astonished that their next door neighbor's son was almost an exact duplicate of their Marcus, it was uncanny. Lucien and his wife, Lisa had one child. It is sometimes known that somewhere everyone has a double. Marcus and Anthony were that and much more.

Lucien unlocked the office door and handed the keys to Charles. "I think I hear the chimes in the front entrance, Charles. Good to see you and we'll catch up later." Charles nodded "Okay, thanks Lucien." Anna and Desmond walked into the office suite after Charles turned the lights on.

The envelope of the telegram was found near his grandfather's settee on small side table. It was addressed to Charles.

Charles...*Found Jeff. We will stop in England to get Aunt Abigail before coming back to States. Hoping to be home June 27th.*

Lucien will be able to be at the shop until June 28th. He needs to fulfill obligations then. If something happens, you will need to go back to work on that day if we are not back in time.

Have a lot to cover with you and the two teenagers when we get back... Grandfather

Charles relayed the message to Anna and Desmond. "We have some more things to tell grandfather when he gets back; also, perhaps he will help us untangle some of the mysteries of the codes."

"And Jeffery Turner is coming with them," Anna supplemented, "which means…"

"….he will tell us all about the codes," interjected Desmond enthusiastically.

"This is beginning to be a marvelous adventure!" Charles moved into another part of the suite, the room of his grandfather's office. Anna and Desmond followed. Oh how he missed Anthony, he mused.

Charles opened the safe where the stones were kept. The stones were glowing in orange & red with elongated brown and white serrations. He remembered them when they were brought to the shop for safekeeping.

Desmond took out the magazine article photograph from his back pocket.

Anna stepped up to take a closer look. "Look at the brown and white lines here." She pointed to the photograph, and then to the lines the stones exhibited on one side. They felt warm and cool at the same time. "See here," She pointed to a circular elongated line on one of the stones, "it's about the same, but the lines change as the stones glow."

"I see that," Charles stood transfixed.

"My guess," Desmond calculated, "is that they are the same as the ones in the museum as in this article from the 1950's."

"And are the same ones from the Andes Mountains that ended up in my driveway, last year," Anne was thrilled.

"Alright then," Charles was coming up with a plan. "Let's leave them here until grandfather comes back. It appears that there is a little mystery here on how the stones ended up in the Andes Mountains, and maybe...wait a minute, isn't tonight the Big Splash at Rose Cottage?"

"Yeah," Desmond replied, "it is! We're all going together." Aunt Ellen, us, and you and your Dad!"

"And...were going to ask Mrs. Perpecuwitz some questions that may fill in some of the gaps," Anna said."

"Hmmm... its 3:00 now, and Dad & I are coming over at 7:00 tonight. Let's go to Café Umbria to appease Desmond's growling stomach," Desmond grinning nodded in appreciation as his stomach growled again, "then I'll take you both home."

Anna was thoughtful on the ride back to the house. She wondered about the mysterious role Mrs. Perpecuwitz played in all of this? The days were moving too fast. Would they be able to accomplish the task that seemed to be given to her and Desmond? And why were they chosen?

So deep in thought, Anna hadn't realized they were back at her house and Charles had opened the door for her. "Are you okay, Anna," Charles looked inquisitive at her.

"Oh, were here," Anna came back from her thoughts. "Sorry, just thinking about some questions I had for Mrs. Perpecuwitz later on. Thanks for the ride home Charles..."

"Yeah, Thanks Charles," Desmond shook Charles' hand.

"See you both tonight. Charles drove away thinking about how all their experiences tied into the mystery of the quest stones.

Chapter 54

Jacques felt relieved to have come out of such a turbulent storm. He thought as the forces of water rushed into the caves, he wasn't going to make it. "Nous sommes tous très chanceux d'être viviant! Very lucky, yes?"

Rene' nodded solemnly. He was so proud of his son. He gave Jacques a he-man hug gruffly, then radioed into shore that the rescue was a success.

As the boat reached the borders of the Reserve Nationale De Camargue, he could see dozens of the wild white horses in the distance. They were beautiful. Jacques sat mesmerized for just a moment, "Cette beauté innocente!"

Bart lingered at the deck watching the horses run into a hidden part of the Reserve. He thought of Elizabeth again, then became focused as he grabbed his duffle bag and walked off the boat with Jeffery.

Jeffery had to return his diving equipment to La Serine' Aquatique, and arrange for someone to pick up the small rented boat anchored back at the underwater caves. Rene' volunteered to take care of returning Jeff's rental after he found the owner of The Colvic Watson 34'6" Motor Sail Boat.

Jacques had an idea; he went and conversed with his father for the duration of all the details concerning the boats. After twenty minutes, everyone gathered back at The Flying Aces Sea Plane for the return trip to Montpellier.

Bart and his nephew Jeffrey were getting reacquainted after so many years. Plans were being made to return to England, then to America. When they reached the city of Montpellier, Bart retrieved his duffle bag, giving Rene' a bear hug, and promised to reconnect soon. He turned to thank Jacques, but he was no were to be found.

"Rene', where is Jacques? Wasn't he right behind us?" Just then, a jeep flew around the bend coming to an abrupt stop.

"Climb in mes amis, I am going with you both!" Jacques had his bags from a previous travel to Languedoc. "A coincidence, eh, Bart? I happen to have my luggage with me? I am coming with you and Jeffery. I will come to America with you, yes?"

Bart let out a bellow of a laugh; Jeff wondered what was so amusing. "Ah Jacques, My Little Pip Squeak, this time you can come with me! "

Jacques chuckled smiling, "He does not know what this is all about, your nephew, Jeffery!"

Bart explained. "Years ago, I had quite a bit of business at some of the museums in the South of France. I had to fly to the Island of Palmer the first time I met Rene' Baigent. We became close friends, and through the years he had three children, Jacques being the youngest one here," Bart nodded to Jacques, and Jacques was grinning ear to ear.

"We were the best of friends, oui?"

Bart just shook his head with a grin. "Well, to finish the story," continued Bart, "every time I would go to leave, Jacques would cling, I mean literally cling to my leg and beg me to take him with me..."

"It was for the adventure," added Jacques, "for a while, I thought you were a spy, and I was quite fascinated at the time with being a spy. I was seven years old!"

"Ah yes, a spy, quite attractive at that age," commented Jeff.

"Of course, I have been to America several times as an adult." Jacques added, "I visited California the first trip, I had my first degree in Physics and in 1989..."

"You're first degree?" Jeffery was curious.

"Actually, I have seven," Jacques answered.

"Seven? How old are you?" Jeff was now astounded.

"I am 37 as of thirteen days ago. I visited California because my cousin was getting married." They went over a few bumps and were speeding around the corners of the narrow roads. Bart was holding on to his seat for fear of falling out.

"Hang on friends, we will make the airport in time, yes?" And with that note, Jacques made it to the Montpellier Airport in exactly 12 minutes from the air terminal of The Flying Aces Taxi Service. They were to board the plane to Paris then to London England. The events were falling into place.

Chapter 55

Lawrence and Charles Edis were at the Belk's front door at 7:01. Ellen greeted them and called for Anna and Desmond. Rose Cottage usually closed at 9:00 pm, but because of the Big Splash, it would close at 10:00 pm and reopen at 11:00 am the next morning.

Charles had mentioned that there were a few new occurrences which happened last evening and in the afternoon with the incident of the mural.

"Almost like a vision, Aunt Ellen," said Desmond, "but it was real."

"We all saw it, Mom," Anna piped in.

"I'd like to hear about it," said Ellen. "Is everyone in a hurry to go to Rose Cottage?"

"Mom I already have coffee prepared ahead in the pot for tomorrow morning, should I turn it on?"

Ellen looked at everyone else, "Yes Anna perhaps that would be a good idea. It should only take a few minutes, and the coffee would be done, or would you prefer ice tea?"

"Well, Ellen, it is warm out and I would welcome some ice tea." Lawrence smiled appreciatively.

"We'll get it Mom." Anna elbowed Desmond to help. Desmond gave Anna the look and retrieved the clean glasses from the dishwasher as Anna pulled out the large decanter of ice tea. She also took the ice container out of the freezer and walked into the dining room.

"Here, let me help," Charles took the container of ice from Anna placing the cubes into each glass and handed them to Anna. Anna smiled and handed Charles the first filled glass. Desmond said under his breath, "Oh brother," took the other two glasses of iced tea and gave one to Lawrence Edis and his Aunt Ellen, then retrieved the last one for himself.

Charles started to relay his dream incident, and Anna and Desmond told their experience the other night of the flyers instructions to place the stones at the entrance of the quarry gate.

"When we got to The Antiquities Shop, we took a look at the one of the murals in the new edition..."

"Yes, I know which ones you are referring to, the large unusual landscapes," Lawrence Edis added.

Anna nodded enthusiastically. "The mural to the left of the large window, the area where the bookcases are, has two medium size orange and reddish stones, with brown serrations on them to one side, Well, we wanted to look at the stones to see if they were similar to the ones that were missing from the Paris museum in the early 1960's."

Desmond cut in, "right and I was able to find the article of the missing stones in an archived report from a museum in Paris on line." Desmond still had the paper in his back pocket. He took it out, unfolded the copy and handed it to Ellen, who in turn handed it to Lawrence after she reviewed it."

"I don't quite understand, what do the stones signify?" Lawrence was intrigued.

Anna spoke up, "Umm, Mom, do you remember the gate incident last year?"

Ellen was taken a little aback, "Yes, but what does that mishap have to do with what we are talking about right now?"

Anna and Desmond took turns conveying what took place, the Shaman, the Andes Mountains, moving the car for the stones to arrive, how the mural became alive before their eyes, the similarity of the stones in the article and how they thought the stones were the ones that vanished from the museum in Paris in the early sixties..."

"And the most amazing thing is," Charles added, "Was that you brought them to the shop.

"Actually, after the Shaman experience, Mrs. Perpecuwitz suggested Mr. Edis," said Anna.

Anna repeated the incident at the Antiquities Shop, how the mural became alive as a hologram right before their eyes, and the mystical Seer who spoke directly at them.

All was silent as the sun hung lower in the warm June sky, with a slight breeze coming through the window screens.

Anna's mother closed her eyes for a moment. "I...I...don't quite know how to take this Anna. Ellen felt overwhelmed with all this new information, especially what transpired a few days ago when Anna and Desmond first told her about their experiences. "If all this is true, Anna, then we will have to get some more information."

Lawrence finished his glass of ice tea. "That was very refreshing, thank you Ellen. Should we go to Rose Cottage now and see if we can get a little insight from Mrs. Perpecuwitz? All the events are a little strange, and I've dealt with quite a bit of peculiar happenings from my boy's anomalies during the past years..."

Charles was about to reply, but decided against it.

Lawrence got up from the table and everyone else followed.

"That's a very good idea," said Ellen. "I think we need to see if Audrey would be available tonight, especially when we're all together."

Anna, Desmond and Charles made quick haste in clearing the table and left the glasses in the sink for later.

"Would you like to come with us? Charles has the jeep and we can all fit."

"That would be lovely, Lawrence," Ellen replied.

With Lawrence and Ellen in the front seat, Charles, Anna and Desmond sat in the back seats in anticipation for a meeting with Mrs. Perpecuwitz. Anna, silently elated, sat in the middle of Desmond and Charles. Her face glowed and was slightly flushed as Charles glanced her way while talking to Desmond.

The Big Splash was in full swing by the time the jeep arrived.

Calla C was with her parents. The twins, John and Josh were walking around with their walkie talkies looking efficient as ever. They were exceptional geniuses. John had developed a new wave color system that ran throughout the whole property. Josh developed the color slides projecting a rainbow effect. The trees were outfitted with fiber optics lights.

Desmond's eyes lit up when he saw Calla C. "Hey, Calla, how's it going?"

Calla C. turned around and gave Desmond a huge grin. "Hi Desmond, hi Anna, we're having a blast. Did you see what Josh and John did with the trees? Isn't that cool?"

Desmond and Anna loved the lights. "I love it, Calla," said Anna.

"How long did it take to get them set up," Desmond asked.

"About five days, and Josh almost broke his leg when he fell from the tall birch near the kayak station"

At hearing his name mentioned, Josh came over and squeezed Calla's hand. Desmond pretended not to notice. Anna aware of his feelings poked him and raised her eyebrows and projected an air of innocence. Desmond sighed.

"The lights are fantastic Josh," said Anna.

"Yes," said Desmond recovering, "it must have been quite a job. How did you think of it, using fiber optics?"

"Pure genius," replied John as he came up to them. Josh grinned from ear to ear.

"We did some research last year for our final Science Project. Adjusted a few tweaks, and voila....the end result!" Josh was quite proud of the effects as he waved his hand around. Ocean blue, green, purple and yellow lights went off and on at different intervals.

There were replicas of waves and mermaids, hidden treasure maps and pirate insignia all over and in and out of the trees. Some were props hanging from the trees; others were staked in the ground.

Just then a voice came through John's intercom announcing a costume contest was to begin in fifteen minutes.

"That's us, Josh," John nodded and answered back. "We'll be there in three." John and Josh were part of the competition. Their costumes were always a mystery, and always worth waiting to see.

Mrs. Perpecuwitz was pleased with it all. Anna spotted her by the ramp near the kayaking station.

"Ellen, Anna, and Desmond, Hello everyone," waved Audrey Perpecuwitz. "How do you like the lights this year?"

"They're great, Mrs. Perpecuwitz, it changes everything!" Anna was having a good time already.

"Just lovely, Audrey, how did you ever pull it off?" Ellen was amazed at the quality of the effects and lights everywhere.

"It was the twin's idea; I think they're on to something this year. Just look at it all!" Audrey was beaming with pride. "How fortunate we are!"

"Yes!" Ellen nodded in satisfaction.

"Hello, Audrey," said Lawrence coming around the corner of the building after parking the car.

"Good evening Lawrence, and Charles, so glad you both could make it!"

"Wouldn't miss it for the world," Lawrence said over the music of the beach boys.

"I have a feeling you all would like to talk to me." Audrey looked at all the anxious faces. "Hmm, it is 8:00 now, how about at ten pm, after the fireworks. Then you wouldn't miss any of the festivities. Its summer and we don't have to worry about school the next day."

Everyone agreed to meet Audrey Perpecuwitz at her office after the fireworks. Anna, Desmond and Charles broke away from Lawrence and Ellen to partake in the Big Splash Ski Lift Ride, overlooking the Cottage and grounds. It would bring them to the costume judging area. The twilight was intensely beautiful as the last of the sun's rays dimmed beyond the mountain. The Color Waves in the trees were exceptional, and you could see the shadow of color in and out of the water.

"CHARLES, HEY CHARLES, OVER HERE," called a voice from behind.

Charles turned around. "Heeyyy, Bryon! How's that new apartment of yours?"

"WHAT," shouted Bryon?

Charles waved to his friend and yelled: "WAIT TILL THE LIFT STOPS!"

"WHAT?"

They were almost at the Landing Pad. Charles was the first one off, then Anna and Desmond followed by Bryon and his girlfriend. Desmond spotted the costume festivities near the swimming area. He nudged Anna to go with him.

"See you at ten, Charles, Anna & I are going to the swimming area", called Desmond as he headed toward his destination.

Charles waved and spoke with Bryon and his girlfriend as they too headed to the costume festivities also.

Chapter 56

Bart sat near the window on the flight from Paris to England. The plane from Montpellier arrived in Paris in no time and he hadn't much time before to think about all that transpired during his flight to England from the United States and the urgency to get to the South of France in time to rescue Jeff.

Bart thought of himself as an adventurous and a fearless man. The rescue unnerved him. He would never admit it to anyone and he didn't like to make reference to it even in his thoughts. But he was "darn right scared!" Especially, when he almost drowned in his own face mask the second time. His feelings brought about the rescue again. "I have to stop thinking about this," Bart thought. "It's over and thank God we're all alive and alright."

This brought his thoughts to the connection with the dolphins. Bart felt the peace and rejuvenation of life within his bones again once more. It seems so unreal, he pondered. He put his head back and smiled as he remembered the ambient feelings that existed on the island. He fell into a light sleep, as he remembered the satisfying breezes and warmth of the sun on his face as he brought back the memories of the beautiful island paradise.

Jeffery was in the adjacent seat. He was very anxious to see his mother, Abigail Turner. After July, he would never see her again, at least physically on this Earth Plane. He wondered how she would take it. "She is a trooper, though," Jeffery mused. He loved her and knew he would miss her tremendously. His life was destined and he knew he had to go back to Neia. Jeffery now in his seventies in this Earth dimension had over fifty years to make up with The Seer and Flyers. One thing for certain, through the abilities of the Seer, Jeffery would still have contact with Abigail; he was quite satisfied with this thought. Guardia would teach him dream transference. It was amazing to him how this could be possible, but being the recipient of this process just recently, gave Jeffery a thrill of anticipation.

His biological parents were waiting for him. Through the years, Jeffery did recall some episodes from his world, but wasn't sure if it was factual or not. He was ready in July to translate; he would miss everyone here. But to see his family in Neia, well, hmmm, he pondered on what it may be like for a few moments. He thought of his earthly father, Walter, smiling to himself as childhood memories suddenly came flooding back. Jeffery would free the collected insecta his father gathered for the University. (His father a Latin scholar, would use the term, insecta when referring to insects, made Jeffery chuckle as he remembered fondly past incidents in regard to the Latin phrases his father would quote.) After a few times, Walter Turner had a talk with him and set him straight in terms he would understand.

After his father had died years ago, Abigail took it very well. She did everything that they use to do together. She missed Walter, but she had promised him to not give up doing their favorite things after he was gone. Abigail encompassed a full life, and had met some marvelous people and became an avid traveler. She was now 83, alert with perfect eyesight, still driving her car and was in very good health.

Nowadays, Abigail lectured from time to time and attended conferences where she was the keynote speaker on Biological Sciences specializing in the Plant Sciences. Her research was always well received.

Abigail Turner became well known when she and a colleague wrote a paper about the synthesis of plant kinetics. They proved that a plant's energy field would change when in positive to negative conditions and visa versa. With special sensory cameras, it was proven that plants had an aura. It was an energy field that gave off light reactions. The cameras would be able to photograph its rate of reactions as the plant was exposed to human conditions and emotions, and also their environments.

As Jeffery noticed Bart slowly falling asleep, he took this opportunity to get his thoughts together for the next part of his journey.

Jacques was able to get a ticket on the flight to Paris, then to London and the United States at the very last minute. He wasn't worried about the cost. He knew for some strange reason, that he was destined to go to America and help in some way. It was a gut feeling. He always had good intuition and it never failed him in the past.

Bart's mobile phone needed to be recharged and in his haste forgot his charger as he hurried to catch the flight from New York City to London, so Jacques volunteered to telephone from his mobile phone. With that done, he boarded the plane just in time.

Jacques now let his thoughts linger on the past. Bart Edis use to come to the house with his father in between his museum trips when he was just a little boy. The first time he met Bart Edis, Jacques was fascinated with the mystique of him. He thought he was a spy. Jacques chuckled to himself as he remembered the briefcases and slick jackets Bart used to carry and wear. He always had unusual devices in his pocket. One time, the most valuable treasure Jacques received from Bart for his twelfth birthday was a Swiss Army Pocket Knife. It was huge. He thought the knife contained the most gadgets he had ever seen on a pocket knife. That year, Jacques pretended he was the elitist of spies! He still carried the pocket knife at times.

And now, well now, he was quite happy with his life. He loved to travel. Jacques decided, he was done with Universities for a while. Seven degrees was enough. "I will travel for a while, before I decide what it is I am to do with my life. Hmmm, one year off will not matter." Jacques smiled as he let his thoughts drift to exploring new avenues.

Chapter 57

The whirr of her DeLonghi permeated the atmosphere with a blend of mocha and chocolate cream, one of Audrey Perpecuwitz's favorite coffees. It was 9:15 and a warm June evening.

Audrey was fascinated by the fast turn of events. She just received a telephone call from a man named Jacques Baigent. Faint persistent ringing from her office suite, caused her to pause when she heard her private line ringing. Sipping her mocha now, Audrey ruminated on the past. That name, Baigent, sounded familiar, but she will find the answer to her curiosity later. All that mattered was Bartholomew Edis was on a plane from Paris to London and soon would be on his way back to America with Jeffery Turner and that strange delightful Frenchman, Jacques who relayed the message she was to give to Ellen and Lawrence.

How remarkable that Ellen Belk met Lawrence Edis. Their meeting would have been inevitable Audrey thought as she glanced toward the clock on the wall. It is time the truth comes out, she reflected. There wasn't much time, just about two weeks before the portal to the old quarry would open.

Audrey finished her mocha and decided to check on the festivities before she met with the Belk's & Edis's. She was very happy about how well the Big Splash went this year. It was a new addition for the month of June and she had been a little apprehensive about it.

After her meeting with the twins in March, they decided to go with the Beach Theme and move The Lights of the Rivera to July. The Big Splash ushered in the beginning of the summer month activities that Rose Cottage is famous for. Recreational bus tours, vacationers, hiking & walking groups, bird watchers come for the fascinating trails, springs, river rapids, and the caverns with the stalagmite formations.

Within walking distance on one of the trails, travelers would come to a natural seashore inlet. Last year a number of naturalists studying the ecosystem and the recent dolphin activity in the fjord had brought various and unique individuals including one character whom no one would ever forget. Audrey met Kevin Branford last year, head of the Department of Ecological Environmental Studies from the Museum. When they had met for tea, Audrey could not stop laughing. Kevin Branford with his slight English accent relayed past episodes of other teammates and the mishaps of various past expeditions. He had to obtain her permission to encamp on her land for an entire month. The Department was part of the scuba diving crew that also took part of the exploration in the water tunnels and caves under the natural stalagmite caverns. They discovered that the tunnels connected into the mountain underground streams and caves near the natural seashore inlet. It was a big to do for the area and good publicity for Rose Cottage also. Visitors to Rose Cottage increased, and the dolphins became one of the highlights along the trail to the natural seashore inlet.

Audrey Perpecuwitz heard the loud roars of laughter and clapping as she opened the side door and stepped out of the Cottage. The twins, John & Josh Bartley, won the grand prize for the best costumes. It was the first contest of the season. The prize for the month of June was a three month pass to Old Seaman's Wharf, one of the best places to swim, kayak and fish. The twins designed a costume resembling stalagmites. The fascinating effects of the costume were images of the caverns and the glowing stalagmites that slowly faded in and out on the front of it.

The rules of the contests were you could only win once for the whole summer season. Next month the contest will entail the theme; Lights of the Rivera. Desmond went to the location where the activities and rules were posted. He grabbed several flyers for Anna and Charles turning around, he accidently bumped into Calla C.

"Sorry, Calla C, I didn't see you, I didn't see...," Desmond stopped short.

"Hi Desmond," Calla C pointed to the girl on the side of her. "This is my cousin Elise, remember from last year."

Desmond turned to Elise, who was smiling. "I think I left before you came last year. Glad to meet you…"

"Hi Elise, wow, you're here early this year," Anna said coming up the path.

Elise and Anna chatted for a few minutes. Josh Bartley came in and joined in the conversation. His brother John called him shortly after on the intercom and the group dispersed.

Anna took a quick look at Desmond, and nonchalantly poked him with her elbow. He was inadvertently staring at Elise as they parted.

Desmond gave Anna the look, "What?"

It was 9:45 pm and the crowd started to congregate near the water for the firework's display.

Sizzzzzzzzssssssphoof the first firework exploded into the night sky. You could hear the gasps and applause from the collected audience all around the park.

Chapter 58

Bart was bewildered when he sat up in his seat with a start. He wasn't quite sure of where he was. Then he saw Jeffery looking at him with his eyes raised.

"You talk in your sleep, Uncle Bart, it's a good thing you didn't divulge any secrets."

Bart smiled sheepishly. "I'd be in a lot of trouble if I did!"

The Stewardess' voice came over the intercom in French, then another in English.

"Attention, s'il vous plaît."
"Attention please."

"Nous approchons de l'aéroport Roissy-Charles de Gaulle."
"We are approaching Roissy-Charles de Gaulle Airport."

"S'il vous plaît attacher votre ceinture de sécurité et veiller à ce que tous les bacs sont en place et vos sièges sont en position verticale."

"Please fasten your seatbelts and ensure that all trays are up and your seats are in an upright position."

"Nous approchons de numéro deux du terminal."
"We are approaching Terminal Number Two."

"Tous les passagers en route pour Londres, en Angleterre sera de nouveau en conseil s'il vous plaît une demi-heure à partir de maintenant."
"All passengers en route to London England will please board again in one half hour from now."

"Merci d'avoir choisi Air Compagnies aériennes France."
"Thank you for choosing Air France Airlines."

As the plane descended to the Roissy-Charles de Gaulle Airport in Paris, everyone fastened their seatbelts and prepared for landing.

Jacques put his newspaper away and made a mental note to get the proper personal care items he lacked for a two week or longer trip. He could purchase the necessary items during the one hour layover in the terminal shopping plaza. He was glad he took his laptop and plug with him on his recent trip to Languedoc. He almost didn't.

Once off the plane, Bart & Jeffery telephoned Abigail Turner. Abigail had a special visitor, whom she knew everyone, would love to see. Jeffery talked to his mother and made the necessary plans for their final flight to America.

Jacques had also contacted Abigail before he put a call through to Audrey Perpecuwitz in the United States, to tell her of their arrival time in Paris, and expected departure flight to London.

Even though they all had a perilous time during the rescue, Bart, Jeffery and Jacques had energy to spare. It was if it didn't happen, a dream in the making, yet so very real. Time was crucial. As the passengers boarded the flight to London, the Stewardess placed Jacques in a seat across the isle near Jeffery and Bart.

Bart explained how his grandson Charles and two younger teens discovered the journal, a small publication of Jeffery Turner's account in the 1940's of a parallel world and Jeffery's part in it. He relayed every detail of all that occurred. Jeffery himself heard first hand of the meeting with Anna and Desmond, Audrey Perpecuwitz's part in it and of his ancestor, Dertia, who came in the 18th century with others to help with the Earth's dimensional changes. When Bart finished one part, Jeffery would add another of his account of his book until Jacques was up to date with what was happening now.

"I am, how you say, accable'!" Jacques hesitated for a second, "...um, oui, overwhelmed! It is incredible, Jeffery, but I expect the story will become more fascinating as we continue on this mystery, yes?" Jacques shook his head, smiling.

A newly married couple sat in the back of Bart & Jeffery. The Maris's had been listening intently to the story. When Bart had finished relaying the account to Jacques, The newlyweds, anxiously said, "What happened next in the story? Don't leave us in the dark!"

"Oh mes bon Amis, you will have to wait until the book comes out, oui? Jacques smiled at the newly weds graciously.

Jeffery thankful of Jacques' tact gave him an appreciative glance.

The flight to London was uneventful, and Abigail and Anthony met Jeffery, Bart and Jacques at the inside terminal gate of the Heathrow Airport.

"Anthony! What are you doing in London; I thought you were in Paris a few days ago? It is so good to see you," said Bart. He gave Anthony the family handshake. Jacques looked at them comically. "Ah ha, et bien c'est maintenant officiel, oui! See the secret spy handshake!" Everyone burst out laughing and Jacques had to explain himself from his childhood reveries.

Anthony found out from Charles there was a mystery surrounding Uncle Jeff, so he cut his Paris trip short and flew to London after his telephone call to Charles. He was due to visit his Great Aunt at some point during the summer, so he decided now was a good time as ever. "I'm coming back to the States with everyone. Aunt Abigail filled me in with the details, Uncle Jeff and I'd like to help if I can!"

Bart gave a snort of laughter, knowing full well that Anthony was going to try to document as much as he could. Anthony, now 32, had passions; for wildlife, UFO's, endangered species, any type of anomaly you could think of, Anthony usually was in the thick of it. Anthony looked at his grandfather and smiled.

Once the necessary bags & duffels were collected, Jeffery took the driver's seat of the rented car and drove everyone to Abigail's home. It was late and the flight to America wasn't booked until the next day at 6:00 pm. There would be five passengers en route to New York City, to collect Jeffery's necessary itinerary then to the state and town Bart Edis lived for the end of the long-awaited journey to begin.

Chapter 59

Anna and Desmond sat near the opened window in Audrey Perpecuwitz's private office suite. It was decorated in a classic yet contemporary style. Anna felt comfortable in this room. She had only been in it once before.

Five spacious rooms outfitted the suite. Three were private quarters. At times when it was very late and Audrey felt too tired to make the thirty minute drive to her home residence; she stayed here, where all her extra comforts were at bay. The other two rooms were set as a lounge and office space, Audrey seated her guests in the lounge area of the suite.

"Thank you for meeting with us Audrey." Ellen Belk was pleased she would finally be able to understand what Anna was involved in. She had some concerns with the discovery of The Epic Catalog and the turn of events that had followed.

"You're welcome, Ellen." Audrey turned to everyone; "I have some lemonade set out here. Anna, would you and Desmond like to distribute the glasses?"

"Oh we love your lemonade, Mrs. Perpecuwitz. It's always so good, thank you," said Anna as she and Desmond handed one to each person in the room. Floating inside the glasses were iced rose petals and lemon slices. And there was always something more, a secret ingredient that Mrs. Perpecuwitz never divulged.

Charles accepted his gratefully. He was very warm and the ice cold lemonade was a welcomed sight.

As soon as everyone had a glass of lemonade, Audrey continued.

"First let me tell everyone that a man named Jacques Baigent telephone not too long ago. He is in the party of your father Lawrence, and Jeffery Turner and from what I gathered from the conversation a long time friend of Bart's."

Audrey took a sip of her lemonade and continued. "They were on their way to Paris, and with a one hour layover continuing to London. A flight will, hmmm, let me see, my notes are around here somewhere. She found her notes on the small table near the side entrance where she kept her telephone, "Ah, yes! It appears they will take a flight from Heathrow at 6:00 pm on the next day to New York City, where Jeffery Turner will collect what he needs and quickly make the necessary contacts to close up his home."

Lawrence cleared his throat. Audrey looked up from his notes. "If I am correct, Audrey, Jeffery hasn't much time. July 11th is in about two weeks, will he get here in time?"

"Yes, I think he will, Lawrence. Jacques said by July first they should arrive here."

Lawrence nodded. "Thank you Audrey. I haven't seen Jeff in years. I would like to talk to him about a few things when he comes. He may have some information about one of the projects we are working on at the museum, and it will be good to see him after all these years."

"Let's take some pictures of Jeff before he leaves, Dad, I am sure Anthony wishes he were here. He always had a special connection with any type of anomaly."

"Yes, he does, Charles..." Lawrence wondered after working with the dolphins in Brazil, if Anthony were enjoying Paris on his bike tour.

Ellen Belk spoke up next. "Audrey, Anna tells me that you have given her the words from last week's assignment which brought up the book The Epic Catalog into her computer. How did you come across it and how does it affect us?"

"I think that it is time for some details and answers. Some things that I am about to tell you may amaze you and some you may find hard to believe."

Audrey looked at all the expectant faces. "Well, by now you have been reading the book of Jeffery Turner, The Epic Catalog. Have you all read it?"

Lawrence spoke up. "Not exactly Audrey. I just found out about it this week, and I believe it is new to Ellen also." Ellen smiled. Lawrence continued, "I find it interesting that my father, Bart, had just found out about it during his vacation earlier in the month. Is it really all true, Jeff is here from a parallel world?"

"Yes, yes it is," Audrey continued, "there is so much to tell, I'm afraid we may not finish it all tonight. I have not read it, but Anna, you first found out about the book on your computer from some phrases I gave you?"

"I did Mrs. Perpecuwitz, Anna started on her part of the story. Mrs. Perpecuwitz would give me words and phrases once a month to write a story with. Anna relayed the story of her illness three years ago, the events that led up to the recent words from Mrs. Perpecuwitz, and how The Epic Catalog appeared on her home computer.

Desmond and Anna became aware of the lettering and number codes from the envelope mentioned in The Epic Catalog when Desmond's computer game froze and brought up the same exact numbers. They told everyone about their dream and The Elder contacting them.

Charles told Mrs. Perpecuwitz about his experience at the old quarry and his dream of the quarry a second time. Charles then relayed the coincidence of Rachel Carde having a dream about him at the quarry, which was written in the journal.

Desmond was quite proud of himself for cracking the puzzle of the cryptogram, and showed Audrey the codes from a pull out in the journal.

Audrey held the book in her hands and felt a slight sensation of energy from it. No one noticed, she wondered why she was the only one who felt it. Images went through her mind and knew it was related to the Seer whom she periodically had contact with in the past.

The clock chimed 11:00. Anna yawned. Audrey took that as a clue. "I guess it is quite late. What is everyone's day like tomorrow? We don't have any tours scheduled tomorrow, and I can be free in the late morning."

"I have a meeting at the museum in the morning and know it will break up by lunch time," said Lawrence.

Ellen spoke up next. "And I'm free for the rest of the summer. Our conferences are over, so Anna, Desmond and I will be available any time."

Everyone looked at Charles. "I think I'm off for a few more days at the Antiquities, I'll check in with Lucien just to make sure."

"Very good then, there is so much to tell you all, about my life and how I came to discover the murals in Bart's shop, so we shall resume the conversation tomorrow say at…..at one in the afternoon. Anna, you may want to tell your mother more about your meeting with Mr. Edis, and Ellen that should explain a little more until tomorrow. Good night everyone! "

Audrey had to admit to herself she was exhausted from all the day's activities with the promotion of campaigning for the opening of the summer season with the Big Splash. She congratulated herself with the people who worked the summer months, mostly implants from all over the country. These people she knew for years and trusted them.

Two college professors who loved to kayak from Wyoming, the Bartley twins from up the road, three nurses from Ontario, computer techies from Nebraska, a film producer from New York City, many, many more from various states and walks of life come to Rose Cottage during their summer vacations for fun, relaxation, work and volunteer.

Audrey plans a huge dinner extravaganza with special "surprise gifts," for everyone at the end of the season to show her gratitude and appreciation.

Even though she was tired, she drove home for the night. She wanted to relax for a few hours in her backyard gardens with a nice glass of chardonnay.

Chapter 60

Artren and Saires looked up into the vast Neian star-lit sky. They were silent for quite awhile. Saires had closed his eyes, listening to the soft melodious droning of the little beetle like species. It was a beautiful sound. The two Anoans had missed their planet, family and friends. It was really a peaceful world, and Artren and Saires were taken aback and shocked at the development of Tegris' behavior, the past two and a half years. The other four seemed to have become just like him.

Saires opened his eyes. He looked at his friend who was deep in thought, gazing at the stars. "What do you think, my friend? Do you believe what the Seer has told us is true? That the Translators of Energy are trying a new approach and may have come to some success. Is it possible that we will be able to see our people soon?"

Artren sighed, "The people of this planet have been kind to us, yet they do not really trust us. With Tegris' and the other's behavior, I do not blame them. But, I do believe the Seer. He has never been one to deceive."

"I do too, Artren. I believe that the Seer said there is another planet, a world like our own that is safe, and a portal opening to both worlds, of Anoa and the other."

"How does he know this? We were not able to contact our planet, do you think they found a way and would we be able to do the same?"

"It is time to go; we must meet with the others, The Elders and the Translators of Energy will be meeting soon with the rest of us and we should find answers soon enough, Artren."

Saires and Artren rose from their sitting place on the rock near their Neian home, hoping in all reality that they would once more see their beloved planet, Anoa soon, or one just like it.

Tegris and the other four Anoans were already at the designated place when Artren and Saires arrived.   Tegris did not notice their arrival. "Greetings Tegris," Artren spoke genially.

The group turned around.   "Artren, Saires, it is good to see you both. We have missed you." Tegris came up to them. The others followed. They all sent their greetings.

"Do you know why we will be assembled with the Elders, this evening, Tegris?" Artren was curious know if Tegris knew why the meeting was assembled.

"We should soon find out, for the Neians are here," Tegris gestured unaware of the intentions the gathering held to the left and everyone present noticed a large group approaching.

Into the great hall came the Translators of Energy, the Elders and the Seer. Everyone greeted each other cordially. Ferian, the highest and most esteemed of the Elders, spoke first. "Please, everyone be seated and we will begin," He looked at the Anoans kindly and addressed Tegris.

"We are assembled here because a great discovery that the Translators of Energy have been working on for almost two and a half years." Ferian focused his attention on the Anoans. "As you know, Lorien will translate from the dimensional Earth plane on July 11th, which to us will be the 30th day of the Season of Warmth and what a joyous day that will be."

Tegris looked a little smug, and what a surprise everyone will have when we thwart your plans, he thought. Thereon was not present, and he was curious to know why, but he did not make it known.

Ferian turned to Orisen, "Good friend Orisen, would you come and tell us of your discovery?"

Artren and Saires were sitting on the edge of their seats. Will this be good news, pondered Saires?

Orisen addressed those who were present in the Great Hall. "Esteemed Elders, our Anoan Friends, and Guardia, we have come upon a discovery that we did not think was possible before." He had a remote that started a hologram in the center of the antechamber.

Orisen looked specifically at Tegris, who felt slightly uncomfortable. "Tegris, we know you and the others had expressed concerns about getting back to your dimension." Tegris nodded in mere functionality. "We have finally found a solution that may prove successful."

Orisen clicked the remote and the hologram changed. "This is a chemical equation we had been working on and mystified us for the longest time. We knew there was more to it, so we broke it down and reassembled it using a modality of data even further. We also recently discovered that your planet is a 4.5 dimensional planet, and we found that inter-dimensionally your planet has a gas in your atmosphere that is dissimilar to ours. We were working with the wrong type of equations. If we change this number here," the remote changed the hologram to another equation.

"What do the equations mean, Orisen," one of the Anoans asked.

"I am glad you asked that question, is it Kiam? "

Kiam nodded. "Yes, it is."

Orisen continued with yet another equation with the remote. "What this means is that matter changes quickly with this equation. When you change the atom, you change matter. Our planet is structured in a similar way as Anoa, but we were missing one element to the equation." He changed the hologram again. "This..."

Everyone gasped. A small portal appeared within the equation.

"This element changes everything. We found a portal that will open a door to your planet, my Anoan friends. Three days hence from Lorien coming back, a portal will open to your world and we had almost missed it."

The Anoans for the first time in 2 ½ years, felt some form of hope. Tegris was taken aback, "Our planet is dying, and we do not even know if it is safe to go back and if our people are still alive."

Orisen spoke then. "We have been told that they are barely surviving. This is why we have been working day and night to find another way and the..." Orisen looked at Ferian.

"Yes, tell them, Orisen, it is time they knew."

At that moment, Guardia the Seer turned it appeared to no one in particular and nodded. Then a Flyer with wings appeared. The Being shimmered with iridescent light, and then his small form came through.

The Anoans were in awe. Tegris, however, was not surprised. Did I not tell the others there were spies around, he deliberated to himself?

"This Being of Light," continued Orisen "is a Flyer. The Flyers are not really from our world, but have come in and out of our dimension for a very long time. They have the ability to go through dimensions and time. You will find his news quite satisfying." Orisen fell silent.

The Flyer addressed the Anoans. "We bid you greetings, I am L'elma, My people and I have been through many dimensions and parallel worlds trying to find a suitable home for you and the inhabitants of Anoa. It was at the request of the Esteemed Elders of this planet, which you have been graciously granted refuge for the time you were here. We have found a planet, Υι Χαπρια. It is similar to your atmospheres that you existed in. It is in the Stellian Galaxy, many light years away from here. A significant portal east of the Caridia Mountains will open to both worlds. We know this because we have the ability to transpose through time.

Artren and Saires were overwhelmed with joy that they both clapped. The others were equally just as happy. Everyone was speaking at once. "This is the best news we have heard," Mernis cried out.

Tegris, not sure if this was all true, resigning to speculative caution, yet cast a shadow of hope. "Have you developed a plan...what must we do to prepare?"

L'elma continued, "The Neians will guide you through the correct coordinates. It is only because of the seven crystals, they have the power within their molecular structures to open the portals. The timing is crucial. The crystals will make it safe for you and the other Anoans to travel through. From an electrical like connection, we have made contact with the people on your planet. They are not well, some have perished. Your atmosphere is letting in too many gasses from your smaller sun, we are assured of your future to be one of great success in this other dimensional world. We have traveled through the future and know this is true."

L'elma looked back at Orisen.

"Thank you friend L'elma," Orisen sifted his stance and continued. We are quite sure that this will transpire on the 30th day of the Season of Warmth, and the crystals will play an important role for the safety of transfer..."

"With that, Orisen, Elders, Guardia, we bid you farewell." L'elma disappeared with just a sparkling of light as a residue and then it was gone.

Tegris still wasn't quite convinced. "You are positive that the crystals will be here. As I remember they are still on the Earth planet. How will you know that you will gain procession of them? Once the Earth inhabitants see the power within the crystals, do you think they will willingly let them go?"

"We are quite sure, Tegris. We will once again gain control of the crystals and the two carnelian-like stones that will translate Lorien back here, we are sure of this. There are many people on earth who are descendants of Neia. Four are in the vicinity where the portal resides, others are friend to us, and so we are confident that the stones will be ours. They are in safe-keeping and hid to anyone else."

Tegris just nodded solemnly, but had the sensation that it may not go as well as Orisen thinks. He let it go for now, and listened to the rest of what the Neians had to say. He will consult with the others later.

Ranier brought up a hologram of the carnelian-like stones. Orisen continued, "These stones have unusual qualities that are different from the carnelian stone of the 3 dimensional Earth." Orisen turned to Ferian & Guardia, "As I have stated before, Ferian, this stone has a slightly altered value, the molecular structure exudes a quality that breaks down electrical energy, or transmutes it. It changes the atom, and in our dimension, changes frequencies in certain areas and opens portals." Orisen nodded to Ferian.

Ferian stood up "The Caridia Mountains are about a three day's journey from our settlement. We will leave the day before the translation to be ready in time. Now it is very late and we will leave any questions for the morrow. Good evening everyone, rest well."

The Anoans, who were grateful for the news, left the meeting happy and full of hope. Tegris left with many things to think about.

Chapter 61

Abigail, relaxed in her seat on the plane headed for New York City, looked out the window and sighed. Jeffrey glancing at his mother of Earth whom he grew to love so much felt she must be battling turmoil within.

A tourist group returning to the United States had a three week excursion of the Sacred and Mystical sites of England. The tour started and ended in London. There were conversations of Glastonbury Tor, Stonehenge, Silbury Hill, and various sites of Crop Circles of the 25 seats around Abigail and Jeffery. Bart, Anthony and Jacques were five rows back.

Abigail turned to Jeffery with a few tears welling up. She knew she must try to keep in control of her emotions, for Jeffery's sake. How I will miss him, she sighed.

Jeffery took Abigail's hand and held it for a few moments. Abigail let the tears flow. Jeffery feeling himself unnerved just barely kept in control, "Mother, I will truly miss you; I am so grateful to you and Father. You know, I think there may be a way to somehow keep in contact with you." He told her about the Seer and how periodically he appeared in his dreams throughout the years.

"I will miss you very much also, Jeffery, and it is a comforting thought. Once in a while I see a Flyer, and just recently one came to tell me of the caves you were going back to in France and assured me you would be safe." Abigail brushed aside the few tears that came, and smiled. She took Jeffery's hand closest to her and held it awhile. "Jeffery, Let me close up the apartment for you. It should be the least of your worries. I may stay a while and visit some places I hadn't been to in quite some time and I think it will help me to adjust."

Jeffery nodded, "Yes that's a capital idea Mother, and how are you physically feeling? Any aches and pains? Eating those chocolate truffles again?" Jeffery feigning humor thought it would help them both release the moment of sadness.

Abigail laughed in spite of herself at their private joke! "Oh Jeffery, you know how much I love them. You still remember that?"

"Most definitely! Whenever you were sick, or so you said, a chocolate truffle would always cure you. I was naïve when I first came here. To think I thought that was medicine, and wished I would become ill so I could have one of them."

"I did tell you after week though and let you have whatever you wanted, even from my private stash. Ohhh Jeffery, what memories we have."

Jeffery and Abigail smiled at each other then each to their own thoughts tried to get some rest on the long flight to New York City.

Meanwhile, Anthony and Jacques talked non-stop for about an hour. Bart and Anthony were sitting together in the row before Jacques. Anthony had to turn sideways to face Jacques and periodically bumped Bart in the shoulder. Anthony related his last visit to Brazil and the pink river dolphin's study and Jacques with his experiences in the recent rescue of Jeffery with Bart.

Bart looking over an Antique Quarterly he purchased in London listened intently and marveled at the passion Anthony showed as he talked about his experiences in Brazil and his research.

"Let me trade seats with you Jacques so you and Anthony can talk more freely and I can read my Quarterly in peace!" Bart emphasized the word peace.

"Oui, certainly Bart, you will not be disturbed, now, eh? Jacques winked at Anthony. Once seated, the conversation was continued with just as much enthusiasm as before. They were both equals in their fields of studies.

Anthony sensed a déjà vu when he was introduced to Jacques, he had the feeling he knew him some time and place before. It was an instantaneous friendship. As soon as one would stop talking to catch his breath the other would jump in. They were in sync to each other's awareness and timing.

"It is like I knew you before, um....you are familiar to me, Anthony. How old are you?"

"I'm 32, and you?"

Oh, *mon ami*, I am 37, is it not likely you had come to Montpellier in your younger years, perhaps with your grandfather..." Jacques accentuated the latter part, "....the spy?"

"I heard that Jacques, I was not a spy and you know that little pip squeak!" Bart laughed while reading his magazine shaking his head.

"I was crestfallen when I found out, my hero was actually an antiques dealer ....how do you say, ah, oui, a let down for an 11 year old boy. I was never the same after that, oui Bart?"

"Just tell Anthony the story and let me read..."

"Oh, yes, yes...in peace," interrupted Jacques in a loud whisper. They all laughed quietly and Jacques told Anthony how his father, Rene' Baigent met Bartholomew Edis for the first time and the famous lost at sea story, and all the adventures he had when he came into the picture at seven years old.

Anthony related some anomalies he experienced and also with his brother Charles. Finally, each passenger settled in for the night and slept for the remaining evening hours until the plane would reach New York City in the early morning.

Chapter 62

Lawrence Edis' meeting went over thirty-three minutes. Lost in the new information received from one of his colleagues, and casually looking at his watch was jolted back into reality. It was 12:33 pm.

"Edmond, have to go, I have another meeting at one, sorry. Mind if I take the last croissant?"

"No, I actually wanted to leave before twelve, but this new feature for the museum is fascinating. Wallace, what do you and Lawrence think about continuing this, say in a day or two?"

"Sounds good to me," Lawrence was almost out the door, "Call me."

"But you hardly ever answer your phone..." Lawrence heard half way down the hall.

The museum was across town and Lawrence would just barely make it to Rose Cottage in time for one o'clock. He thought of all that had transpired in just one week. Meeting Ellen Belk again, and the two teens, Anna and Desmond, Charles's incident at the old quarry and his dream. His cousin Jeffery's secret previous life and now the journal, and what was it about the two stones? It was a mystery; he digested all the information and tried to make some sense of every part of it. After all, he'd always been a practical man, but now, well, now it seemed he was opening a door to something new and fascinating. He now understood Anthony & Charles' fascination to the anomalies they would uncover. He was starting to feel alive again. Too long had he felt the inertia of life, this was, well, damn exciting!

Lawrence never made much of the peculiarities with the topics and instigations Anthony and his younger brother Charles would get into. He stopped at a red light. A horn blared in back of him. How did the light turn green so quickly? Unaware of his preoccupation in thought, he passed Rose Cottage and had to turn around a half mile down the road.

"Okay," he said aloud as his blinker signaled a left hand turn into the Rose Cottage parking lot. "I got here in twenty minutes!" Lawrence parked his car and went into the side entrance where he would meet the others.

It was just about one o'clock and Charles wasn't there yet. It wasn't like him to be late. He was always very punctual. Now Anthony, he was always late for everything. Lawrence saw Ellen and his heart leaped when she saw him and gave a wide smile. He passed by Anna and Desmond, said "Hello'" to everyone and the two adults were in conversation when Charles rushed in.

"Sorry Dad, Lucien had an appointment in the late morning and I had to cover for him at the shop." It was 1:10pm.

"Oh my goodness gracious," Audrey Perpecuwitz came flying around the corner and opened the door to her office suite. "Come in everyone. Well, we had some unexpected visitors this morning. A magazine called Old Style Living came around 10:00 and interviewed us. Rose Cottage will be the feature article next month, in August. Many years ago it was regarded as an historic landmark, which became of a particular interest to one of the contributing editors; Lidia Walker. She came last summer for one of the events. She suggested Rose Cottage at an editorial meeting and arranged to come today with her staff. I had completely forgotten. I hope you weren't waiting too long."

"We arrived about ten minutes ago, Audrey," Ellen assured, "not to worry. What exciting news, later you will have to tell us how the interview went!"

Audrey smiled and nodded. "Desmond and Charles, would you both be so kind to get the sandwiches and ice tea I have in the refrigerator. Arlis, one of the chefs, made some little sandwiches. I for one am staving! Let's sit at the table. There are just enough seats. Anna, would you please get the glasses in the cupboard? I wanted to have everything out before you arrived, but I just barely made it back myself.

The platter that was set on the table contained little sandwiches, veggies, berries and an organic nut mixture. They had a pleasant conversation recalling some of the pertinent points covered in the evening before, and new additions forgotten. After the late lunch, the teens had cleared the table and the adults helped put the dishes in the dishwasher and everyone gathered in the lounge area again.

"It is about time that I tell everyone my story, and it is important that you tell no one. It is about my private life and I think relevant to what will be happening in a few weeks from now. Are we agreed?" Everyone agreed.

"I shall start when my mother met my father...

Chapter 63

Bart thought Central Park in New York City couldn't have been more beautiful when they stopped for a moment in the rental car from the airport. Paddle and row boats on the lake made an ideal picture as they followed the green oasis. Abigail looked younger than her 84 years, thought Bart. He studied her as his nephew Jeffery made comments about the scenery and buildings on the way to his apartment home. It was really a pent-house redesigned and refurbished from the 1940's.

In 1978, Jeffery and Rachel Turner acquired the location after a long dig in Nepal. A senior editor for a local publishing company had arranged for them to see the pent-house. Rachel fell in love with it and they lived there on and off when time allowed. Jeffery kept it after Rachel died. He turned into the parking garage and drove into his parking space.

Bart's telephone rang. "Hello. Lawrence! Why yes, yes I did telephone earlier. We've just arrived at Jeffery's place. I called because I knew you were worried about Anthony when you tried to get in touch with him a few days earlier. Well, rest assured, he's fine. Yes, I did speak to him....in fact...um...I'll tell you about it when I see you. Yes, I accidently called him instead of Charles. He was on the bike tour, and he's going to call you in a few days. Uh-huh, the time frame is different there. Well, he left his telephone at a restaurant and had to go back to retrieve it..." Bart chuckled, "Oh yes, that truly is Anthony!"

"We should be at your house in three to four days, oh, and Aunt Abigail is with us. I have a lot to tell you, and don't worry; Anthony will call after his bike tour is over. I love you too son. G'bye."

Anthony grinned as Bart closed his cell phone.

Jacques and Anthony were able to secure a rental car. They were going to head out in a few hours. As they took the elevator up to Jeffrey's home, Bart cleared his throat, "So Jeffrey, we actually had you declared as a missing person. Where were you for the seven days prior to your rendezvous in France?"

Looking surprised, Jeffery coughed, the doors to the elevator opened, "Ah...well, hmm, where to start!" They arrived at the front door and Jeffery unlocked it.

"Whoa, Uncle Jeff....this place is fabulous!" Anthony took in the surroundings as the doors opened to Jeff's inner sanctum, and went from room to room.

"Jeff-er-y extravagant, oui?" Jacques followed Anthony.

"Jeffrey, let's sit down in the living room, and we can talk." Abigail sat near the window. There was a chorus of sparrows singing in the trees and garden on the enlarged patio, an occasional dragon fly whizzed by.

Jacques and Anthony found comfortable chairs and joined the discussion.

"I started thinking about Rachel," Jeffrey said solemnly, "I missed her. I know it's been four years since her death, but I had her on my mind for quite sometime. She loved this room you know, one of her favorite things to do was to sit and watch the birds. She planted all the trees and flowers, especially ones that would attract butterflies. When she..." Jeffrey paused, looking out the window reminiscing, "passed, I thought of selling the place...I just couldn't. She was still here, in every nook and corner..."

"I know what you mean, Jeffrey, I felt like that when your father died. I still miss him!"

Jeffery smiled and patted his mother's hand, "I know, I do too...I do too!" Everyone was quiet for a moment, each to their own thoughts.

"Beautiful up here, Jeffrey, and it's still as I remembered it." Bart stood near the largest of the beveled sliding glass doors. The view from up here is absolutely phenomenal, haven't been here in quite a while."

"It is charming here, that's what attracted Rachel at first, but then it started to be home once we had both retired. I had decided to go to some of the old haunts Rachel and I use to frequent. It was refreshing to live them again and imagining her by my side. I was lost in her memory for a while. I actually had been gone a month or so. Then I had the dream from I thought to be from Rachel and went to England to collect some information and on to France about the same time you must have filed the missing person's report, Bart. I can feel her around me less and less now. It is as if we had finally said our goodbyes, I had to finally let her go.

Bart nodded his head, smiling hesitantly, "Yes I understand, it's hard. Even though Elizabeth and I had divorced, I found I had missed her, and when she perished in the car accident, I was beside myself with grief. Time heals all wounds, Jeffrey, yes, time heals all wounds."

Chapter 64

Audrey Perpecuwitz paused. Everyone was in awe. Lawrence Edis couldn't help thinking how preposterous this all seemed, and yet, a parallel...real parallel world. Proven to exist, not just some random philosophical talk about one, almost hard to believe, but Audrey was the amplifying truth behind it

A Holding Place, Shangri-la, the Himalayan Mountains, extraterrestrials, portals, dimensions, and his cousin Jeffery, not really from Earth. Audrey half human and how old is she really? She would be well almost 67 years old, at least. It's inconceivable...Lawrence took a quick peek at Audrey again; she looked not a day over 40.

"I will tell you now why some of you are so important in getting Jeffery Turner back to his home in Neia." Audrey turned to Ellen Belk, "Ellen how long have you lived here?"

"Henry & I lived in New York State, We had vacationed here one year and after the accident, I resigned my teaching position and found a house and teaching position here. Anna was about 6 years old. I felt really drawn to the place. It's been about 8 years now."

Anna shifted and sat forward, something was happening. Something important, she felt a small tingle and shivered slightly. Desmond noticed and gave Anna a questioning look. Anna just shrugged the 'I don't know look' and left it at that.

"Do you remember anything about your great, great grandparents, Ellen," Audrey continued, "two relatives, on your mother's side? Rudolf and Dertia Steiger were pure Neians. They came in the early 1800's when the last portal was opened to help with the Earth's magnetic transition. They were here before Lorien's spontaneous appearance. Their real names were Roln and Eriana. They are only known in Neia by one name. Neia is a small planet. They only have four nations. Each nation has an Elder. Jeffery or Lorien's father is the highest Elder. The Elder's keep the seven atmospheres in balance from each corner of the planet. It is in their genetic code. They are in harmony with all nature of the planet. If storms or any other types of anomaly upset the balance of the planet, the Elders can fix it. That is why it is so important for Lorien to go back. All of the other Elders had transcended their place to a younger descendant; Lorien is the last and the most important. He will be the Highest Elder. The Elders only have that life force for so many years, and then the office goes to the next descendant, who has the equilibrium and DNA codes that agree with the balance of the planet.

Ellen sat amazed with all this information. "How do you know all this Audrey?"

"One of The Flyer's, L'elma and my mother Lanaia told me. You wouldn't have believed me if I had told you a year ago. It is when my mother had come in her last visit. She told me not to tell you until this year."

"Well, you are absolutely correct Audrey; I would have thought you lost your mind. But, now, with all this happening, the journal, and what Anna and Desmond have been through and uncovered, it's just, well really seems far-fetched, and all the while, quite fascinating."

"You and your sister Lenora carry your ancestor's DNA in your blood. Anna and Desmond have the same genetic code in their blood. That is why they are so important in helping Jeffery get back to his world. Rudolf and Dertia were Jeffery's great aunt and uncle. You and your sister and Jeffery are really related in a way."

"Wow! Aunt Ellen is that true, Anna and I are related to Jeffery?"

"Yes, Desmond...I think so! It is hard to believe, but I really think Mrs. Perpecuwitz is right."

"Which is why Desmond and I have to be the ones to help Jeffery get back....our birthdays and the codes in the book match. Jeffery's birthday is July11th. Mine is the 10th and...

"Mine is the 12th," Desmond jumped in.

The clock on the mantel chimed at 4:00 pm.

"Well, Audrey," Lawrence got up to stretch his legs. "It is July 2nd, if all this is happening July 11th, time is quickly running out. What should we do, what is our part in it, I mean Charles and I. To put it bluntly, we're not really related."

If I am correct, Lawrence, Charles has had dreams and then saw that vision of the portal at the old quarry..."

Charles spoke up, "...and Rachel Carde dreamt about the dream I had the other night, Jeffery wrote about it in his journal"

"Tell me Charles about the dream other night." Audrey sifted the cushions on her comfy chair.

Charles stood up and slowly paced. "The dream was related to the vision at the old quarry, only it seemed so lucid and real...."

Anna took out the Epic Catalog from her backpack and looked for Rachel's description and read to herself: 'A young man stood outside a gate, shouting at someone on the other side. Lightening and torrents of rain came in such force with the rushing wind...'

Charles relayed the whole episode to Mrs. Perpecuwitz. Anna read Rachel's account in the journal.

Lawrence stood up again and stretched his legs, "I have an idea, I sure would like to see the Murals at Dad's store again, but won't be able to get away for a couple of days. Can everyone meet there, say Monday the 4th? It will be closed and we can have the place to ourselves."

Everyone agreed. Audrey spoke up, "I am sure that we all play a major role in this, I for one am a messenger and I believe we all are a support team. She sighed at the intensity of it all.

Chapter 65

The rental car secured, Jacques and Anthony said their goodbyes and headed toward their destination, which was a four hour trip. Jacques comfortable in New York City, reminiscing of Paris, was quite at home.

Anthony relayed about his hometown and the Gorges around Rose Cottage, the coming of the dolphins in the inlet, and the caverns with the iridescent stalagmites. Jacques thought the Gorges reminded him of the Languedoc Coast in France.

Anthony heard about Jacques' driving to the French Airport from his grandfather Bart, and decided to drive while hearing about Jacques' recent vacation in Castlebouc, a small village in the Gorges du Tarn, part of the Languedoc-Roussillon region.

Jacques had rented a small villa with some friends for almost two weeks and went kayaking, hiking, spent a day on the rapids and camping. One of his friends from Italy had an old school bus converted into a sage green camper. Jacques met him at Castlebouc. They went camping for the first week on the trails of the

Gorge du Tan, then stayed at the villa for 12 days, with two other college friends and participating in medieval tournaments during the Renaissance week in the village.

Anthony was amazed at how Jacques kept going. "Jacques, how do you do it? You had come from an exciting vacation, only to rescue my cousin, in a tropical depression battling fierce winds and turbulent waters from an underwater cave, and now, here you are, like nothing ever happened?"

"Oh Anthony, it excites me, another adventure, I would not miss this for the world!"

"Well that explains it then, you are definitely a Type A."

Jacques, smiled widely, turned his head and caught sight of a coffee sign. "...And now, Mon Ami, we go to your Rose Cottage, but first, we need coffee, oui? I think I saw a small café....yes, back there...down the road?"

Anthony turned the rental car around and stopped at an old Victorian café that had a sign in front painted in bold letters: Ernest Hemingway Stopped Here! They had been on the road for a little over an hour.

It was a quaint café in an old restored Victorian home converted into a coffee/pastry/sandwich shop many years ago. And yes, Hemingway did stop there. In the hallway photographs lined the walls as well as the main room of Hemingway, and other authors, actors and the general public. It was called The Victorian Travelers Café.

After a chat, coffee and a bag of pastries, the two travelers were on the road again, for a three hour drive.

Not much happened along the way. The July sun bore down on the roof of the car. The air-conditioning in the car was a welcome commodity. Anthony finally pulled into his driveway. No one appeared to be at home. It was 5:30 pm and usually his father was home from the museum by now, unless they had a meeting or a new program going on. Charles' jeep was not in the yard either. They stopped by the Antiquities Shop to see if Charles was there, but Lucien was just closing up for the day and no sign of Charles around either

Anthony and Jacques took their luggage into the house. Anthony opened the refrigerator door to see if any remains of supper were left, nothing much in there. Anthony broke down and dialed his father's cell phone number. He did want to surprise him, and all he heard was a recording. So he left a message that he was returning his call. There was a guest room upstairs across from Charles's bedroom and Jacques put his bags, computer and backpack in there. Then he took a quick shower adjacent the guestroom while Anthony showered in the downstairs bathroom.

"HELLOOOO!!! Hello? Who is here?" Anthony heard his father's voice through the house as he stepped out of the shower, and bathroom door.

"DAD, IT'S ME ANTHONY! I'LL BE RIGHT OUT."

"ANTHONY? I don't believe it, your home?"

Anthony dressed and refreshed opened the bathroom door and there stood his father.

"It is really good to see you son! Why are you home so early from your trip? We didn't expect you for another two weeks." They gave each other a bear hug.

Just then an energetic Jacques came around the corner. "Ah, Monsieur Edis, I am Jacques Baigent, Bart Edis' long time acquaintance. He knows my father Rene' very well!" He shook a confused Lawrence's hand and continued, "This part of the country is very beautiful. Oui, very beautiful!

"Ah, yes! I remember now, my father's friend. He telephoned and said he was going to see him. What brings you to the States Jacques? "

"Well, I could not miss the adventure about to happen and I am here to help."

"Dad, Jacques is the one who rescued Jeffery. Let's go to The Bistro, we're starving and we'll tell you all about it."

Charles walked through the kitchen door. "Dad, whose car is out back?" He did a double take, "Anthony!"

They were all sitting at The Bistro, when Ellen Belk walked through the door with Anna & Desmond. Charles caught sight of Anna, she didn't notice. "Dad, look, Mrs. Belk is here…"

"Oh good, I telephoned her before we left. Thought it would be good for every one to meet" Lawrence stood up and waved an arm in the air. Charles thought that was a great idea, and started to bring three chairs from the nearby tables. Ellen looked his way and came to the table.

"Thank you Lawrence for inviting us tonight." Ellen sat down in one of the chairs, Anna and Desmond followed suit.

"You're Welcome, Ellen; this is a good way for every one to meet"

Lawrence introduced everyone. After two large pizzas, salads, deep fried battered mushrooms, potato skins and beverages were decided upon, the conversations began.

Lawrence initiated the dialogue. "Anthony has come back early from his vacation in Paris to help with Jeffry's …is it translation they call it? Jacques was Jeffery's rescuer in the underwater caves in the south of France…."

Anna perked up...."You mean the underwater caves near Saintes-Maries-de-la-Mer?"

"Yes," smiled Jacques, "the very same."

Lawrence continued, "We are not quite sure how and what happened over there, would you tell us, Jacques?"

Jacques in his element was pleased to tell everyone of the rescue. He started with the events when he responded to a telephone call from his father's receptionist about the patron cat. He had his audience captivated with his wit, charm and humor, and had them on the edge of their seats as he expounded on the sudden fierce storm during Jeffrey's rescue, and the underwater experiences.

"......there was a time I did not think either of us could go on. Your father Bart, Lawrence, a very brave man! He led the way through the fiercest of the storm." Jacques made it apparent that Bart was the hero. "I would not have found my way back if not for the guidance of your father."

Everyone was in awe.

"What was it like, meeting the dolphins, Jacques?" Anna thought this would make a great story and was in her reporter mode. Desmond recognizing the signs, seeing her take out a pencil and pad, sighed as he thought to himself that she would be grilling him for hours for information.

The waiter came with the pizza, "...it was something I had never experienced before." Jacques cut a slice of pizza, tasted it, and continued. "I felt, how do you say...um, ah yes, in tuned with them, I understood their motives. The Island was ...um...seemed...ather...uh, ethe..re...al? Oui, very dream like!" Jacques out of the corner of his eye saw Desmond frown at Anna's drilling, winked at him. "And now, we eat," said Jacques lightheartedly. Yes, Desmond liked Jacques very much!

During the meal, Anthony wanted to hear all about the journal and how it came to the knowledge of Anna and Desmond. As they settled into dessert, Charles told Anthony and Jacques about his experience at the quarry and the two dreams; the dream he had and the discovery of Rachel Cardes dream in the journal. It was uncanny! The Bistro, heavy with the evening crowd was fading. The party of seven was there for three hours.

It was after 10:00 pm and they had all decided to go home and meet again. Jacques wanted to see the journal and Anthony wanted to see the stones at the Antiquities Shop. Anna and Desmond never got around to telling the episode about the murals. It was decided that everyone would meet at The Antiquities Shop in the new edition after lunch on July 4th since it was previously decided before.

Chapter 66

Tegris sat outside his dwelling and viewed what looked to be a meteor shower. He had much to think about. It was late and the other Anoans had already retired. "Suppose….. The information from the Flyers was true?" Tegris had a complex nature; and he questioned everything, and was unsure of what they called feelings, or emotion. The Anoans learned emotional behavior in Neia. What was it they called hope? It meant many things, yet one thing for sure, he wanted to have hope, and he wanted to be able to feel it, like his fellow companions who started to have a measure of hope.

Soon it would be the time of the Translation. Tegris now thought differently about his previous plans to thwart the operation. He had to think this through, if it doesn't go as plan, they would be at the mercy of the Neians, because Lorien would be back. He rose from his seat and walked to the glistening lake. The stars electrified the water. He sat down deep in thought and was startled when L'elma appeared beside him ten minutes later. The Flyer appeared as a spark of light, and then took form, still suspended in the air.

"Greetings, Anoan."

"Why have you come?"

"I have come to warn you. We Flyers know of your plans. If you try to take over the planet, it will die. We have foreseen it. You and everyone else will die. The planet is in equilibrium because The Elders have coded within their bodies to work with the elements of this planet. Long ago they have been created in such a fashion to be the stabilizers of this planet. They are of an ancient race. The atmospheres are living organisms which are of the same substance as the ancient race of the Elders.

We have traveled through time and space. We found a planet not because of your threats to Thereon," Tegris raised his eyebrows ready to speak, but L'elma continued on, "we know well of your plans. It was not the Neians who pursued it, but because of our allegiance and friendship to them that we had continued our search."

"Why are you here now?"

I am here to let you know that we are more powerful than you. We will defeat you if you try to thwart Lorien from coming back. The planet depends on it. You do not have the body to sustain this planet. Your body has tolerated the atmospheres, but it is not really akin to it. You are a little weaker and grow weaker the longer you stay here. Your own dimension has slight differences. The planet we found is of the same dimensional vibration as your bodies. It is a new planet and is highly sustainable for all your race of people."

Tegris looked L'elma in the eye, "You were spying on us, I felt it."

"It was from this that prompted us to find a better home for you. If you try to take over, you will become prisoners of this planet, instead of roaming at will. The Neians are a kind race, but when it comes to threatening their existence, they will not look kindly upon you."

Tegris sighed. "I am tired, I will think on your words."

L'elma circled in the air. "We will speak again, I bid you farewell."

Tegris lost in his thought for awhile, heard a twig break in the distance. He saw a form slowly walking toward him. The figure resembled The Seer.

Guardia taking a late night stroll happened to notice a movement at the lake. A spark of light disappeared. "I wonder..." He looked closer and recognized the outline of the Anoan, Tegris. He strolled slowly toward him and sat down on a nearby rock.

For a long time, no one spoke. Each content with their own thoughts as a gentle breeze made wave patterns on the water. Then at last, Guardia spoke. "Tegris, I hope you know we are your friends, and that we want only to help you. We know you miss your home and family. It will not be long.   We hope this new world will accommodate your people.   It is the best we can do."

Tegris, not use to being addressed in a familiar manner, cleared his throat, "We look forward to when the time comes, and it will be a great celebration for those of our planet.   Our planet has been slowly dying, I fear for my people."

"We understand your fear Tegris. The Translators of Energy have researched and tested their theories, for many years, and they are theories no longer."

Let us meet with Orisen on the morrow and he will speak to us about how the translations will occur.   Will you come?"

Tegris was silent for a half of minute.   "Yes."

Guardia rose, "Farewell, I think I will continue on my stroll.   The moons and stars are especially beautiful tonight."

Tegris nodded in acknowledgement, "Farewell." He sat in silence for a while, feeling the light wind upon the water, and thought, just maybe, there was hope.

Chapter 67

The last week flew by. Anna finally met Jeffery Turner. Even at 73, he looked to be in his early 50's or younger. He exhibited an air of elegance and a graceful manner she had never witnessed in a person. Desmond was in awe. It was uncanny the difference, especially to the character she read in the journal. He was in his early twenties, and here, now, he still looked to be in his late forties to early fifties. Anna looked at her mother. She looked younger than her age. Ellen Belk turned 42 a few months ago. Her parents were married in their thirties, and Anna was born in 1997. Her thoughts turned to her Aunt Lenora, who was a few years younger than her mother. She didn't look her age either.

Anna was enthralled with Abigail Turner. She wondered why she looked younger also. There wasn't any blood relation that would tie her to Lorien, yet having him in her life may have had an effect on her. She remembered a part in the journal when Lorien healed some of the Flyers while he was part of the Neia Culture, many, many years ago, and Abigail Turner talked about the 7 crystals. What were the qualities; did they give you a better quality of life? Anna thought about this as she entered the new addition of the Antiquities Shop.

They were all there, Bart Edis, Abigail and Jeffery Turner, Jacques Baigent and Anthony Edis, Audrey Perpecuwitz, Ellen and Anna Belk, Desmond Shay, Lawrence and Charles Edis. Bart, along with Jeffrey and Abigail Turner arrived in the area early on July 3rd.

So being a Holiday, July 4th, and the Antiquities Shop was closed, everyone met without interruptions. Bart Edis introduced his sister Abigail Turner, and his nephew Jeffrey.

Jeffery spoke up. "It is extraordinary, the turn of events in my life since I boarded the Queen Mary. Earth has been a wonderful home for me," he smiled at Abigail, who returned the smile.

"Well the secrecy surrounding you in the past Jeff, has had its element of mystery lately to say the least." Bart with intense unruly hair stood with his arms folded and a slight smile.

During the banter that flowed freely in the room, Ellen noticed a faint light on one of the murals, flickering across it once. She steadied her gaze, nothing. It must have been a reflection from outdoors somewhere, so she just sat listening to the cordial banter. It was very pleasant. Then after a while, the first mural began to glow, Ellen Belk noticed it again, and there was something different about it. No one observed her stand up and slowly walk to the mural, except for Anna, who followed her.

"Mom, you see it too, don't you?" Anna's voice was barely audible.

"What is it Anna," whispered her mother? "Are we seeing things? Is...is it normal?"

"It is sort of paranormal, Mom," Anna looked back at the group, they were laughing, still bantering; when Lawrence suddenly notice Ellen wasn't seated next to him. He stood up and walked over to Ellen and Anna and all of a sudden a bright light flashed in the mural. He stood there with his mouth a gaped. Everyone in the room suddenly became aware of an odd light emanating from within the mural. The group started to congregate toward it. Images flashed by until beautiful brilliant lights started to form pictures.

Audrey Perpecuwitz recognized part of the scenery. "I know that place, I've seen it before. I've been there!"

"C'est extraordinaire," Jacques loved being in this experience.

"Holy Cow," Anthony was excited. Charles was right beside him in an instant.

"This is what I was telling you about at The Bistro Anthony," Charles moved closer to touch it. "Touch the mural, Ant, do you feel it?" Anthony touched the mural and was immediately satisfied...another anomaly!

"Can this be the portal? It doesn't seem so though, the date is wrong." Jeffrey seemed perplexed.

Bart touched the mural; he also felt the slight tingling sensation. "I'll be darn!"

Then Ellen had a vision of a mysterious elegant woman encircled in yellow, white light. She smiled at Ellen. "I am here for Sephiria..."

Audrey saw her too, "Oh my, oh my goodness!" Tears of happiness stream down her face, and she became ecstatic. Her mother stepped into the room and Lawrence Edis fainted.

Lanaia walked to Lawrence lying near the mural and touched his forehead. She smiled at Ellen, whose attention was on Lawrence as he stirred. This was beyond anything that Ellen had ever seen. Anthony took his father's arm and helped him up.

"What just happened?" He looked at Lanaia curiously who was embracing her daughter, Audrey.

Charles spoke up, "No broken bones, Dad."

"Yeah, thanks Charles. Lawrence fixed his glasses, as he glanced at Ellen. Another fumble in front of Ellen, he thought and was slightly embarrassed.

Jeffery examined the mural. "Who are you, you don't appear to be from Neia," What is that place?"

"I am Lanaia, Sephiria is my daughter. I came through The Holding Place from a planet in another dimension," She took Audrey hands. "The Holding Place is an inter-dimensional portal that allows certain planets access to this place and others deep within the Himalayan Mountains. Neia is not one of them. I can only stay about an hour dearest Sephiria. She placed something in Audrey's opened palms. "This is an equilateral stone. All the sides are even. It is a similar base chemical as of the orange brown stones to be used for Lorien's translation. The stone's properties vary. It will allow the user to become acclimated to the energy around the portal quicker than normal. The Flyers foresaw something in the future where you may need this energy. Having a sampling of the Neian blood in your system, Sephiria, the stone will help equalize the energy so you can be more effective in its use." Lanaia, not wanting to alarm Jeffrey whispered, "I will tell you more in private," then raising her voice, slightly exclaimed, "Oh, dearest one, it is so good to see you and to be able to touch you my dear daughter."

Lanaia turned to the group, and spotted Jeffrey Turner. "Lorien, it is good to finally talk to you. The Flyers send you a message. Be aware of the time as you go through the portal. It must be at 11:45pm to be successful and that the portal is only open for translation up to three minutes..."

Jeffrey nodded his head. "Yes, thank you."

Lanaia reached inside her pocket. "This medallion is from your family. It is your heritage. It is from Thereon, your brother who insisted you have it now, does it bring back any memoires? The flyers brought it through."

Yes, yes it does. It is mine, I remember that I had it on before I came through, and it had broken when my brother and I had a disagreement. I had forgotten all about it! Thank you and if you can, please thank my brother." Jeffrey held it in his hand and moved around to Abigail to show her. It glowed as if it were alive.

Bart amazed had never seen any metal like it. Jeffery put it around his neck. He felt different at once, more energetic, and alive.

"This medallion will help your body system balance as you enter Neia, which has become slightly acclimated to Earth's gravity, but you will be like your old self when you are ready to walk through the portal."

"I am feeling a difference already!"

Lawrence feeling a little sheepish for fainting moved closer to take a look at the medallion. "Dad, do you see it? Have you seen the inscription? It looks like the piece you brought to the museum the other day."

Bart took a closer look, "May I Jeff?"

Jeff took off the medallion and handed it to Bart, who held it in his hands and felt a slight tingling sensation. "I have seen these symbols before, Jeff... when I went to a museum in Palma, Spain, years ago to buy a piece that came from an estate. It held something of a mystery dealing with the area around Saintes-Maries-de-la-Mer. By the time I got there, it was acquired by a museum in Paris. Just a few weeks ago, the same piece was up for auction at the very same museum. The symbols appear to have some connection to Neia.

Everyone moved over for a closer look.

Tηε σεϖεν ατμοσπηερεσ οφ Νεια
Tηε φιρστ Ελδερ χοντριβυτεσ

"Look Anna," Desmond pointed to the inscription, "it's in code as the others from the journal."

"It is interpreted as: The Seven Atmospheres of Neia. The First Elder Contributes." Lanaia came up from the rear holding her daughter's hand. She continued. "An Elder would use his energy to funnel through the eye of the medallion." She pointed to the middle of the medallion with deep blues flashing through the center. Everyone was fascinated. Jeffery put the medallion back on. "There are always two medallions per family of Elders. At the birth of the first male, a medallion is tested to see if the child is the one who would begin training at age thirteen. This medallion belongs to your family line Lorien. The flyers told me that as a child, you were secretly chosen and tested through out your childhood. You were told you were chosen when you were about ten years old. The medallion had energized your body with codes enhancing your DNA. The energy funneled ionizes a level of the atmosphere..."

"...And thus equalizes the atom or molecules in the air," Bart contributed.   "As far as the connection to Saintes-Maries-de-la-Mer, I am not sure."

Audrey revealed what she knew about the murals and its connection to the Saintes-Maries-de-la-Mer surrounding area. "Tens of thousands of years ago, the sea level was lower in that area. The monks of Tibet had told me this in my earlier years of travel. It was written on one of their earlier cylinders. They had found the writings secreted away in one of their libraries. One of the monks knew my body was biologically unusual and suspected I had some connection to this area, I had forgotten all of this and it is just now coming back to me."

Audrey looked at all the murals and mused over her travels before she ever lived in the States. "The land mass was quite different. It was one of the areas that had an open portal lasting for about 300 years. This area was one of the major portals and many Neians had come through and ended up staying to help our world progress to what it is now. The portal was opened to other worlds and dimensions. The Ustellia Galaxy with a myriad of worlds in an alternate dimension has allowed several species of plant and animal life to co-exist with the natural vegetation and animals of Earth. There was a mountain range close to the shore with various caves, and through a period of years, earthquakes leveled the mountains. Now it is a beautiful inlet on the south shore, where the caves are under water. There are other mysteries the monks would not reveal. I am not sure why but….."

Lanaia started to disappear. "Goodbye, Sephiria, I will see you later in your dreams…"

Audrey sighed. "Goodbye." She felt her mother's hand start to evaporate.

Chapter 68

The evening started out calm and anxiety was soaring. Anna was prepared; she went over the instructions numerous times in her head. She knew exactly what to do. Desmond kept checking his notes. He was elated and nervous at the same time. The day became hot and the humidity was almost unbearable, but the evening was cooler and the breeze was welcomed. The stars were just starting to become visible.

It was 9:09 pm and at 11:00, there would be a gathering of a small party of people to see Jeffery Turner, Lorien translate into another dimension. Jeffery had some trepidation, yet within the communications of his dream state the evening before, and the medal he wore, Ferian had reassured him that the Translators of Energy had tested the portal with extreme care. It was happening! It was really happening!

Among those present were Ellen & Anna Belk, Desmond Shay. Bart, Lawrence, Anthony & Charles Edis, Audrey Perpecuwitz, Jeffery's long time friend, Marcel Laurent, who wouldn't miss this for anything! Abigail & Jeffery (Lorien) Turner and Jacques Baigent were present.

Everyone talked well into the night. The party became jovial, yet solemn at times. A police car drove to the gate area. The officers wanted to know what was going on. Bart Edis, a prominent citizen in the community explained they were taking night photos for a project they were working on and his friend Joe Evans, one of the officers answered a dispatch message and wished him luck. The officers drove on responding to a call in another part of town.

It was 11:30 pm. The forecast for July 11th late evening was stormy. Dark clouds had moved in about an hour before. No storm activity was prevalent yet. Bart had obtained the keys of the quarry from his friend Ben Tucci who still owned the property. His great grandfather started the quarry business in 1949. Ben needed photographs of the ornate antique cast iron molding and trim on the main building on the quarry grounds. The quarry building structures were built in 1948.

Antonio Tucci, 47, who was already a multimillionaire from Italy, married a famous playwright's daughter Melody Wilson from America. Melody, 38, and who had never been married, vacationed in various places in Italy. One favorite place she frequented was Cinque Terra, on the coastline of the Italian Riviera. It was there she had met Antonio Tucci, and they both fell head over heels in love. They were wed in 1940 and moved to the United States. Melody had several investments and one was the land containing beautiful and rare granite. They employed workers to dig up the granite and sold it all over the world. In 1978, Antonio and Melody Tucci retired to Cinque Terra, Italy. They left the quarry to their son, Garret, who didn't want anything to do with it. It was locked and abandoned. Garret left the quarry to his daughter's son, Ben, who was a Bank Vice President in his will. Ben really wanted to sell it. Just the property, the artwork on the buildings and the ornate fence alone may entice a buyer. Ben was happy to have his old friend Bart Edis' grandson Charles photograph the property and buildings. Being able to have the keys ready for July 11th had worked out perfectly for Bart. He didn't have to explain why he really wanted the keys.

Cautiously unlocking the gate, and walking around the grounds, Charles invested time during the day to go to the quarry and was amazed at the stunning architecture on the buildings. Sometimes you can feel a prominent energy when you go to a place that has been abandon. Charles didn't know what to expect. As he opened the gate, guardedly, remembering the experience the last time he was there, decided to walk through and survey it first. He didn't feel anything, only a sadness of the quarry being forgotten.

He wished he had the money. He would have loved to purchase the property. Charles took several hundred photos with his digital camera, a Canon Power Shot SD600 6MP Digital Elph Camera with 3x Optical Zoom. He found some angles were a little difficult without a ladder, so he went back to his jeep to get the one he thought of at the last minute before leaving home. He was satisfied with the photographs and secured them on his computer into a flash drive. During the week, Charles would select the best shots and put them into slides and deliver them to Ben Tucci

Now back at the quarry Charles felt a quiver of anticipation brewing. It was time and it was decided that Charles and Lawrence would opened the first initial quarry gate. Once the stones activated the opening, no one but Dertia's descendants could actually touch the gate without being harmed. Lightening shadowed the sky. To the left of the tallest trees, a patch of sky with twinkling stars broke through. Passing clouds quickly covered the display.

Anna and Desmond were ready. They opened their backpacks, carefully taking out the orange stones and placing them on each side of the entrance gate. The stones became enlarged and activated an energy field. Charles remembered how the energy around the gate looked like heat rising on a hot humid summer's day from his first encounter at the gate. The energy field was similar.

Another gate appeared, and Jeffery handed Ellen Belk the three keys that had been forgotten so long ago. They vibrated with light. Ellen was nervous, but excited at the same time. Lawrence patted her shoulder, and let her know that he had her back. Ellen walked over to the gate, and opened it, immediately the air was filled with exotic perfumed flowers. The old quarry slowly disappeared.

Jeffery handed Anna the fabric to place on the ground. It fit perfectly between the two sides of the gate. The fabric between the stones appeared as a luminous liquid substance, and hovered slightly off the ground. Moonlight, galaxies, brilliant stars and other planets far off in the sky started to appear, like a motion picture. Jeffrey opened the box of crystals and handed it to Desmond. Desmond was amazed at how extraordinarily beautiful they were. He had never seen anything like them. The wind increased, Desmond worried that the cloth would take off, saw that it settled in between the doorway of the quarry gate.

"Anna, I see the formation of the constellation, the seven stars, look, there is a faint impression of light on the cloth."

Anna looked at the cloth and then into the sky beyond the gate. Desmond knelt down beside her. "Ok, I have to touch each one with my energy then hand them to you..."

"I'm ready Des..." Every one was silent, again, you could feel the anxiety as Anna accepted the first crystal and laid it on the cloth. A star beamed from the constellation in the sky from the other side of the gate and lit up the crystal.

Every crystal Desmond handed to Anna, responded in the same manner.

Seven filaments began to form one by one in the upper atmosphere beyond the gate. Desmond and Anna rose up and backed away as the last crystal was placed on the fabric. Ellen, her arms around Anna and Desmond gathered them close to her as they watched.

A surge of energy lit the night sky, clouds, stars, moons, and galaxies rushed by slowly illuminating into another world. Now, you could see clearly into the other dimension, the lake, trees, beautiful flowers and all the people there waiting to welcome their next Elder.

It was 11:37 pm. Bart stepped forward and took hold of Jeffery. "Jeffery, Lorien, I have seen many anomalies during my years as a rare antiquities dealer. I wish we had more time. I never would have thought in my wildest dreams that I would be participating in such an historic moment..."

"And it must remain secret Bart, no one outside of this party here must know."

Bart sighed, "Yes I know," He gave Lorien a hardy handshake then hugged him goodbye.

Abigail next, hugged her adopted son tightly. Goodbye Jeffery, I will always remember you as that little boy who was given to Walter & me as a beautiful gift. You will always be kept dearly in my heart. Remember I will always love you."

I love you too, Mother, and I shall never forget you. Abigail noticed a movement in the other dimension. A woman full of light came near the gate. She smiled at Ellen Belk and said, "You can take this from our dimension. Please give this to Lorien's Earth Mother. Ellen cautiously walked closer to the gate and put her hand out. She was not affected by the energy glowing around the gate. Meriasa, Lorien's true mother, dropped a beautiful pendant of exquisite stones set in something that looked like silver. "This gift is the least we could do for her love and support of our son. It will extend her Earth years and will be a connection to Lorien whenever she wishes." Meriasa looked directly at Abigail and gave her a loving smile. "Thank you Abigail. You have already met The Flyers long ago. They are willing to come back and forth now and then with messages from Lorien." Abigail, with tears in her eyes, accepted the gift graciously.

After all the farewells, as Jeffery turned to the gate, the brewing storm released with a fury and the wind whip around the gate furiously. Jeffrey's shirt wildly flew around his waist.

Jacques yelled out, "Mes amis, Look at the clouds. Are they forming a funnel?"

Every one went into action. Jeffrey stumbled and his shirt snagged on a hinge of the gate leveled with the back side of his torso. The clock in the distance showed 11:45 as lightening lit the evening sky.

"I'm stuck, can't get loose." It was hard to maneuver, Jeffrey couldn't quite reach it.

Jacques ran over to help and was zapped by the electrical charge around the gate. He looked wildly around. "I can't touch him..."

Audrey knew in an instant what she must do. She started to run to the gate.

"No," yelled Jacques, "you will be harmed by the en-er-gy..."

"I have the stone from my mother..."

"The what?" Jacques couldn't quite hear her.

Bart ran over and stumbled to the ground by a broken tree limb. He had trouble getting up because of the force of the wind, and tripped over the branch again. Lawrence, Anthony & Charles ran over to help, and Lawrence fumbled over Bart.

The Neians panicked. There was nothing they could do on their side; it must be done on the Earth plane.

Audrey made it to Jacques. Jeffrey still couldn't free himself, Audrey looked at her watch. One minute left. She was nervous. Audrey extended a hand quickly toward Jeffery.

"I can't get loose, I can't free myself!" Jeffrey wildly trying to yank himself from the gate couldn't get free. The cloud funnel made its way over to the eastern sky line. It was getting dangerously close.

"I have the stone, I can help," Audrey showed the stone to Jeffery and the wind blew it out of her hand to the ground. Desmond ran to pick it up and handed it to Audrey.

"Quick Audrey," yelled Ellen, "23 seconds left."

Audrey quickly grabbed the back of Jeffrey's shirt with such force, and ripped him free. She pushed him through the gate with three seconds to spare. The portal remained opened, but a shield of a glasslike material had closed the opening. You could still see through the gate which was phenomenal.

A younger Jeffery of 25 years, who now is known as Lorien turned after greeting his parents of Neia. He smiled a boyish smile that always held Abigail's heart with tears in his eyes as he turned to her. Even though the opening was sealed off, Abigail could still hear him. "Thank you dear one for all your love, support and keeping me safe. I love you." His parents overcome with joy bowed their heads slightly to Abigail with gratitude and happiness for their returned son. Lorien's twin Thereon hugged him and was grateful that his brother was safely back. Thereon would talk privately with him after and show his support for him as well.

Everyone was in awe, Jacques, Anthony and Charles, stepped closer for a better look. Charles accidently touched the gate. "Ohhhh...not again!" It felt like a small bolt of electricity had seized his hand.

"Are you alright, Charles?" Lawrence rushed right over.

"Yes," Charles answered a little weakly, "I forgot about the gate." He shook his hand slightly.

The cloud funnel in the eastern skyline miraculously dissipated. The Seer came forward and thanked everyone, especially Anna and Desmond. Flyers flew in and out of the portal even with the shield. Everyone was amazed and fascinated.

Oh mon Dieu, je ne le crois pas, mais je le vois ... il est sensationnel, les petites fées! Jacques was astonished by the Flyers.

Bart came closer and looked into the parallel world. It looked remarkable. Even in the evening, the colors and the textures shimmered ethereally. He couldn't take his gaze away. The whole planet of Neia took everyone's breathe away!

Anthony took out his digital camera, and left off the flash and started taking photographs. No one was sure how long the portal would remain open; everyone was prepared to stay until it closed.

"Wait a minute, I have a premonition, and I'm feeling like...there is a plane going down.

Jacques turned his head slowly, "What?   A plane..?"

Audrey Perpecuwitz holding on to the closet person next to her suddenly had a vision; "a plane.... going down in a mountainous region." She reiterated as she saw the pictures in her mind. "Two orange stones appeared on a path and there is an explosion. The plane had the emblem of an Ace with wings, and a parachute in the sky far off in the distance and two strangely dressed people appeared on the path...."

A freak lightening bolt flashed from the sky, a rainbow ray that bent with the violent thunder and lightening storm, it was refracted and the two orange stones disappeared, and the vortex was suddenly closed.....the whole evening felt ethereal.

After many questions and answers, Jacques was sure it was his father's plane that had gone down.   He made plans to leave as soon as possible.   Bart asked Charles to look after the Antiquities Shop until they found his friend, Rene' Baigent. He was going with Jacques, "But I'm driving this time, Jacques!"   Jacques laughed, thankful for the humor.   Anthony decided to go as well.   So began the party of three on a new adventure, which is actually the beginning of another story!

Until then, I bid you farewell!

Glossary of French Phrases

"Chambre des Antiquités International"
International House of Antiques

"La Serine' Aquatique"   The Aquatic Mermaid

"mon tres bon ami, Bart!" My very good friend
Bart!

"J'essaie de mon mieux." I try my best!

"Regardez...la'-bas"   Look...over there!

"Oui"...Yes

"Je ne le crois pas.!"   I do not believe it!!

"C'est assez incroyable!"   That is amazing!

"Cette beauté innocente!"   Such innocent
beauty!

C'est extraordinaire.....This is extraordinary!

"Nous sommes tous tres chanceux d'être vivant!"
We are all lucky to be alive !

« oh mes bons amis. » oh my good friends

ah ha, et bien c'est maintenant officiel, oui!
ah ha, well it is official now, yes!

Attention, s'il vous plaît. Nous approchons de
l'aéroport Roissy-Charles de Gaulle. S'il vous plaît
attacher votre ceinture de sécurité et veiller à ce
que tous les bacs sont en place et vos sièges sont
en position verticale. Nous approchons de
numéro deux du terminal. Tous les passagers en
route pour Londres, en Angleterre sera de
nouveau en conseil s'il vous plaît une demi-heure
à partir de maintenant. Merci d'avoir choisi Air
Compagnies aériennes France.

Attention please. We are approaching Roissy-
Charles de Gaulle Airport. Please fasten your
seatbelts and ensure that all trays are up and
your seats are in an upright position. We are
approaching Terminal Number Two. All
passengers enroute to London England will please
board again in one half hour from now. Thank
you for choosing Air France Airlines.

Oh mon Dieu, je ne le crois pas, mais je le vois
... il est sensationnel, les petites fées!......
Oh my God, I don't believe it, but I see it...it is
sensational, the little fairies!

Coded numbers"

7101999-7121999-7112011

ABDSUSA RCJT2011

Author Information

Denise Gadreau is the Author of various articles and four books.

"Crystal Meditations, The Inward Journey," takes you through guided meditations with the use of crystals and common stones. With today's busy schedule and on the go lifestyle, learn to de-stress and go within for release and relief.

"Points Of Light, A Poetic Journey," is a poetic journey of love, spiritual, and relative living; words of passion and healing. Through this book, you will feel the love for the earth, within yourself as you visualize and feel it extracted from the vivid adventure of words into something beautiful and alive.

"The Miracle is You, Life's Journey" is a series of articles to relieve stress, beautifully written and to the point.

"Light Wisdom, A Journey of Positive Quotes," is a photographic masterpiece. She includes her talent for artistic design with the pages of her positive quotes and affirmations. Photos and links of trails & State Forests, brooks and Floral included in the last 10 pages.

Her aesthetic photos bring illusionary and abstract perceptions through out her books.

The Reflections of the Norwich State Mental Hospital, 2008-2010, is a joint publication, in which she is a co-author. The book includes many photos of the deterioration of a once thriving era of 1904 through 1996 when it was finally closed.

Contact Information:

dgadreau@live.com

Web Page of various articles:

http://renememlight.wordpress.com/

To the Reader,

Thank you for purchasing this book. I hope you enjoyed reading it as much as I had writing it.

I am currently living in Connecticut and love to walk and hike when I am not busy. I love to take nature photos and was once entertained by a little squirrel that let me pass into the entrance of The Mohegan Park in Norwich, Connecticut. He did put up quite a fuss when he found out I was without a token of food. (However, I did have a chocolate bar from Trader Joe's but kept that quiet!) I did offer to take his picture and he graciously posed for me.

I do get a little busy and if you e-mail me, I will eventually answer your query in adequate time.

Look for the sequel: "The Flying Aces Taxi Service, The Himalayans" in the future.

Denise Gadreau

Preface

It was at a turning point in my life when I started writing fiction; The Epic Catalog is the first one. I had just moved back to Connecticut and was staying with a friend until I decided what I was going to do and where I would like to live.

One day, bored out of my mind, I sat down to my computer and just started to write anything that caught my attention. I am generally a no nonsense type of individual, usually writing non-fiction books.

When I reread the first four paragraphs, I thought, "Hmmmm, it looks like a murder mystery, and that something really dreadful had happened." I left it for a while and then a bright idea came to me after a month or so involving the 14 year old Anna Belk, and then it seemed like it was just taking off.

The story developed into a genuine full-fledged sci-fi-ish mystery adventure with very authentic and eclectic characters.

For a long time, I didn't have a title, which didn't faze me too much. I figured later on I'd think of one. You always want to have a really fantastic title to impress the media crowd.

Sooner than later, I stopped in to see my good friend Steven Gosselin, who happened to do a reading for me. We were trying to think of a catchy title for my book when out of the blue, he blurts out…"The Epic Catalog!"

I said," That's it, the title for my book! I was very excited. You know when you have that feeling inside that something is coming together, how excited you are? That is exactly how I felt. I knew that day the title was born.

Thank you, Steve, for your quick thinking and your wonderful friendship!

I am not really sure how I came up with all the characters in my book except for an over indulgent imagination. I would be writing along when an idea would spark and I would do some Google and internet research and go with it.

The places I decided to use in France were a mere whim. I researched areas of where a hospital or airport would be with the idea of a character that happened to be in a surrounding area. The idea of the caves near Saintes-Maries-de-la-Mer, along the coast of southern France, came from the Cosquer Caves in Marseilles, France. Prehistoric paintings really intrigued me, and I tried to be as realistic as I could. I also used certain events in Paris that were on going to make the characters participating in them more credible.

Denise L Gadreau

Acknowledgements

I wish to thank Cam Fogg for your continued support and enthusiasm during the process of writing this book and who encouraged me to finish it!

Thank you so much Annette Gelinas for your constant cheering as you reviewed the contents of this book in little increments. It was so helpful to have your input!

Special, special thanks to Louise Walkup for all your wise encouragement and friendship. Thank you for the editing the book! I very much appreciate your time, wisdom, and kindness.

Thank you to Carmen Gray for also reading the book and sharing some of your valuable thoughts. They were very helpful and I think the readers will be more appreciative of your input at the end.

Thank you Steve Gosselin for your continued friendship ...loved the suggestion for the title and the help from the other side for the ending! It was marvelous!

Thank you Venus Andrecht, yes I am mentioning you, for the reading you gave me on the Holly

408

Hall Show back in October, 2011. Still trying to figure out who the dressed up lady is who has encouraged me to go with the 1950's, but I have a feeling I may know in the future.

Thank you Josh Downing, my favorite son, for your love and support. I am very fortunate as a mother to have you in my life!

Last, but not at all least, special thanks to Florence Kelly for being there for me, Love your spontaneity and how you look at life. It is an inspiration to us all!

www.ingramcontent.com/pod-product-compliance
Lightning Source LLC
Chambersburg PA
CBHW070803030726
47504CB00003B/679